A FABULOUS SHARP VIEWCAM!

This month, as a special surprise, we're giving away a Sharp ViewCam**, the big-screen camcorder that has revolutionized home videos!

This is the camcorder every-one's talking about! Sharp's new ViewCam has a big 3" full-color viewing screen with 180° swivel action that lets you control everything you record—and watch it at the same time! Features include a remote control (so you can get into the picture yourself), 8 power zoom, full-range auto focus, battery pack, recharger and more!

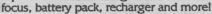

The next page contains two Entry Coupons (as does every book you received this shipment). Complete and return *all* the entry coupons; **the more times you enter, the better your chances of winning!**

Then keep your fingers crossed, because you'll find out by November 15, 1995 if you're the winner!

Remember: The more times you enter, the better your chances of winning!*

PRIZE SURPRISE
SWEEPSTAKES

OFFICIAL ENTRY COUPON

This entry must be received by: OCTOBER 30, 1995
This month's winner will be notified by: NOVEMBER 15, 1995

YES, I want to win the Sharp ViewCam! Please enter me in the drawing and let me know if I've won!

Name_____

Address _____ Apt. _____

City   State/Prov.   Zip/Postal Code

Account #_____

Return entry with invoice in reply envelope.

© 1995 HARLEQUIN ENTERPRISES LTD.   CVC KAL

PRIZE SURPRISE
SWEEPSTAKES

OFFICIAL ENTRY COUPON

This entry must be received by: OCTOBER 30, 1995
This month's winner will be notified by: NOVEMBER 15, 1995

YES, I want to win the Sharp ViewCam! Please enter me in the drawing and let me know if I've won!

Name_____

Address _____ Apt. _____

City   State/Prov.   Zip/Postal Code

Account #_____

Return entry with invoice in reply envelope.

© 1995 HARLEQUIN ENTERPRISES LTD.   CVC KAL

"You're the first kangaroo I've spoken to all day."

Susan solemnly addressed the furry brown kangaroo standing on her porch.

The kangaroo giggled, a warm, throaty sound. "He's not really talking. It's me."

"I see. And who are you?"

The kangaroo moved aside to reveal a little girl with dark eyes and shining brown hair. "I'm Emma," she said. "This is Gerald. He's three, just like me."

"I'm pleased to meet you, Emma. Where do you live?"

The little girl made a face. "We live in an ugly place with a dirty bathroom. But Daddy says we're going to live here now."

"Here?" Susan gazed at the child in astonishment.

Just then Mike Murphy moved out from behind the forsythia at the bottom of the steps and smiled at them. "Emma's my daughter," he said, coming up to stand beside the child, who slipped her hand into his and leaned against his leg.

Susan shook her head. "This really isn't fair," she muttered.

"I'm sorry," he said, looking decidedly unrepentant. "I thought I'd give it one more try. You said you wanted a female housemate and Emma qualifies...."

ABOUT THE AUTHOR

In *Man of My Dreams,* bestselling author Margot Dalton explores the world of dating services. "As a romance writer," she says, "I have always been curious about personal ads and dating services. People always seem so definite about the type of person they're looking for." Certainly, Susan, heroine of *Man of My Dreams,* has a clear picture of her ideal man. But, as often happens, that picture doesn't quite match the reality.

Margot Dalton has written thirteen Superromance novels and seven titles for the Crystal Creek series. She is now writing her first mainstream title in the category of women's fiction. Watch for *Tangled Lives* by Margot Dalton, available from MIRA Books in February 1996. Superromance readers can also look forward to upcoming titles from this talented author.

Note to Readers: Margot Dalton welcomes your letters and will try to answer each one personally. Letters can be sent to her c/o Harlequin Reader Service, P.O. Box 1397, Buffalo, NY 14240, U.S.A.

Books by Margot Dalton

HARLEQUIN SUPERROMANCE
558—ANOTHER WOMAN
576—ANGELS IN THE LIGHT
622—KIM & THE COWBOY
638—THE SECRET YEARS

Don't miss any of our special offers. Write to us at the following address for information on our newest releases.

Harlequin Reader Service
U.S.: 3010 Walden Ave., P.O. Box 1325, Buffalo, NY 14269
Canadian: P.O. Box 609, Fort Erie, Ont. L2A 5X3

Margot Dalton

MAN OF MY DREAMS

Harlequin Books

TORONTO • NEW YORK • LONDON
AMSTERDAM • PARIS • SYDNEY • HAMBURG
STOCKHOLM • ATHENS • TOKYO • MILAN
MADRID • WARSAW • BUDAPEST • AUCKLAND

ISBN 0-373-70664-2

MAN OF MY DREAMS

MAN OF
MY DREAMS

CHAPTER ONE

"I LIKE all kinds of sports, and I have quite a few hobbies, and I love listening to music, and..."

"Too general. Lick your lips."

"What?" Susan glared at the boy behind the video camera. He was wearing a baseball cap with a ragged ponytail hanging through the opening at the back, and a single long earring shaped like a cross.

"It looks sexier if you lick your lips so they shine a little. Like this."

Susan watched as he ran his tongue over his mouth, then gave her a damp, gap-toothed smile.

"You've got to be kidding," she said, thinking how much she'd like to wring her friend's neck for talking her into joining this video dating service. She looked over at the adjoining cubicle where Betty was making her tape. "Can we stop and check how my friend's doing?"

"Don't worry about her. We gotta get through this. Now, back to your interests. Try to be a little more specific, okay? Listening to music doesn't actually cut it."

"Specific? How?"

"Like for instance, you can say something like this. 'On a cold rainy night, I like to...'"

The boy leered at her and ducked behind the camera again, then gave her a stern glance over the viewfinder.

Susan sighed and began. "On a cold rainy night, I like to build a big fire in the fireplace, make a bowl of popcorn and curl up with a good book."

Her tormentor frowned and turned off the camera. "Not totally thrilling stuff," he commented sadly. "But then, I guess you're not in the market for a real exciting guy, are you?"

"Why would you say that?"

He gave her a pitying glance and consulted a file card. "High school English teacher, twenty-eight years old, who took French lessons for *fun* last year..."

Susan laughed. "Hey, don't make me sound like somebody's maiden aunt. Twenty-eight isn't ancient, you know. And I do other things for fun. I'm taking rock-climbing lessons this fall, and I play baseball during the summer in a teacher's league, and two years ago I went hiking and backpacking in the—"

"Okay, okay, I get the picture. Let's finish up by telling the people what kind of man you're looking for." He switched on the camera.

Susan turned back to face him. "What happens when you stop the camera and talk to me? Or when I make a mistake and have to start again?"

"We'll edit all of it," he said. "When you see the final tape, it'll be a flawless production, like you're a pro."

"I hate this whole thing. It wasn't my idea, you know. Betty dragged me down here."

The young camera operator gave her an impudent grin. "Yeah, sure she did."

"It's true! The idea of using a video dating service had never crossed my mind."

"Video dating is the only way to go," the boy said, frowning at a tape cartridge. "You have a chance to see what you're getting into before you commit yourself. Besides, you can learn a lot about a person in a ninety-second video."

"Yeah, right. This video isn't going to tell anybody a single thing about me that really matters."

"You'd be surprised," the boy said cryptically, vanishing behind the camera again. "Now, what kind of man are you looking for?"

Susan hesitated, not sure how to respond, while the camera operator made a series of impatient hand signals. "The kind of man I like..." She stopped and cleared her throat.

The teenager sighed and lifted his eyes heavenward in eloquent silence.

"Lick your lips."

Susan glared at him again, then began speaking, suddenly anxious to get the whole thing over with.

"I like powerful, boardroom kind of guys," she said. "Men in suits who...play raquetball on their lunch hour."

"Okay, now we're getting somewhere. This is the kind of stuff we want," the cameraman said approvingly. "What does he look like, this dream man of yours?"

"He's tall and strong, and very well-groomed. He wears custom-fitted suits and gets fifty-dollar haircuts." The boy gave a silent whistle and whipped his hand in a circle, gesturing her to continue.

"He's well educated and widely read, likes good music, probably has season tickets for the symphony and isn't ashamed to attend a ballet." Susan continued, beginning to get into the spirit of the thing. "But he also plays a competition-level game of tennis and he's a scratch golfer."

"And what do you want to say to him?"

"I beg your pardon?"

"The man of your dreams. He's watching your tape and deciding whether or not to call you. What do you want to tell him?"

Susan stared at the red light on the camera, seeing a man's confident, handsome face. "I want him to know..."

"Talk directly to him."

"I want you to know that I'm lonely," she murmured softly. "I want to tell you that I've been waiting a long time and I'm really anxious to meet you, because ... because there are so many things I'd love to share with you."

Horrified at her words, she stopped, feeling hot and embarrassed.

The boy gave her a casual smile and removed the tape from the camera. "Great. I'll have it edited in an hour or so. You wanna come back and check it before I start running it?"

"No!" Susan said too quickly. "I couldn't stand to look at it. Nobody's going to call, anyway," she added. "Not in a million years."

"Maybe not," the boy agreed, making her feel even worse. She wandered out to the reception area and sat down to wait for Betty.

"I'M GOING to kill you," Susan said coldly when they were driving toward her house. "First I'm going to kill you, and then I'm never going to speak to you again as long as I live."

Betty chuckled and gripped the steering wheel, apparently not at all troubled by these dark threats. "It's going to be fun," she said cheerfully. "Besides, why are you so worried?"

"I sounded like a complete idiot! You should have heard me. I was babbling."

"So what? These guys only have to look at you on the tape and they'll be falling all over themselves to get your phone number."

"Oh, sure," Susan muttered. "My phone is always ringing off the hook."

"You never let anybody know you're available, that's all. Look at you, kid. If I had that honey-blond hair, and those eyes, and that *figure*..."

"I probably should have mentioned that I'm intending to lose seven pounds this winter."

Betty laughed. "You've been intending to lose those seven pounds for the past five years at least, and you never do. Face it, Susie. You're perfect just the way you are."

"I wish I were like you. You could probably live on chocolate cheesecake and never gain an ounce."

Her friend seemed to run on stored energy, like a hummingbird. In fact, the two of them were an interesting study in contrasts. Betty was vivid, witty and quick-moving. She was tiny with bright dark eyes and a glossy black ponytail, while Susan's nature was more contemplative and gentle. She had a tall shapely figure, thick blond hair trimmed casually short, gold-flecked hazel eyes and a round, sweet face.

But despite their differences, she and Betty had been close friends for more than ten years.

"What kind of man did you say you wanted?" Susan asked, glancing again at Betty.

"I said it didn't really matter as long as his fingernails were clean. I can't stand a man who has dirty fingernails, can you? I also mentioned," Betty added, "that I like men with big ears. I think they have more generous personalities. They're better lovers, too."

Susan laughed. "You're great. You're just great, you know that?"

"I thought you were planning to kill me."

"I must admit the idea is often extremely tempting. Without you, my life would be much saner. Far more civilized and genteel."

"But?"

"But dull," Susan admitted. "Very dull."

Betty flashed a smile at her, then concentrated on her driving again. "How about you, Susie?"

"Hmm?"

"What kind of man did you say you wanted? Were you specific at all?"

"Pretty specific," Susan said. "And you know what? After I was finished, while I was waiting for you, I realized that the man I'd described was exactly like Jerry."

"No kidding. Now, isn't that interesting? You dumped Jerry, practically jilted him at the altar, and here you are looking for him all over again. We never learn, do we?"

"I can't help it," Susan said. "Men like Jerry are the only kind of men I'm attracted to. It's just that *he* wasn't right for me, that's all."

"I'll say he wasn't," Betty muttered, then fell silent as Susan gave her a warning glance. "Well, here we are," she announced, pulling up in front of an elegant old house fronted by a pair of enormous weeping willow trees, their long branches trailing gracefully onto the lawn.

Susan reached for the door handle. "Can you come in for a minute, Betts? I made a banana-nut bread this morning, and I have some—"

"What about those seven pounds?" Betty asked.

"I fully intend to lose that weight, you know. It's just that the world is so full of good things to eat."

Betty followed her up the walk to the backyard, pausing by the gate to pat a big golden retriever who galloped up to them with his tongue lolling and his head tilted cheerfully to one side.

"Hi, Buster," she said. "How are you? Chased any butterflies lately?"

"Buster's a very good watchdog," Susan said with dignity. "He barks at everything."

"Including baby strollers and best friends."

"So he isn't perfect. You're a good boy, aren't you, Buster?"

The dog whined in delight and ran in a tight circle, his tail waving erratically. Susan smiled at him, walked past a lilac hedge and unlocked the back door.

Betty followed her inside, looking around with pleasure at the old house. "I love this place," she said, sighing. "You're so lucky to own it, Susie."

"I own about two percent of it," Susan said dryly. "Last time I checked my equity, I owned the back door, the front steps and one of the hallway light fixtures. Everything else belongs to the bank."

"Whatever." Betty gave her an airy smile. "This is Vancouver, kid, the costliest housing market in the country. Nobody owns more than two percent of their house. You're probably lucky to have the light fixture."

With the ease of long familiarity, she went down the hallway and into the sunny kitchen where a freshly baked nut bread sat in its pan on a yellow gingham cloth. Plants crowded the windowsills and the kitchen sparkled with rainbows from a hanging prism in one of the tall windows opening into the backyard. The white curtains stirred quietly in a breeze that was gentle and mellow with the warmth of late summer.

"Oh, my, this smells delicious," Betty said. "I'll eat half of it, and you eat the other half. Quick, Susie, get the butter."

Susan moved across the room to fill the kettle while Betty rummaged idly through a pile of books and papers on the table.

"Thank God for Saturday, right?" she said. "How do your classes look this year?"

"My timetable seems pretty good. Mostly grade ten English, and I really like that. There's a big emphasis on literature and writing in the tenth grade. But I haven't seen any of the kids yet, you know. We don't have our first class until Tuesday."

"Teaching high school would be a great job," Betty commented, looking greedily at the slices of nut bread that Susan placed on the table, "if it weren't for the kids."

"Isn't that funny?" Susan sat opposite her friend and reached for a slice of bread. "I feel the same about your students. I can't imagine anybody, let alone *you*, having the patience to teach first grade. Those little kids have the attention span of a mosquito."

"That's what I like about them. We never get bored with one another. Susie, this stuff is delicious! It's like heaven."

"Thank you." Susan looked wistfully at the plate. "And also about a thousand calories a slice."

"When did you start getting all concerned about calories, anyway? Remember in college, when we practically lived on chocolate shakes and fries?"

"*You* did." Susan smiled, remembering. "Although I could afford to eat like that sometimes, too. I was on the track team in those days, running the ten thousand-meter."

"There's not a thing wrong with your figure, Susie. You look great."

"Jerry always wanted me to lose a few—"

"Don't tell me! If you tell me, I'll just get mad and say really nasty things. Like, do you remember the way he used to..."

"Betty, don't. I hate talking about him now that he's ... now that we're not together anymore."

"I don't know why we let men do this to us." Betty got up to fetch the steaming kettle along with a couple of mugs. "We give them our undivided attention, submerge our tastes for theirs, endure their nasty personal attacks and then enshrine their memories after they're gone. It's crazy."

Susan accepted a cup of coffee and patted her friend's arm. "Look, give me a break. I went with you and made your damn video, didn't I? Even though I hated the whole idea?"

Betty's face softened. "Yeah, I guess you did. Hey, Susie," she added, brightening, "how soon do you think they'll start calling?"

"I don't think anybody's going to call." Susan stirred powdered milk into her coffee. "What kind of person uses a video dating service, anyway?"

"Us," Betty said.

The two friends looked at each other and laughed.

"You probably have three calls waiting on your machine already," Susan told her.

"It can't happen *that* fast, dummy. For one thing, they don't give out any phone numbers until we've seen the guy's video and given the okay."

"Really? I'm not even sure how it works."

"Didn't the kid tell you?"

"I didn't pay much attention to what he said," Susan confessed. "I was too busy worrying that he might turn out to be one of my students."

Betty laughed. "Don't worry, I saw him. He's at least nineteen."

"So are quite a few of my students."

"The way it works," Betty went on, "is this. A guy comes in, checks the card and picks you as a good prospect. The service lets him watch your video and if he likes you, they pull his video and call you down to watch it. Then if you approve of him, they call you and arrange a contact. It's all very safe and secure."

"And completely terrifying. Betty, did you know there are more than a hundred teachers at my school, and half of them are men?"

"Yeah? So what?"

"What if one of those guys uses the same service and happens to see my video?"

"Maybe you'll get together," Betty said comfortably. "Would that be so bad?"

"I'd be so embarrassed if he told everybody in the staff room, and people found out that I..."

"What? Found out that you're lonely and want to meet someone? There's nothing sinful about being lonely, Susie. Almost everybody I know is lonely." Betty gazed at her earnestly. "Look at you. You're twenty-eight and beautiful, and the nicest person I've ever met. You live all alone in this big old place except for Buster out there, and I bet you haven't had a serious date in two years since Jerry left. Is it so bad to want to meet someone and share a bit of your life?"

Susan shook her head. "I guess not," she said in a low voice.

"Damn right it isn't," Betty said. "What are you doing tomorrow?"

"Painting the fence in the backyard. I want to finish it while the weather's nice. How about you?"

"I'm taking Connie down to Bellingham to do some shopping and get her mind off things. She's having another crisis."

Susan grinned, thinking about Betty's younger sister. The two of them shared an apartment in Burnaby, and Connie regularly went through crises involving men, heartrending emotional problems that Betty endured with surprising patience.

"You're a good person, Betty," she said gently. "You're always doing nice things for people."

"I'm okay," Betty said with a placid smile, gathering up her handbag and sunglasses. "Call me Tuesday and tell me what your classes are like, okay?"

"All right. Give my love to Connie. Hey, tell her she should take up needlework. Or rock climbing."

"Maybe both."

"If Connie ever gets her life straightened out, you could come and live here with me. I'd really love that."

"Oh, sure," Betty said. "And I'd have to drive twenty miles to work every day, and cross the Second Narrows Bridge at rush hour . . ."

"You could get a job over here in North Van, couldn't you?"

"No way. I like my school. Everybody's a little crazy over there. It suits me fine."

Susan smiled at her. "I posted an ad in the staff room yesterday, asking for a housemate. There seem to be a lot of new women on staff this year, so maybe somebody will be interested." She sighed, looking around at the gracious old house. "I could sure use a little help with the mortgage now that interest rates are going up again."

"Ah, the joys of being a homeowner. I think I'll stick with Connie. She's just annoying *some* of the time." Betty paused in the doorway. "If the dating service calls you," she said, "don't you dare go down there without me."

"I wouldn't think of it," Susan assured her.

She followed her friend to the door and watched as Betty ran down the walk to her car and drove off in a swirl of leaves. Then she wandered back inside, wrapped the nut bread and put it away, snipped a couple of dead blossoms from the geranium in the window and watched Buster chasing butterflies across the yard.

THE BIG high school was in the thick of opening-day confusion. Everyone seemed to be running around shouting questions to which nobody had any answers.

"Where's the *gym?*"

"Who knows? That other place is full of guys in hard hats, knocking out walls. Hey, man, do you know where the gym is?"

"Where's the freshmen orientation class? Where's the math office? Where's the women's bathroom? Where do I get my textbooks? Where do I get a deferral on my student fees? Where do I get my timetable changed? Hey, where do we..."

"Who's handing out the lockers?"

"I am." Susan pushed her hair back from her forehead with a weary gesture. "Don't you have one yet?"

"Yes, but I don't like it. My locker's next to that creep over there, and I can't stand him. He keeps staring at me. I want to be moved."

Susan looked at the girl standing by her desk. She was wearing a skintight black bodysuit, a red leather miniskirt and short black lace-up boots.

"You're a beautiful girl, Lynnette," Susan said, aware that the other students were waiting for her response. "The thing is, when something attractive is displayed, you really can't be surprised if people look."

The girl's face softened. "Beautiful?" she echoed. "Hey, Teacher, you think I'm beautiful?"

"My name is Miss Adamson. And yes, Lynnette, I think you're very beautiful. I think you should take your locker assignment and ignore your neighbors."

"Right on," a boy murmured approvingly as Lynnette accepted her combination lock with scarlet-tipped nails, tossed her head loftily and swayed off in her dainty boots.

"Yo, Teach," another boy said, looking at Susan with interest.

"Miss Adamson," she said calmly. "My name is Miss Adamson. Please get used to it, or *your* name will be mud."

"Hey, Mud," one of his friends said, chuckling and elbowing him. "Hey, Mud, you're looking slimy today."

"Miss Adamson," the first boy went on, standing wide-eyed and innocent next to her desk. Susan measured him with practiced ease, instantly recognizing him as the class clown and troublemaker. This boy could be a thorn in her side for the whole term if she didn't handle him properly from the outset.

"Yes, Jason?" she asked, frowning as she sorted through the piles of locker sheets and textbook rental lists.

He moved closer, looking interested. "Hey, how'd you know my name already? You haven't even called attendance yet."

"Your fame," Susan said, "has preceded you."

"No kidding." The boy grinned at his friends, clearly delighted. He looked back at Susan. "Hey, Miss Adamson, you smoke a lot, right?"

She looked up in surprise. "I've never smoked. Why do you ask?"

"Well, look at all them nicotine stains on your fingers. It looks bad, Miss Adamson. Real bad."

She glanced down at her hands, still covered with brownish stains around the nails even after diligent scrubbing.

"I was... I was painting the fence in my backyard yesterday," she said, briefly taken aback. "It's really hard to wash that stuff off."

"Yeah, right," the clown said, laughing noisily. "Painting a fence. That's the story they all tell when they get up to three packs a day."

The rest of Susan's English class straggled in and began to settle in their desks, obviously interested in the conversation between her and Jason. She got up and moved around the desk, standing in front of the class in a soft flowered dress that hung loosely on her tall body.

"Hey, Miss Adamson," Jason went on, "I heard you used to be some kind of track star back in college. Right?"

"I was on the team," Susan said. "Do all of you have your English texts with you?"

"And you run here on the track every morning before school, right?"

Susan sighed. "That's been my habit," she said. "Why do you ask, Jason?"

"Well, I used to run a real fast three thousand meters at my old school," the boy told her. "Now that you're a heavy smoker, Miss Adamson, I bet I could take you. How about tomorrow morning?"

"Jason, I have no desire to compete with you in a race. I've been just a recreational runner for years now."

"Yeah, I know. Ever since you started smoking, right?"

Susan knew this was an important moment. The other students were listening with breathless interest, their eyes turning from the grinning boy to their new teacher at the front of the room.

"It's an open track," Susan said at last, moving back to her desk and picking up a textbook. "I suppose that anybody who shows up can use it in the morning. Including you, Jason."

The girls cheered as Susan flipped through the book. Many of the boys, too, gave her private smiles and small thumbs-up signs.

Susan wondered if Jason was really a competitive runner. She remembered his name on the list of freshman candidates for the track team, but she was also fairly sure she'd seen the boy during the summer, smoking with his friends in front of a downtown hangout...

Finally, she put Jason's challenge out of her mind and prepared to read from the text.

"This is the 'Lady of Shallot,' by Alfred Lord Tennyson," she told the class. "It's one of my favorite poems. While I read, I want you to listen to the flow and rhythm of the words and then tell me what you think the story is about."

She began to read, thrilled as always by the beauty of Tennyson's words and images...

"All in the blue unclouded weather
Thick-jewelled shone the saddle-leather
The helmet and the helmet-feather
Burned like one burning flame together
As he rode down to Camelot . . ."

The sun glimmered through the window blinds, and insects drowsed and hummed at the sills. Students listened to the poetry, their faces displaying a full range of emotions: interest, boredom, bewilderment, tiredness and pleasure.

Near the front, Lynnette buffed her scarlet nails and gazed at the teacher with shy adoration. A few rows behind her, Jason slouched in his desk with folded arms and watched Susan, a faint smile on his face.

Somebody coughed, somebody dropped a book, somebody giggled and fell abruptly silent. Feet scraped, books shifted, chair legs were dragged across the floor.

A new school year at Whittier High had begun.

"GOOD CLASSES, Susie?"

Susan nodded, sipping a carton of orange juice and sorting through a pile of student record sheets. "Not bad. What are we supposed to do with these? Does the office want them back, or do we keep them with our files, or what?"

Allan Hamilton, one of the math teachers, leaned over to look at her papers. "Oh, those. We fill them out and give them to Gloria, and then we get issued with duplicates."

"It's different every year, isn't it? Why can't we ever develop one system and then stick with it?"

"Because that, my dear, would not be a proper bureaucracy." Peg Smith, the girls' physical education teacher, crossed the staff room in a pair of shorts and a white sweatshirt, munching on an apple. "Hey, Susie, what's this I hear about you challenging Jason Caine to eight circuits tomorrow morning?"

Susan held up her hands, displaying the stains around her fingernails. "He challenged me. Said he could probably beat me now that I'm a heavy smoker."

"No kidding. What a little brat." Peg shook her head in amazement. "So, what did you tell him?"

Susan shrugged. "I said it was an open track. What else could I do?"

The other teachers looked at her with evident enjoyment. "Can we all come and watch?" one of them asked.

"Better not," Allan said. "He's going to be humiliated enough, the poor boy. Susie just wants to teach him a lesson, not destroy him."

"She's so soft," Peg said.

"It's part of my charm." Susan gathered up her books from the worktable, waved to her colleagues and left, hurrying through the crowded halls and out to the parking lot.

THE MESSAGE LIGHT was blinking on her phone when she came in, and Buster whined outside the back door, informing her that his water dish was empty. Susan dumped her books on the hall console, hung up her sweater and pushed the message button.

"Miss Adamson, this is Melanie from Sweet Dreams Video Dating. We just had a customer watch your video and he really liked it, so could you call and make some arrangements to see his video? Thank you.''

Susan looked at the phone, feeling sudden panic. "Dammit, Betty," she muttered. "Sometimes ... I'm coming! Buster, be quiet!" she shouted as the dog's pleas escalated into an uproar.

Just as she started toward the back door, the front doorbell rang.

Susan paused, looked toward the kitchen, then went down the hall to the front door. She opened it and blinked in the afternoon light.

A man stood on the front porch, the sun's rays surrounding him in a halo of misted gold. But this man looked anything but angelic. He wore dirty blue jeans, a gray plaid shirt with a rip in one sleeve and heavy work boots with the laces untied. His face was lean and tanned, with a square jaw and the bluest eyes she'd ever seen. They contrasted startlingly with his sun-browned skin. His dark hair was long and untidy, curling down onto his collar, and his face and hands gave evidence of having been hastily and inadequately scrubbed.

He smiled, teeth flashing white in his tanned face. "Miss Adamson?" he asked. "Susan Adamson?"

Susan hesitated, increasingly distracted by the racket that Buster was making in the backyard. "Yes, that's me," she said. "What can I do for you?"

"I saw your ad a little while ago," he said. "It was so perfect, I couldn't wait to call you. I just came right over."

CHAPTER TWO

SUSAN'S MOUTH dropped open. "My... my ad?" she faltered. "You're the one who... you saw my..."

"Yeah." He smiled at her with warm speculation. "I think you've got exactly what I'm looking for, Susan. Pretty much all my dreams come true."

Susan looked at his soiled clothes, his sweat-dampened hair and the spot of dirt on his neck. "But there has to be... I mean, this is some kind of mistake. I specifically mentioned that I..."

He began to look concerned. "There's no mistake." He reached into his shirt pocket and consulted a scrap of paper with some penciled markings. "Susan Adamson, 920 Birch Drive. That's you, right?"

"But I can't believe..." Susan's head whirled. How could the people at the dating service have made such an appalling mistake? More important, what was she supposed to do about it?

"Can't believe what?" he asked.

"That they... they gave you my address. I mean, they're supposed to call me first and ask me if I want to..."

His eyes rested on her with thoughtful appraisal. "Your address was on the ad you posted," he told her.

"It was not!" Susan protested. "I didn't even give my phone number! I just talked about my hobbies and interests, and the . . . the kind of man I . . ."

He grinned suddenly, a lopsided sparkling smile that made her feel even more unsettled.

"I think," he murmured, "that maybe we're talking about two different things here. I saw your ad on the bulletin board in the high school staff room, asking for a housemate. That's why I'm here."

Susan stared at him, openmouthed, her face and body turning hot with embarrassment.

His eyes danced with a teasing glint. "So how about it?" he asked. "Can I have a look at the house?"

"No!" Susan said, then shifted awkwardly on her feet. "I'm sorry, Mr. . . . ?"

"Murphy," he said, extending a hand. "My name's Mike Murphy."

Susan shook his hand reluctantly, almost wincing at the strength of his callused grip. "Well, Mr. Murphy," she said, trying to recapture some of her dignity, "if I'm not mistaken, I believe I specifically mentioned in my ad that I was looking for a female housemate."

"That's unconstitutional," he said placidly. "You're not allowed to specify gender in an advertisement, so I just ignored it."

Susan examined him with sudden suspicion. "What were you doing in the staff room? Are you a teacher?"

"No," he said. "I'm on the construction crew working on the new gym. I went to the staff room for water to make coffee, and read the ads on the board while I waited for the kettle to boil."

"Well, I'm afraid I'm not able to—"

"What's wrong with that dog?"

"He's thirsty. He wants his water dish filled."

"Then let's fill it, okay? I hate to hear an animal suffering like that."

Susan watched in alarm as the man moved past her into the house and strode down the hall in the direction of Buster's mournful howls. After a moment's hesitation she turned and hurried after him.

"Hey, boy," the man said, opening the back door and smiling at Buster, who barked a couple of times, sniffed the stranger's denim-clad leg and then pressed forward to lick his hand.

"Good boy," the man said approvingly, fondling the big dog's ears. "I like golden retrievers," he said to Susan, who was unrolling the hose to fill the water dish. "I had a dog just like this when I was a kid."

"He's not really much of a watchdog," Susan said, watching as Buster fawned on the stranger again, then galloped toward her to lap noisily at his dish.

"Sure he is. He's just a good judge of character, that's all."

"Look, Mr. Murphy, I—"

"Mike. Do I look like a guy who should be called mister?"

"No, I guess not," Susan said.

He smiled, apparently untroubled by the edge to her voice, and strolled around the yard to examine the hydrangea bushes, the tidy flower beds and trimmed lawn. Finally, he squinted up at the rear facade of the big, old clapboard house, eyeing the gingerbread moldings with approval.

"It's in really good shape," he told Susan. "How old is the house?"

"It's Edwardian," Susan said, warming slightly. She loved hearing people praise the house. "It was built around 1908."

"How's the roof?"

"Not great. It leaks in a couple of places. I'll probably have to get it repaired before winter."

"I'll do it for you," Mike offered. "Just let me move in, and I'll look after all that stuff."

"I can't possibly let you move in," Susan said.

"Why not?"

Susan took a deep breath. "Because it's a...a roommate situation."

He raised an eyebrow and gave her a lazy grin, which she ignored.

"I mean," she went on, "there's a couple of rooms upstairs and a private bath, but we'd have to share the entrance, the laundry facilities and the kitchen. I'm sorry, it's just not possible."

"I'm a terrific guy to share a kitchen with," Murphy said. "I'm compulsively neat. I even label shelves and rotate leftovers."

In spite of herself, Susan glanced at his dirty hands.

He smiled, unruffled. "I've been working hard all day, Susan. We're knocking out walls and hauling away junk, getting ready to build the new gym. It's not a nice clean job like teaching school."

"Look, Mr. Murphy..."

"Mike."

"Look, Mike, I'm very sorry about this misunderstanding, but I don't want you to move into my house, and I'm afraid that's the end of it. Now, if you don't mind..."

She walked around the house toward the front, motioning him to follow.

But Murphy stood near the hydrangeas, patting Buster who had trotted over to stand beside him. "What happened to your last housemate?" he asked.

She paused and looked at him in surprise.

"Did you have somebody sharing the house with you before?"

Susan felt suddenly chilled, though the sun was still warm. She hesitated, rubbing her arms in the slanting afternoon light.

"Not for... I've lived alone here for two years. I just... things are kind of hard now," she murmured. "I need some help with the mortgage payments and there's a lot more room upstairs than I need, so I thought..."

"What happened two years ago?" he persisted, his blue eyes fixed on her with steady interest.

"I was... living with someone. A man. We were about to be married, and we bought the house together."

"And then what?"

Susan looked away from him to the vivid blue of the hydrangea blossoms, a color that was, she realized absently, quite similar to Mike Murphy's eyes. "I broke it off."

"Why?"

"I got scared at the last minute," she said in a low voice, wondering why she felt compelled to answer the man's questions. "I just didn't want to go through with it. But there were still a lot of expenses to cover."

"What was his name?"

"Jerry Samuel."

"And what does Jerry do?"

"He's a stockbroker. He moved to Toronto last year."

"I see." Mike bent and picked up a twig from the lawn, threw it and watched as Buster galloped happily across the yard to pick it up. "Didn't good old Jerry feel that he should help with the expenses?"

"Since I was the one who canceled the wedding," Susan told him, "Jerry felt that it was my responsibility to pay for it."

"So he moved out and left you with all that expense, plus the mortgage payments. That's why you're looking for a housemate now?"

She turned away to open the latch on the gate.

"Look, Susan," he said with sudden earnestness. "Let me move in upstairs, and I promise you'll never regret it. I'll be unobtrusive and easy to get along with. I'll fix everything that needs fixing. I'll pay right on time every month and I won't interfere with your personal life in any way. Please, just give me a chance."

Susan almost wavered when she heard the powerful intensity of his plea. She had a sudden wistful image of what it would be like to have a man around the house, tending to loose shingles and broken eaves troughs, coming downstairs at night to check when there were suspicious noises . . .

"I'm afraid not," she said, pulling herself back to reality with an effort. "I'm afraid it just isn't possible. I'm sorry."

She moved forward with decisive steps, held the gate open and watched as he passed through it to stop on the other side.

He turned and looked at her with frank speculation, staring so intently that Susan began to feel uneasy. At last he shook his head.

"That other ad you talked about," he began. "It
was a dating service, right? There's sure something
wrong with the world when a woman like you has to
use a dating service to find a boyfriend."

Susan's cheeks flamed. "Look, I don't care what
you think! I'm not..."

But he was already walking away from her, striding
across the street to his dusty pickup truck.

STUDENTS MILLED and shouted around the quarter-
mile track early the next morning. They cheered wildly
as Susan arrived in a navy blue warm-up suit, carrying her gym bag. Jason strutted into view a few moments later, surrounded by a solemn group of cohorts
who formed an impromptu honor guard. He wore
surfing clothes—a brilliantly dyed tank top, baggy
knee-length shorts made of burlap tied with string,
high-top runners and a bandanna around his head.
The boy's tanned body was skinny but his legs looked
muscular.

"Yo, *Teach!*" he called impudently, catching sight
of Susan near the fence. "Ready to be totally humiliated, you poor nicotine fiend?"

Susan looked at him calmly. "I'm ready for my
morning run, Jason. Same as always."

As she'd done hundreds of times before races, she
stripped off her warm-ups to reveal a white silk running suit emblazoned with the red and gold of the
University of Calgary track team. She handed her
jogging pants and sweatshirt to Lynnette, still in her

leather miniskirt and lace top, who was apparently acting as cheerleader and wardrobe mistress.

A slight, dark-haired young man, a little older than the high school students, stood at the edge of the track with his hands in his pockets, watching Lynnette. Susan glanced at him, then at the girl.

"Who's that fellow in the black jacket, Lynnette? Is he your boyfriend?"

Lynnette's cheeks turned pink. She murmured something, her voice so low that Susan leaned closer to hear.

"His name's Danny Clammer," the girl said. "He drives a cab at the taxi stand where I work nights."

"Why is he here?"

Lynnette shrugged. "He wanted to watch the race, I guess."

"That's not all he's watching."

"He just gives me a ride to school sometimes in his cab," Lynnette protested. "He doesn't *like* me or anything."

Susan glanced at the young man again. He had a shy, pleasant face, and his expression when he looked at Lynnette bordered on worship.

"Could have fooled me," she whispered, causing the girl to blush even more furiously.

Finally, Susan fitted a white headband in place over her hair and moved onto the curving track, taking a position on the outside in one of the forward blocks used for the sprints. She nodded back at Jason and waited for the starting call. The boy grinned and blew a cheery kiss, which Susan ignored, though she couldn't help smiling.

"On your marks. Get set. Go!"

Jason exploded from the blocks like a cheetah, pounding off down the cinder track in a blur of neon orange and green. Susan let him go, settling into a steady long-legged stride that ate up the distance. Students from other classes, hearing about the fun, had wandered over and were positioned around the circular track, shouting insults and encouragement.

"Miss Adamson, he's blowing you away. Pick it up, lady! Don't let him beat you!"

"Hey, Jason, she's right on your tail, man. She's eating up your sneakers! Give it some gas."

"Go, Teach, go! Jason Caine, he don't know spit about running. He just thinks he's so great."

Jason finished the first two circuits about fifty paces ahead of her, but Susan was fairly pleased with the progress of the race. At the reckless speed her opponent was maintaining, he'd probably be tired by the last few laps, while she was still holding a lot of energy in reserve.

She settled into her running form, loving the way the wind mingled with the shouts of the students and the world flashed by in a whirling kaleidoscope of color. Her lungs filled and expanded, her heart pumped strongly and power flowed into her legs, carrying her forward with so little effort that she might have been flying.

It was one of her favorite sensations.

On the seventh lap, she finally began drawing closer to Jason who was breathing raggedly, his face red and mottled. He cast her a terrified glance as she closed the gap, then tried to smile over his shoulder.

"Saving some kick . . . for the end," he gasped.

Susan gave him a brief nod of encouragement, settling down to run for a few paces behind him. He was stronger than she'd thought, and she had to admire his spirit. Especially when she could see how much effort it took for him to maintain his pace.

Several of the onlookers tooted bicycle horns to mark the bell lap, and Susan surged past Jason to move into the lead. The shouts grew into a roar. Susan glanced back at Jason, still running doggedly behind her. She was a little concerned by his ghastly color and uneven pace, but it was clear that he intended to finish the race.

She crossed the finish line and stood running in place for a while, then bent to grip her knees and breathed deeply as she cooled down. Jason floundered to the end and collapsed on the grass, moaning pitifully.

Lynnette hurried up, carrying Susan's warm-up suit and bag. The girl's young admirer seemed to have vanished, but Lynnette glowed with pride and excitement. Susan walked with her to the group of boys attending their fallen comrade.

"Are you okay, Jason?" she asked, kneeling to examine his pinched nostrils, his scarlet face and blue-tinged lips.

"Fine," he gasped, trying to smile. "Just...fine. Let's run it...again. I'll win...next time."

Susan laughed and ruffled his damp hair. "You're pretty good, Jason," she said. "If you ever decide to quit smoking and go out for track, I'd be glad to be your faculty sponsor, okay? I think you've got championship quality."

She went back and stepped into her warm-up suit, took her gym bag and started off toward the school, smiling as a lusty cheer went up behind her.

Less than twelve minutes on the quarter-mile track, Susan thought, and she'd probably have no trouble with these students in English class for the rest of the year. Not such a bad investment.

As she neared the school, she suddenly became aware of a well-built man in jeans, work shirt and a yellow hard hat who had apparently been standing near the edge of the field, watching the event. By now, Susan was close enough to recognize Mike Murphy's blue eyes and teasing smile. He raised his lunch box to her in an admiring salute and called something, but she hurried across the student parking lot and through a side door before he could approach her.

"*FOUR GUYS?*" Susan said in disbelief, cradling the receiver against her shoulder while she searched for money to pay the paperboy.

It was later the same day, but with all the tumult and confusion of school opening, her race with Jason already seemed to be lost in the distant past.

"Look, that's all I've got," Susan said to the boy, adding a dollar to the pile. "I'll give you a double tip next week, Jody. What?" she said into the phone, watching as the boy clattered down the steps with obvious good cheer.

"Who are you talking to?" Betty asked on the other end of the line.

"My paperboy. Now, you said *four* guys have watched your video and want to meet you?"

"Yep. And apparently you've got a couple of interesting prospects, too. So let's go down there now, okay? You doing anything?"

"Not really," Susan said, "but I'm not dressed or anything, Betty. In fact, I'm wearing my oldest khaki shorts and my Mickey Mouse T-shirt, the one with the hole in the—"

"We're not dining at the Sheraton, kiddo. We're just watching a few videos. What does it matter how you look? Now, I have to drop Connie at her gym so I'll meet you over at the dating service in an hour. Say, about eight o'clock?"

"Fine," Susan murmured, with the futile sense of being steamrolled that was always part of life with her friend. Susan had long since discovered that it was easiest just to relax and let Betty's plans flow over her. Things tended to be less painful that way.

Still, she couldn't forget the sting of Mike Murphy's parting words the previous evening, when he'd questioned out loud why a woman like Susan would need to use a dating service.

She wondered the same thing. But it seemed so hard to meet a nice man, someone who shared her tastes and understood her feelings. Susan didn't think she was unduly demanding, and yet the men she encountered were all so completely wrong, so incompatible in every way that she was seldom interested in a second date.

Not that she believed the men from the dating service were going to be any different, in spite of Betty's optimism.

The doorbell rang, startling her as she stood brooding in the hallway.

Susan glanced at her watch, went to open the door and stood gazing blankly into emptiness.

"Hello," a husky voice said from somewhere around her knees. Susan looked down and saw that she was being addressed by a furry brown kangaroo with bright eyes and a bland smile.

"Hello," she said solemnly. "You're the first kangaroo I've talked to all day."

The kangaroo giggled, a warm, throaty sound in the quiet evening. "He's not really *talking*. It's me."

"I see. And who are you?"

The kangaroo moved aside to reveal a little girl with big dark eyes and shining brown hair falling in a smooth cap to her eyebrows and the nape of her neck. She was wearing a clean pink T-shirt, flowered shorts and socks that were dazzling in their whiteness.

"I'm Emma," the little girl said. "This is Gerald," she added, holding up the kangaroo. "He's three, just like me."

"Is he? My goodness, he's big for three," Susan said, wondering which of her neighbors this enchanting little girl belonged to.

"I know," Emma said solemnly. "He eats carrots and cereal."

"Those are very healthy foods for Gerald. Where do you live, Emma?"

The little girl made a face. "We live in an ugly place with a dirty bathroom. But Daddy says we're going to live here now, and that's nice because there's a yard and flowers and it's all clean."

"You're going to live *here*?"

A man moved out from behind the forsythia at the bottom of the steps and stood smiling up at them.

"Sorry," he said, looking distinctly unrepentant.

Again Susan was taken aback by the startling blue of Mike Murphy's eyes and the easy confidence of his smile. But the man looked different tonight. He was as clean and neat as the little girl on the veranda, wearing a fresh white shirt and faded jeans, with his dark hair shining.

Gradually, the reality of the situation began to dawn on her. "You're . . . this is . . ."

"My daughter," he said, coming up the steps to stand beside Emma, who slipped her hand into his and leaned against his leg.

Susan shook her head. "This isn't fair," she muttered. "This really isn't fair."

"Sorry," he said again. "I thought I'd give it one more try since you said you wanted a female housemate, and Emma qualifies."

"Look, Mike, I really can't—"

"Do you know how hard it is?" he asked with sudden intensity, leaning toward her. "Do you have any idea what it's like to look after a little kid under the conditions we're living in? All I could find is a single room in a place that's just about one step up from a shelter. I'm afraid to let Emma go to the bathroom alone because we share it with three other tenants and I'm not sure what they do for a living."

Susan's head whirled. She looked at the hard planes of the man's face, then down at the quiet little girl who stood next to him clutching her stuffed toy.

"Daddy says there's a big dog that lives here," the child ventured, her eyes fixed on Susan's face. "And there's a magic thing in the kitchen that makes rainbows."

Susan nodded with a growing sense of helplessness. She looked back at the man, trying to think. "There are two bedrooms and a little sitting room upstairs," she said. "And a full bath and a small alcove with a hot plate and a bar fridge. But it's certainly not equipped for making or serving meals, and there's no private entrance . . ."

"I'll take it," he said instantly.

"Look, you haven't even seen the rooms. We haven't discussed price or terms or anything."

He raised an eyebrow and smiled. "Well, let's look at the rooms, shall we? And then we can discuss terms, if that's what you want."

Susan stepped aside and watched as Mike Murphy and his daughter entered the house.

"Look, Daddy!" Emma said, gazing around in delight. "Look how nice it is, and there's stairs going up to a colored place in the sky!"

Susan and Mike stood together in silence, looking up at the stained-glass window on the landing. Fading rays of sunlight streamed through the glass, scattering bright fragments on the landing and the gleaming oak stairs.

Emma started upward, clutching her toy kangaroo. She paused near the landing, tense with excitement, and looked back at her father.

"It's okay, honey," he said in a gentle voice. "We're right behind you."

Susan walked up the stairs next to him, watching Emma's white socks and flowered shorts as the child edged onto the landing.

Emma stopped and gazed at the stained glass for a moment, then continued her climb. "It's got flowers on the walls!'' she reported to her father from the top of the stairs. ''And pretty curtains. Oh, and look at the little room! Daddy, can this be my room?''

''We have to wait and let Susan decide,'' he called to his daughter. ''It's her house, Emma. She gets to say who lives here.''

''A little late in the day to be telling her that, isn't it?'' Susan muttered.

Mike smiled. ''You won't regret it,'' he told Susan. ''I'm really a clean, handy kind of guy, you know, and Emma's a good little kid. We won't cause you any problems.''

''But I...'' Susan fell silent, watching as Mike went into the room where his daughter stood by a small ruffled bed, tucking her kangaroo under the covers.

''You go to sleep now, Gerald, and pretty soon I'll come to bed with you,'' the child crooned. ''I just have to see the big dog and the rainbow thing, and then I'll be—''

''Sweetheart, we're not staying here tonight,'' Mike said quietly, stroking her hair. ''I have to talk to Susan about things. And even if we do move here, it won't be for a while.''

Emma looked up at him, her eyes filling with tears. ''I don't want to go back to that other place, Daddy!'' she whispered passionately. ''The bathroom smells, and there's bugs, and Gerald gets really scared at night. We want to live here!''

Susan looked at the tears rolling down Emma's cheeks and her heart melted. She knelt and put her hands on the little girl's shoulders. ''You can live here, dear,'' she said gently. ''Your daddy and I will make the arrangements and you can move in here just as soon as we get things worked out.''

She got to her feet, avoiding Mike Murphy's bright glance, and moved out into the hallway. "This is the other bedroom,'' she said, indicating a larger room with a braided oval rug and a window seat in an alcove draped with yellow chintz to match the bedspread. "And here's the bathroom, with one of those big old cast-iron tubs, and this is the—''

"Where's your room?''

"Downstairs.''

"Look, Susan, I'm sorry to push you into a corner like this.'' Mike touched her shoulder. "I really am. But I'm desperate for a place to live, and I promise you won't regret it.''

Susan looked up at him, unsettled by his nearness and the warm sincerity in his eyes. "I hope not,'' she muttered. "I sure hope not.''

"SO HE'S GOT a little kid?'' Betty leaned toward her with breathless interest.

Susan nodded gloomily. They were sitting in the reception area at the dating service, surrounded by artificial plants and posters depicting romantic, faraway places.

"Yes, apparently he does. I had no idea, Betty. He certainly never mentioned a child when he came the first time.''

"So when are they moving in?''

"Tomorrow night,'' Susan said, nervously fingering the strap on her handbag. "The place he's in now,'' she added with a bleak smile, "doesn't exactly sound like the kind of situation where you have to give a month's notice.''

"I can't believe you're being so impulsive. You, of all people, actually letting a stranger move into your house without running a two-month security check on him.''

"He has references,'' Susan told her. "He gave me phone numbers from his last two jobs, and the place they were living in Calgary before he moved here, and Emma's day-care supervisor.''

"Emma's day-care supervisor,'' Betty echoed in wonder. "Truly amazing. So, kid, where will Emma go for day care after she moves into your house?''

"There's a day care at the school,'' Susan said. "Mostly for the children of teachers and students, but other employees can use it, too. It will be ideal for Emma because Mike's crew is going to be working on the new gym for quite a while.''

"What happened to Emma's mother?'' Betty asked.

"It's a sad story. They must have been married quite young, because Mike can't be more than my age and Emma's almost four. Her mother was killed in an accident when Emma was just a few months old.''

"What kind of accident?''

"A bus crash. She was on her way to Montana to visit her sister. The bus skidded on an icy patch in the highway and went over an embankment.''

Betty looked shaken. "Was Emma with her?''

Susan nodded. "I didn't ask Mike too much about it, because I could tell he didn't want to talk about the accident in front of Emma. Apparently, his wife died instantly but Emma was found on a snowbank about a hundred yards away from the bus, still wrapped in her blanket, hardly even bruised.''

"God,'' Betty muttered. "The poor guy. What's he like, Susie?''

Susan frowned, trying to think how to describe Mike Murphy. "He's sort of...good-looking,'' she said at last. "In a shaggy, diamond-in-the-rough kind of way, you know? But he's annoying, too. He has this confident swagger, and he always looks as if he's enjoying some kind of private joke. He seems really...''

"You're falling for him,'' Betty announced smugly.

"I am *not!*'' she said.

"He's good-looking, right?''

"Sort of.''

"And masculine, and confident, and he tugs at your heartstrings because he has this cute little kid and you're a sucker for kids and animals.''

"That doesn't mean I'm attracted to the man. He's absolutely not my type.''

"What do you mean, not your type?''

"Just what I said. When he first came to the house, and I thought the dating service had sent him over, I couldn't believe they'd made such a ridiculous mistake,'' Susan told her. "The man was so completely *not* what I wanted, it was almost funny.''

"Adamson?'' a girl asked, pausing in the doorway with a clipboard. "Susan Adamson? And Betty Morrell?''

"That's us,'' Betty said cheerfully. "Come on, Susie, let's see what kind of terrific guys they've found for us.''

Susan followed the girl to a viewing cubicle, while Betty vanished down the hallway with another employee.

"This is the easy part, Miss Adamson," the girl said. "All you have to do is watch their videos and decide if you like them. No pressure."

Susan smiled gratefully and seated herself in a chair facing a big television screen. "There are two tapes here for you to view," the employee said. "One guy's a teacher, like you, and the other's a chartered accountant. Which would you like to see first?"

"The teacher, please," Susan murmured.

She settled back in the chair and watched nervously as an image flashed on the screen. It was a youngish man, dark-haired and slightly plump, with his hands folded tightly in his lap and his feet placed close together on the floor.

"I'm a primary-school teacher," he said, smiling awkwardly. "I like children and intellectual pursuits, so my job is perfect for me. I'm also a Scout leader in my free time, and I do volunteer work at the hospital on weekends. I'm pretty shy and it's hard for me to meet people, but I think I'd be a good companion for the right woman because I..."

The image blurred. Susan glanced at the woman by the video machine and shook her head. "No," she said apologetically. "I mean, he seems like a really nice man but he just doesn't... appeal to me. I'm sorry."

"No need to be sorry," she said cheerfully, punching buttons on the machine. "The whole idea is to get people together who appeal to each other. Here's the accountant."

Susan looked up with sudden interest as another image appeared on the screen. This man was tall and slender, with smooth fair hair and broad shoulders under a well-fitted suit. His tie was expensive and perfectly knotted, his face tanned and handsome.

"I'm a CPA," he said with an engaging smile at the camera. "But I like strenuous physical activities when I'm away from the job. Last year I was part of a five-man team that climbed Mount McKinley, and this fall I'm going river rafting on the Colorado. I play a pretty good jazz piano and I'm fluent in Spanish. The woman I'm looking for will be attractive and confident, both physically and mentally. She'll be a perfect companion for all the things I like to do, and I'll treat her very well."

He leaned forward and gave the camera a warm, intimate smile that made Susan feel a little dizzy. Then he settled back in his chair and went on speaking. "I grew up in central British Columbia and got my master's degree in business from Simon Fraser University. Since then I've been . . ."

Susan watched as the video ended, swallowed hard and looked at the young woman next to her. "This man saw my video and wants to meet me?"

"That's why I'm showing you his tape," the girl said. "At his request. Do you like him?"

"*Like* him?" Susan breathed. "He's . . . he's absolutely perfect. He's the man of my dreams."

CHAPTER THREE

ON FRIDAY MORNING, Susan woke to the smell of fresh coffee wafting into her room. She frowned, staring at the ceiling, then remembered and sat up.

Mike Murphy and his daughter had been living in her house for more than a week, but it was still hard to get used to waking up and finding other people in the kitchen. Susan cherished her privacy, and it was a little disconcerting to hear the voices and footsteps of strangers.

Nevertheless, she had to admit that the situation wasn't entirely unpleasant. Especially when the new occupants were as delightful as Emma, and as efficient and tidy as Mike.

Her tenants were also unobtrusive, just as Mike had promised. Emma went to bed early and her father either worked on his old truck or remained upstairs, reading and watching television in his little sitting room, making coffee and snacks on the hot plate. Most days, Susan only saw them at breakfast and dinner.

And though occasionally she suffered from the loss of privacy, Susan's diet had certainly become a lot healthier since Mike's arrival. He cooked on alternate days and, like everything else, he did it well enough that Susan felt obliged to compete.

She got up and padded into her bathroom, brushed her hair and applied a little makeup, then pulled on a skirt and blouse and hurried toward the kitchen where the smell of pancakes now mingled with the aroma of coffee.

"Where's Emma?" she asked, coming into the room with her shoes in one hand.

As she stepped into them, she smiled at Mike who stood by the stove with a bowl and spatula, wearing work clothes and heavy gray socks.

"She's outside with Buster." He gestured at the terrace with his bowl.

Susan moved across the kitchen and looked through the doorway at Emma who sat cross-legged on the flagstones in the morning sunlight, her stuffed kangaroo beside her. She was feeding Buster handfuls of cereal from a plastic cup.

"Buster's getting really spoiled," Susan said, coming back into the kitchen. "He's never had so much attention."

She seated herself at the table and began to eat the fruit salad at her place.

"This is so good," she said. "I never used to eat a proper breakfast, you know. I just grabbed a pastry or something."

"Emma!" Mike called through the door. "Come in and eat. Wash your hands first," he added sternly as the little girl burst into the room with her kangaroo under one arm.

Emma nodded, kissed Susan's cheek and ran from the kitchen, heading upstairs in a flash of denim overalls.

Susan sighed with pleasure as Mike set a plate of pancakes in front of her. "I really shouldn't eat all this," she protested. "I'm still trying to lose seven pounds."

"I can't see why," he said calmly, lowering himself into the opposite chair and reaching for the syrup. "If there was ever a woman with a perfect figure, it's you."

Susan shifted in her chair, unnerved at his frank praise. By tacit agreement, she and her new housemate avoided this sort of personal conversation.

"I'd just be more comfortable if I could lose a few pounds," she said.

"Why?" He handed her the syrup jug.

"I don't know. It's just that some people have told me I'd look better if I were..."

"What people? Nice, supportive guys like your boyfriend, Jerry, who wanted you to be a model?"

"Who told you that?"

"Betty. Did I mention that she stopped by last night while you were at your needlework class? Emma really loved her."

Susan's cheeks warmed with annoyance. "Well, Betty shouldn't be telling you details about my private life. It's none of your—"

"Gerald's got a tummy ache," Emma announced as she came into the kitchen and climbed into her chair.

"Does he, sweetheart?" Susan asked. "Poor Gerald. Did he eat too much cereal?"

Emma nodded, her mouth full of fruit salad. "He doesn't want to go to day care today. He says he's not afraid to stay home by himself."

Mike and Susan exchanged a glance. This was the first time Emma had shown a willingness to leave her kangaroo behind when she went to day care. It was an indication that the little girl felt comfortable and secure in her new home, and it warmed Susan's heart.

"Do you like the day care, honey?" she asked gently.

Emma nodded, watching as her father put a couple of small pancakes onto her plate. "It's fun. I *love* Carla," she added.

"I'm glad, sweetheart," Mike said, stirring the last of the pancake batter. To Susan, he said, "She's the dark-haired woman I spoke to, right? The one who runs the day care."

"Yes. She's the pregnant one. And she brings her other two kids to work with her," Susan said.

"Tommy and Steven," Emma contributed. "Tommy's my boyfriend."

"How about Steven?" Mike asked with a smile.

Emma shrugged. "Steven's just a little kid. He wears diapers."

"And she's having *another* one?" Mike asked.

Susan smiled. "Carla likes kids."

Emma finished her second pancake, climbed down from her chair and headed for the terrace. "I'm going to fill Buster's water dish," she told them. "Can I use the hose?"

"Make sure you turn it all the way off when you're finished," Susan said. "Mike, this is *so* delicious."

"Thanks." Mike poured himself a cup of coffee and glanced at his watch. "We have to leave in a few minutes. Do you want a ride?"

"No thanks. I need my car to go over to the mall on my lunch hour. I'm shopping for a new dress."

"For the big date?" he asked with a grin.

"Never mind." She got up and began to stack dishes in the dishwasher.

"Will you still have time to go running this morning?" he asked. "Or will you need lots of time to prepare for... what's his name?"

"His name is Graham McBride. Not that it's any of your business. And I'm thinking of running in the evenings now. It takes too much time to get over to the park and then back to school before my first class. Besides, that way I can take Buster with me."

Mike frowned. "I don't like that idea."

"What idea? Taking Buster with me?"

"You know what I mean. I don't think you should be running alone in the park at night. It's not safe."

"Don't be ridiculous. This is a quiet residential area. Besides, I'm not planning to run after dark. I thought I'd go right after school and be home around five."

"If I could find someone reliable to stay with Emma, I'd go with you."

Susan looked at him in astonishment. "You want to *run* with me? After working all day?"

"Not really. But I don't want you to go alone, and you're too stubborn to reason with."

"Look, you just happen to live upstairs, Mike," she told him quietly. "You're not responsible for my welfare, okay? If I want to run alone in the park—or anywhere else, for that matter—I'll do it."

He was silent for a moment. "I saw you blow that smart-aleck kid away on the track last week," he said at last. "It was a joy to watch. You're quite a woman, you know."

Susan turned aside, both warmed and annoyed by the man. She began to fuss with the dishes, conscious of him watching her as she worked.

THE DAY flew by with alarming speed. Just before seven o'clock, Susan looked anxiously at her reflection in the long mirror as she fastened one of her silver earrings. She turned slowly in front of the mirror, squinting over her shoulder at the fit of her new dress across the hips.

For this first date—they were going to a jazz concert—she'd chosen a plain black jersey with a draped collar and a skirt that swirled gracefully around her legs. The salesperson had assured her that the dark color was slimming, announcing that Susan looked "thin as a rail" in the flared skirt.

The other earring seemed to have vanished in the depths of her jewelry box. Susan riffled through the trinkets, wondering why she was taking such pains with her appearance. It's just a blind date, she told herself. She found the earring, then wandered across her bedroom to look out the window.

Mike, who had taken over most of the yard work since his arrival, was trimming the lilac hedge at the front of the house. He was barefoot, wearing white cotton shorts and a faded navy T-shirt.

His body looked lean and muscular, his shoulders broad and powerful under the thin fabric. His upper body was darkly bronzed from working in the sun without a shirt, but his powerful legs were pale. Mike

Murphy was hardly the kind of man to lie in the sun on weekends and tan his legs . . .

Susan watched him absently. Even doing something as commonplace as trimming a hedge, Mike had an air of physical ease, a kind of flourish that made the job look effortless. His hands were strong and brown, surprisingly graceful as they flexed and tightened on the wooden handles of the clippers.

While Susan watched, Emma came bursting around the corner of the house, accompanied by Buster who was barking joyously. The two of them sped past Mike in a blur of color and sound. Emma wore shorts, a yellow raincoat and a red plastic fireman's hat, and Buster was on his red leash.

Emma carried a watering can which she paused to sprinkle on one of the flower beds, all the time shouting with a shrill, steady wail that almost drowned out the sound of Buster's barking. After a brief pause, the two of them were off again, hurtling down to the corner of the hedge.

Susan laughed aloud, understanding instantly what game they were playing. Emma was a fireman, and Buster was the fire engine. For a dog unaccustomed to small children, he was playing his part with admirable enthusiasm.

As Emma and Buster roared toward the edge of the lawn, a low-slung silver sports car pulled up to the curb and a man got out, obviously taken aback at the boisterous scene in the front yard. Susan tensed and ducked behind the curtain. She lifted a bit of the fabric aside and peered at the newcomer.

Graham McBride was even more handsome in person than he'd looked on videotape. He wore gray

flannel slacks, a navy blue blazer and a white shirt with
a dark gray tie. His blond hair glistened in the waning
sunlight as he came up the front walk. Emma and
Buster paused by the hedge and watched him in silence.

As Graham McBride neared Mike and stopped to
talk, Susan couldn't help noticing the difference between the two. But Mike, with his bare feet and un-
tanned legs, his faded, sweaty T-shirt and hair still
damp from his evening shower, didn't seem troubled
by the contrast. He lowered the hedge clippers and
spoke to the visitor with his usual easy confidence,
resting one hand gently on Emma's red plastic hat as
she edged close to her father and pressed against his
leg, staring up at the stranger.

Mike gestured toward Susan's main-floor window.
She drew aside, took a deep breath and fitted her earring in place. With a final glance in the mirror, she
smoothed her dress over her hips again, gathered up
her handbag and sweater and hurried down the hallway, where her date stood waiting by the front door.

Susan went out onto the veranda and smiled at him,
her heart hammering so noisily that she was afraid he
could hear it.

"Hello," she said, extending her hand. "You must
be Graham. I'm Susan."

"You certainly are," the man said, his eyes warm
with admiration. "Even more beautiful in person than
you looked on your video."

"I was just thinking the same thing about you,"
Susan told him, returning his smile.

This wasn't so hard, she thought. In fact, it was going really well. "Well, shall we go?" she asked.

He offered his arm and escorted her down the steps and past Mike, who was impassively clipping the hedge. Emma and Buster had retreated to the corner of the yard where they sat together on the grass, watching in silence.

Mike turned as they passed, his eyes widening as he saw Susan's sleek black dress, her silver jewelry and high-heel shoes.

Susan blushed, more conscious of his scrutiny than she had been of Graham McBride's. She waited tensely for Mike to make one of his teasing remarks. But he said nothing, just waved the clippers at her and went on working.

"The front door's unlocked," Susan said to him as they moved toward the car.

"I'll look after it. Have a good time." Mike turned to the other man. "Don't forget to drive real carefully, son. And have her home by midnight, you hear?"

Susan gritted her teeth. Mike Murphy really was intolerable. She forced herself to smile at Graham, who was looking a little puzzled.

And who can blame him? Susan thought. As they drove off, she glanced over her shoulder at the front yard where Emma and Buster had resumed their noisy game, careering around the lawn with the watering can. She watched until the car turned the corner, then focused her attention on her date.

"Don't mind Mike," she said. "He's my tenant. He lives in the upstairs suite."

"And the little girl?"

"His daughter."

"Ah." Graham nodded, looking relieved. "Where's the mother? Does she live in your house, too?"

Susan twisted her hands in her lap and forced herself to relax.

"Mike's wife died when Emma was a baby. This is really a beautiful car, Graham," she added, looking at the soft leather interior, the wood-grain dashboard filled with lighted dials and silver buttons.

"It's a British make. There are only four others like it in the whole city."

Susan tried to look impressed. But for some reason, she had a sudden vision of Mike Murphy's dusty old pickup truck, with the patch of rust on a rear fender that he'd spent the last two evenings sanding and repairing with body filler.

She forced the image from her mind. "So, you're a chartered accountant," she said. "That must be... really interesting."

I'm an idiot, she thought in despair. *I'm completely, utterly hopeless...*

"It pays the rent," Graham said with a polite smile. "How about you? Do you like teaching school?"

Susan nodded. "It's a pretty good job," she said lamely. "I enjoy the students."

Their conversation was like a bad tennis game, Susan thought. Both of them kept laboring to get the ball back over the net without losing points.

But what could she expect? She'd just met the man. They still had so much to learn about each other. It wasn't reasonable to think the conversation would flow effortlessly right from the first meeting.

Again an image of Mike Murphy popped into Susan's head. She recalled his first day as a tenant in her house, when they'd become absorbed in a heated political argument at the breakfast table that had almost resulted in their both being late for work.

But that was different, she told herself firmly. She was able to be relaxed with Mike because he was so obviously not her type. There could never, ever be any romantic involvement.

Graham McBride, on the other hand, was *exactly* the kind of man she dreamed of. She felt nervous just looking at his tanned profile, his smooth golden head and well-cut jacket.

"What kind of music do you like? My guess would be jazz," she ventured.

"You'd be right. I like classic jazz, ragtime, swing, free-form, third stream, all kinds. But the Bird is my hero."

Susan, who preferred folk and county music, had no idea what he was talking about. She nodded, trying not to look like an idiot, and afraid she was failing. "I guess it's becoming really popular, isn't it? Jazz, I mean."

Good going, Susan, she thought. *That's a really intelligent statement.*

Graham wheeled his powerful car around a corner. "Too popular," he said, frowning at a station wagon that tried to cut him off. "Too many people think they understand jazz these days, don't you think?"

"I don't know," she said awkwardly. "I know what I like, that's all."

"Tell me, Susan, why did you go to a video dating service? A beautiful woman like you must have no shortage of interested guys."

"I guess I could ask you the same thing, couldn't I? You're suave and handsome, so it shouldn't be hard for you to meet attractive women."

"I like the video service. It's really up front and honest. Neither of us has to waste an evening with someone who's going to turn out to be totally unsuitable. We both know in advance exactly what we're getting."

Susan looked out the window, wondering exactly what *she* had gotten.

"Is that kid always so . . . noisy?" he asked, pulling up by the curb in front of the theater.

"What kid?" Susan asked.

"That little girl who was running around with the dog. I don't know much about kids. Does she yell like that a lot of the time?"

"She's a lovely little girl," Susan said. "I really love Emma."

"I guess you've got more patience than I do." Graham gave her another admiring smile.

She watched in silence as he got out of the car, tossed the keys to a valet and strolled around to open her door. Suddenly, she wondered how Betty was getting along. Betty had a date tonight, too, with "this really cute little guy with big ears who runs an antique shop and collects Donald Duck memorabilia," as Betty had described him.

I'll bet she's having a lot more fun than I am, Susan thought. She forced a smile at her handsome date as he took her arm and escorted her into the theater.

The jazz concert was a blur of noise and confusion to Susan, who really didn't understand this art form at all. Graham, on the other hand, seemed to be absorbed in the music.

By the end of the performance, she was so bored that she was reduced to mental diversions like trying to recall recipes or the words to old country songs, and idle speculations abut Mike Murphy's past, like where he'd gone to high school and what kind of girls he'd dated . . .

She pulled herself together with an effort when the houselights came up and Graham got to his feet, smiling at her.

"Wasn't that *great?*" he asked. "The sax was fabulous, didn't you think?"

"Yes," Susan murmured. "Very nice."

"I come to these concerts as often as I can," he went on, escorting her into the mellow autumn evening. "Jazz concerts and foreign films are pretty much my main kind of entertainment. What about you, Susan?"

Susan thought this over. "I like films," she said at last.

"Would you like to see *My Turkish Uncle* next weekend at the gallery in Gastown?"

Susan's mind raced. "I think I might be...not next weekend," she said at last. "I promised my girlfriend we'd go to a film together."

At least that was the truth, Susan thought. For weeks she and Betty had been planning to see the latest Harrison Ford movie as soon as they got a chance.

And if Betty's date had been as unsatisfactory as hers, maybe they would both be at loose ends next weekend. The only thing she knew for sure was that she wouldn't be dating this man again.

You certainly couldn't go by looks, she thought sadly as he held open the door to his elegant little car. Graham had seemed so perfect in his video, but he was no more her type than . . . Mike Murphy was.

WHILE SUSAN was experiencing dubious reactions to the first candidate from the dating service, Danny Clammer was wandering along the winding, leafy trails of the park near the old brick apartment building where he lived.

He paused by a spreading oak tree and thought about Lynnette Campbell. Danny was really attracted to her, though he was too shy to say anything.

He'd learned a lot about her in recent weeks, like the fact that she lived in a shabby apartment building much like his own, and provided most of the care for a houseful of little brothers and sisters. She never said much about her home life, but Danny got the impression that her parents weren't around a lot.

And in spite of her seductive clothes, she seemed gentle, almost shy. She avoided the rowdy banter that went on among the cabdrivers and the other dispatchers, and resisted all kinds of advances. She just did her job, collected her pay and went home, the same as Danny did.

He recognized Lynnette's flamboyant style of dress as a defense, something that helped her cope with a world that was harsh and difficult. It was a feeling that Danny understood all too well.

At the edge of the park he saw the bus approaching down the street and ran to catch up with it, shouting and waving his arms. He settled in a rear seat and folded his arms, ignoring the giggles of a group of little boys in Cub Scout uniforms who sat nearby.

The bus lurched to a stop near the big hospital downtown. Danny entered the lobby and chose an elevator, feeling a rising tide of emotion. As he rode to the floor where they'd moved his great-aunt, he sent up a quick prayer that some kind of miracle had happened since yesterday.

She'd be better now. When he went into her room, she'd sit up in bed and smile at him, looking the same as always, and she'd say...

But she didn't.

When he tiptoed into her room, his heart sank and he had to choke back a sob. Rosa lay against the pillows with her eyes closed, looking gray and tired. Her hair, usually so tidy in its little bun, stood up in thin silver wisps all around her head.

Danny edged close to the bed and sat down, taking her veined hand in his. Rosa Clammer, his father's aunt, had raised him since infancy. She was Danny's last living relative, the only connection to a sunny, distant childhood filled with music and laughter and the warmth of their colorful immigrant neighborhood. Danny didn't think he could bear the pain if Rosa died.

But she'd had a massive heart attack a couple of weeks ago, and then another soon after she was admitted to the hospital. The doctor said it didn't look good.

Rosa's eyes fluttered open and focused on the dark-haired young man sitting on the edge of the bed.

"Beanie," she murmured.

Danny cast a nervous glance at the empty doorway. He'd hate anyone to know that his aunt still called him by that baby nickname. But he didn't correct her, just squeezed her hand and bent to give her a kiss.

"Hi, Rosa. You look real good tonight. Pretty soon you'll be out of here. You'll be home in your kitchen, making me some cannelloni and apple dumplings. I can hardly wait."

Rosa sighed impatiently and waved her hand to silence him. She gazed at him with unashamed hunger, taking in every detail of his face.

"That silly mustache," she whispered fondly. "You're too young to grow a mustache."

He touched the dark wisp above his upper lip. "It's getting thicker," he said defensively. "Everyone tells me it makes me look older."

"Why do you want to look older?"

"People take a guy more seriously if he's mature. I hate looking like a kid. I'm almost twenty-three."

"You're still driving your cab?"

"Most days. I get a lot of the early shifts. But I wish..."

"What, Danny? What do you wish?"

Danny avoided his aunt's gaze. He turned and looked out the window at the darkening sky.

"I dunno," he said at last. "I wish I had enough money to buy my own cab, that's all. Working for other guys, there's no future in it. I wanna start building something. I'd like to...be somebody," he finished. "Somebody who... You know what I mean."

"I know," his aunt said.

Danny stroked his mustache awkwardly and looked out the window again.

"Beanie, are you staying out of trouble?" Rosa asked. "None of those old problems?"

"No!" Danny said. "Never. I swear it. All that stuff, it's over now. I'll never be dumb like that again."

"Because you don't want to go to jail again," Rosa said. "And you know what the judge told you. Next time, it would be a lot more than two years."

"I know." Danny shuddered at the memory. "Believe me. Auntie, I'm never going there again. Never. I don't even double-park my cab or jaywalk. I don't do anything to even make a policeman look at me twice."

"Good boy," Rosa said. "That's a good boy."

She closed her eyes and sighed, looking so frail that Danny felt a sudden clutch of panic.

"So," he said loudly, forcing himself to sound bright and full of energy, "how you feeling, anyway? The doctor said you're getting a whole lot better," he lied. "Pretty soon you'll be up and around. Maybe you and me, we'll start jogging together like a lady I saw the other day. She runs in the park at night. You should see her, Rosa. She's a schoolteacher, teaches English where a . . . a friend of mine goes to school. And she runs races, too. My friend says—"

"I'm dying, Danny," his aunt said quietly.

"Tell you what," he said, ignoring her words. "I'll buy you some of them new high-top runners like the basketball players wear, okay? Real fancy ones. And you and me, we'll go running every night. We'll—"

"Danny," she said, frowning at him. "Stop talking nonsense. Stop it right now."

Danny was silent. His heart pounded, and his throat felt dry and tight.

"I'm dying, my dear. I'm not going to make it."

Tears stung his eyes. "Please don't...don't say things like that."

Rosa reached up with a trembling hand and stroked his hair. "Always so curly," she said fondly. "Such a lovely little baby you were. I loved you like you were my own."

"I know you did," he said, his voice muffled and husky. The tears were running down his cheeks now, and he didn't bother to wipe them away. "I know you did."

"And you were a good boy. You made some bad friends and did foolish things, but you were always a good boy at heart. I was proud of you."

"Were you?" he whispered.

"Always," she said firmly.

"I wish I'd—"

Rosa made another impatient gesture, cutting off his words.

"Don't wish, my dear. Wishes about the past are foolish. The past is gone." She fell silent and her eyes closed wearily. After a few moments' rest, she looked at him again. "All we can do is try to make the future better. Promise me you'll try."

"I promise," Danny said.

"Good. Now, Danny, listen to me."

Her voice was growing so faint that Danny had to lean closer, almost resting his cheek against her soft wrinkled face. He choked back a sob as he smelled the familiar scent of her, a pleasant fragrance of lavender and sunshine that had been part of his life for as long as he could remember.

"I'm listening, Rosa."

"There are...things in my apartment, Beanie. There's something under the bed."

"Under the bed?" he asked cautiously.

Again she made that brief gesture with her hand. "Don't argue. Just look under the bed. And remember that everything you find in my apartment is yours."

Danny thought about her shabby little downtown rooms with their sparse furnishings, the bright hand-knit afghan and secondhand television set.

"You'll be going home again soon," he said. "You'll need your things."

"I haven't made a will," she whispered. "But whatever you find in my apartment, it's all yours. Don't forget that. Take it with my blessing."

"Rosa," he said wildly. "Look, I can't..."

Her eyes closed again. She stopped speaking and rested against the pillows, but her weariness seemed to have vanished. To Danny's tear-dimmed eyes, she looked happy and full of anticipation, like someone about to embark on a long-awaited journey. After a moment, her lips moved again and Danny leaned close to make out the words.

"I love you, Beanie," she whispered.

It was the last thing he ever heard her say.

ROSA CLAMMER'S DEATH was a tragedy to her grieving nephew, but it made no other impact on the beautiful waterfront city that blazed and glistened with autumn splendor.

Early the next morning, in the old house across the city from the hospital, Mike Murphy finished shaving, cleaned the sink carefully and put his razor away. He looked around the bathroom, catching sight of a smear of blue foam on the edge of the bathtub where Emma and her plastic ducks had cavorted the night before in a froth of bubbles. Mike knelt to wipe the tub and polish it, then went back into his own room, moving quietly in case Susan planned to sleep in on this Saturday morning.

He stood on the braided rug near his bed, thinking about her. Everything in the room reminded him of the woman who owned it, from the yellow chintz curtains to the framed flower prints on the walls.

Susan's bedroom was directly below his, removed from the kitchen by a short hallway. Mike, who found himself increasingly curious about her, had stolen a couple of glimpses into her room and been charmed by the ruffled curtains, the antique rocker and four-poster bed with a handmade starburst quilt and brass-cornered chest at its foot.

He wondered what she wore to bed. Probably a chaste white cotton nightgown, buttoned to the neck, with long full sleeves. . . .

He banished the wayward image. Mike realized that he couldn't give way to these speculations about his landlady. If he let himself think too much about her, he'd eventually find himself making some kind of move toward her.

And that would be disastrous.

For Emma's sake, it was important not to upset the delicate balance of this relationship. Emma loved everything about their new home—the stained-glass window on the landing, Buster, her friends at the day care. She was happier and more settled than she'd been in a long time. It would be unforgivably selfish of him to risk spoiling everything for the little girl just because he couldn't keep his hands off the landlady.

Mike sighed and leaned over to smooth the yellow comforter on his neatly made bed. He straightened the curtains, dusted the dresser top and padded downstairs to the kitchen, taking care to be quiet on the stairs.

But his caution was unnecessary. Susan was up and dressed, standing by the counter as she whipped something in a blue enamel bowl.

"I thought you might decide to sleep in this morning," Mike said, struggling not to show how powerfully he was affected by the sight of her.

She was wearing a yellow T-shirt with the sleeves rolled up on her tanned arms, and a gingham apron over jeans. Her slender feet were bare, and the only makeup she had on was a dash of lipstick. She was like a tall golden iris, so fresh and beautiful that, despite his best efforts, it was all he could do not to take her in his arms and kiss her.

"It's my turn to make breakfast," she said cheerfully. "What am I supposed to do? Loll in bed while you and Emma eat cornflakes?"

"We've eaten worse things." He crossed the kitchen to pour himself a mug of fresh coffee. "Need any help?"

She shook her head and opened the lid on the waffle iron. He swallowed hard, watching how the motion set her hair swinging. The nape of her neck was slim and white, so delicate that it looked childlike. If a man were to drop a kiss there, her skin would probably be as soft and fragrant as Emma's . . .

Abruptly, he pulled out a chair and sat down at the table. "Eleven thirty-two," he commented, searching for something to get his mind off the idea of kissing her.

Annoying the woman, Mike had discovered, was safer than yearning for her all the time.

She paused in the act of pouring batter onto the sizzling metal surface. "What?"

"That's what time you came in last night. Eleven thirty-two."

Her hands tensed on the edge of the mixing bowl. "How do you know?"

"I was reading. I heard the front door open."

She closed the lid carefully on the waffle iron. "I'm always afraid this thing is going to stick. It's an amazing invention, a waffle iron, isn't it? By the way," she added, "I'm picking up groceries this afternoon. Be sure to give me your list, okay?"

He nodded and dug a serrated spoon into the halved grapefruit sitting on his plate. "Eleven-thirty, that's pretty early to be getting home," he observed.

"Is it? How many waffles can you eat?"

"Quite a few. Emma will probably just want a couple of squares."

"Buster can eat the leftovers. He loves waffles."

Mike watched as she lifted a golden-brown waffle onto a plate and carried it to the table, setting it by his elbow.

"Thanks," he said. "So, did you and Graham enjoy the concert?"

Susan paused and looked at him directly. "What is this? An inquisition?"

He shrugged, spreading butter on his waffle. "I'm merely expressing polite interest in your evening," he said mildly. "I've never been to a jazz concert. I wondered what it was like."

"It was interesting," she said, returning to the counter, "but not my style. I don't understand jazz. I prefer my music more straightforward."

Mike nodded agreement. "So, how was Graham?" he asked. "Did you like him?"

Susan turned away, concentrating on the waffle iron. "He was nice," she said in noncommittal voice. "Very courteous and sophisticated."

"I thought," he ventured after a moment, pouring syrup carefully, "the guy seemed a little stiff."

"What do you mean?"

"Just . . . stiff. Sort of humorless, you know?"

Susan brought another waffle to the table and hesitated, toying with the fringe on Emma's place mat.

"He sent his meal back," she said abruptly.

Mike gave her an inquiring glance.

"To the kitchen," she explained. "He said the vegetables were cold, and the steak was overdone."

"Was it?"

"I don't know. I thought the food was just fine. I almost caught myself dealing with him like you do with Emma. You know, saying, 'Be quiet and eat your supper, or you won't get dessert!' ''

Mike grinned. "Why didn't you?"

"He was...kind of intimidating," Susan said reluctantly. "Not really the sort you kid around with."

Mike relaxed and began to feel comfortable again. He watched as she seated herself opposite and shook out her napkin. "Maybe not your dream man, after all?"

"Maybe not," she said, ignoring his teasing look. "But," she added, "Betty called the dating service yesterday and there's another guy who's probably going to be perfect for me. He's just my type, a college professor who teaches political science at Simon Fraser. We're going down to the agency today to watch his video."

"That sounds nice," he said in a neutral tone, causing Susan to give him another suspicious glance.

"What are you and Emma doing today?"

"Shopping for new shoes and clothes. She's growing out of everything."

Susan picked up a spoon and tackled her grapefruit. "Can you manage all that by yourself?"

"I always have," he said.

She nodded, then lifted her head as a sound came from overhead, a rhythmic creaking noise accompanied by a muffled hum.

"I'll be right back." Mike got to his feet and placed his napkin carefully on the table. "Don't let Buster have my waffles, okay?"

He ran lightly up the stairs and went into Emma's room. She was sitting up in the ruffled bed, clutching her kangaroo to her chest, her big dark eyes still wide with dreams. She was rocking and humming a tuneless song, swaying rhythmically until the little bed creaked and strained on the floorboards.

Mike smiled tenderly, marveling at the little girl's ability to wake up and be excited about the day ahead almost before she had her eyes open. She was wearing a pair of pink flannel pajamas covered with blue kittens, and her hair was standing straight up, glowing in the early-morning sunlight like a halo.

Love swept over him, an emotion so pure and powerful that he was briefly shaken. Tears burned in his eyes and he turned aside for a moment so she wouldn't see them.

"Hi, punkin," he said gruffly, turning back to her and sitting on the edge of the bed. "What's all this noise?"

Emma wound her arms around his neck and kissed him, almost toppling him in her exuberance. "Today, Daddy!" she shouted. "Today we're going shopping. New shoes, Daddy! Pants and shirts and everything. Daddy, I want a red T-shirt with the Warrior Heroes on it, and pants with a little pocket on the side to carry my gun. Brown ones."

"You aren't allowed to play with guns," Mike said automatically. "You know how much Daddy hates guns. So does Susan."

Emma climbed from the bed, ignoring him. "And I want a shirt like Tommy has. A lumberjack shirt. I'm going to be a lumberjack when I grow up."

"I thought you were going to be a fireman." Mike followed as she marched off to the bathroom.

"I'm going to be both," Emma told him serenely, closing the door and leaving him outside. "I'm going to be a fireman *and* a lumberjack."

Mike sat on a blanket chest in the hallway, thinking this over. "Well, you're going to be busy," he remarked to the closed door. "Those are both pretty demanding careers."

Emma opened the door and smiled at him, then stood on a little stool to wash her hands at the sink. "Is Susan coming with us when we go shopping?"

"She and Betty have their own plans for the day."

"I want Susan to come with *us*. I want her to watch me picking out my new clothes."

Mike stood up and walked into the bathroom. "Sweetheart," Mike said gently, lifting her down from the stool. "Susan can't do things with us all the time. She has her own life to live."

"But I *love* Susan." Emma gave him a questioning look, her face puckered with concern. "Don't you, Daddy?"

Mike's heart lurched and steadied. "I think Susan's a really nice person," he said calmly. "But we just rent part of her house, sweetie. That's all. You have to remember that Susan isn't...part of our family. There's still just you and me in our family, the same as it's always been."

Emma watched him a moment longer, her eyes wide and unfathomable. Then she ran down the hall to her room, where he heard her scrabbling busily among her clothes and toys, getting ready for the day.

CHAPTER FOUR

SUSAN SAT on a bench in the mall, surrounded by the bags and packages she was guarding while Betty shopped in a bookstore nearby.

The flagstone walkways echoed with hundreds of passing feet as shoppers hunted for back-to-school bargains. Susan rested her head against the bench, enjoying the filtered warmth from a skylight overhead, watching the crowds. People-watching was one of her favorite hobbies.

On the bench across from her, a little boy sat next to his harried-looking mother and a couple of other small children. He was about two years old, even smaller than Emma, with a mass of golden curls and eyes as blue as the stripes on his kid-size baseball uniform.

He caught Susan's eye and gave her a shy smile. She smiled back. He lowered his head, covered his face with his chubby hands and looked up, spreading his fingers to give her another enchanting grin. Susan responded by bending a branch from a nearby potted palm over her face. His eyes widened in alarm. She leaned out to peek at him and he chuckled.

They continued their game for a little while, until the boy's mother gathered her parcels and bundled him into a stroller to wheel him away. Susan could hear his shouts of protest carrying faintly through the noise and bustle.

She settled back to wait again, but Betty appeared almost at once, lugging a huge bag emblazoned with the bookstore logo.

"My goodness, I thought you were just browsing," Susan said. "What's all this?"

Betty plopped onto the bench and opened the package to reveal a number of books on antiques. "Barney's driving up to Squamish next weekend to shop for antiques at an estate sale, and he asked me to go with him."

"I can't believe that's really his name. I've never met anyone called Barney."

"It's short for Barnaby. It's his mother's maiden name. The family's Irish. I think that's where he gets his boyish charm."

Susan grinned. There was no doubt that Betty was smitten with her very first date from the video service. She radiated a kind of incandescent excitement, and she'd already reached the stage where she wanted to talk about the man all the time. No detail about the life and times of Barnaby Evans was too insignificant to be mulled over and discussed.

"So," Susan said, "how come you're building an entire library on the antique business? I mean, it's *his* job, not yours, right?"

"I told him I was an expert on nineteenth-century furniture," Betty said glumly.

"Betty! You don't know an armoire from an antimacassar."

"I know. But somehow I sort of gave the impression that I knew something about it, you know? And he seemed so interested, I didn't have the heart to tell him I was just a big phony."

"'O, what a tangled web we weave,'" Susan quoted, laughing.

Betty glared at her, then smiled. "Hey, how complicated can it be?" she said cheerfully. "I just have to read these books in my free time before next weekend, after I finish marking two hundred little exercise books and building sixteen hand puppets from papier-mâché. Piece of cake."

"I'll help you. I took a couple of courses on antique furniture and decorating right after I bought the house, remember?"

"Thanks, Susie. It's too bad you didn't like your guy," Betty added with sympathy.

"Not everybody can be lucky the very first time like you were. Besides, the college professor seems like a really good prospect. I think he'll be much nicer."

"What's he like?"

"Well, in the video he looked kind of broad and rugged, thick brown hair graying a little at the temples. Tweed sport jacket with elbow patches. Enjoys hiking, reading and listening to opera."

"*Opera?*"

"So he's not perfect," Susan admitted.

Betty, never content to stay long in one place, jumped to her feet and gathered some of the packages, then watched while Susan did the same.

"Hey, Susie, have you heard from your mom lately?" she asked as they began walking.

"Actually, she called this morning, right after we finished breakfast. They've got an electric-powered wheelchair for Daddy, and a ramp so he can get in and out of the house easily. Mom says he's feeling much more cheerful.''

"That's great," Betty said. "I'm really glad to hear it.''

Susan's parents lived in Victoria, on Vancouver Island, and her father had been battling Parkinson's disease for years. But the Adamsons were a happy couple, so absorbed in their books and shared artistic pursuits that they seemed virtually unaffected by their problems.

"Actually, Mom seems more worried about me than she is about Daddy.'' Susan paused to admire a window display of autumn leaves and fruit.

"She's worried about you? How come?''

"They both love my house. They're so afraid I'm going to lose it.''

"Lose your *house?*" Betty turned to stare at her friend. "Susie, why would you lose your house? I mean, sure, things are a little tight, but . . .''

"It's the mortgage," Susan said, biting her lip as she studied the window display. "Interest rates have gone up so much, it was a real shock when I had to refinance my loan last month. If I didn't have the extra income from Mike . . .''

She fell silent.

"Well," Betty said with determined cheerfulness, "you've got it, right? So what's the problem?''

"For one thing, I don't know how long they'll stay. Mike's job isn't a permanent one. He goes where the work is. When the school gym's finished, he'll have to move on to another construction site, and if it's not in the city, I'll be making those big payments again.''

"You can always find another tenant, can't you?''

"Probably, but I wish I didn't have to," Susan said gloomily. "I wish I could get my hands on enough money to buy down the mortgage. Then I could handle the payments on my own and I wouldn't need tenants."

"You know I'd help if I could," Betty told her. "But after putting that new transmission in my car, I've got about three hundred dollars in the bank and I still need a muffler."

"Oh, Betty, you don't have to worry about my problems." Susan gave her friend a hug. "I'll manage somehow. Like you said, I've got tenants now, so there's no immediate problem. And if they have to move out, I'll cross that bridge when I come to it, right?"

"That's the spirit. Maybe you'll fall in love with the professor and he'll pay off your mortgage. College professors are notoriously wealthy."

"You know, I've heard that." Susan laughed, feeling much better. "Do you think plaid will still be in style this winter?" she added, looking at a window full of clothes.

"You're too tall to wear plaid. It looks best on little people like me."

"You little people," Susan complained, "get to have all the fun." She scanned the crowd, turning quickly to watch a laughing little girl with short brown hair and a red jacket.

"Sure we do," Betty said. "We get to wear vertical stripes and four-inch heels all the time. It's great. Susan, you're not even listening. Are you looking for somebody, or what?"

"I just thought Mike and Emma might be here somewhere," Susan said casually. "They're out shopping today, too. I wonder how he's managing, buying clothes for her."

Betty gave her friend a shrewd glance and shifted the load of books to her other arm. "Why? Is it any of your concern?"

"Of course not," Susan said. "I just wondered, that's all."

Betty frowned at a huge pyramid of tennis balls in a sporting-goods window. "Doesn't it ever seem a little odd to you?" she asked with studied casualness. "That whole situation?"

"What situation? Hey, Betty, I'll bet those things are glued together. Otherwise, what keeps them from falling down?"

"Don't change the subject. Isn't it kind of strange, a guy like Mike raising that little girl all by himself with nobody else involved?"

"What do you mean? Emma's his daughter. Who else would be involved?"

"Other people," Betty said with a shrug. "Family. Aunties and grandparents, people like that. Has he ever mentioned a family?"

"We don't talk much about our personal histories."

"You don't know where he grew up? Whether he finished high school? Whether his family lives far away from here, or what?"

Susan shook her head.

"Does the guy have any friends?" Betty went on. "Does he go out with anybody?"

"He looks after Emma. He's very protective of her. I can't imagine him going out and leaving her with a baby-sitter, and he's certainly never asked me to look after her."

"He takes her to day care, doesn't he?"

"That's different," Susan said with some exasperation. "He has to *work,* for goodness' sake."

"Does he ever get any mail?" Betty persisted.

Susan began to feel troubled. "No," she said slowly. "Not really. Nothing personal. Just bills and circulars, stuff like that."

"And that's never struck you as being just a little odd?"

"What are you saying? Do you think he..."

Betty waved a hand. "Nothing," she said abruptly. "Forget it."

"No." Susan paused by the entry to a department store, its windows crowded with displays of schoolbooks and supplies. "You started it. Now, tell me what you're thinking."

"Well, I just wondered..." Betty looked around, then turned back to Susan. "I work with little kids all the time, so maybe I'm kind of paranoid. We hear about so many cases of people kidnapping their own kids, and then going into hiding with them. It happens all the time."

Susan's mouth dropped open. "You mean 'kidnap' as in take the child away from the other parent?"

"Correct."

Susan looked at her friend in horror. "And you think *Mike*... But his wife is dead. She died when Emma was a baby."

"That's what he told you. And you're such a trusting person, Susie, you can never bring yourself to think that maybe other people are lying to you."

"He told me the whole story of how she died. All about the bus crash in Montana, Emma in her blanket on the snowbank, everything."

"But you have no way of knowing whether his story is true, right? And you have to admit, the whole thing looks pretty suspicious."

Susan kept walking. "You mean," she began slowly, "the fact that Mike and Emma don't have any contact with family? You think maybe he's hiding from everybody because if they knew where he was..."

"They'd come and get the kid," Betty concluded. "Look, don't get all upset," she added. "I could be way out in left field. Maybe he really is a poor young widower raising his kid all alone, exactly like he says. I wonder sometimes, that's all."

"He never mentions relatives, either his own or his wife's. I just assumed he didn't have any."

"I know you did. But everybody's got family. Look at us. We're both single, but you've got your parents in Victoria and your aunt Janet right here in Vancouver, and Alison down in Washington. I've got my dad out in Surrey, and my two brothers at the community college, and Connie in my hair all the time. Everybody's got somebody."

"So if he took Emma and ran away, then maybe there's a poor mother somewhere who's dying of worry, not knowing where her little girl is?"

"It's been known to happen," Betty said quietly.

Susan bit her lip. "How awful," she said. "Betty, I can't imagine how a mother would feel, not knowing where her child is or what's happening to her."

"To say nothing of the fact that it's illegal," Betty said. "If Mike's really a runaway parent, you could be harboring a fugitive, kiddo."

Susan sank onto a nearby bench with her packages, staring blindly at the passing shoppers.

Betty's suspicions, she realized, hadn't entirely come as a surprise to her. In fact, they'd served to re-inforce some deep fears of her own, feelings about Mike she'd been reluctant to analyze...

"I'm going to ask him," she said firmly. "Right away. I'll confront him with it as soon as I get a chance, and make him tell me the truth."

Betty sat next to her. "How?" she asked gently. "Will you wait till after he serves the mashed pota-toes some night and then say, 'Oh, by the way, Mike, I've been wondering. Did you by any chance kidnap this little girl, or do you really have legal custody of her?'"

Susan rested against the bench, closing her eyes briefly. "I'm not sure how I'll do it," she muttered. "But I will. I have to find out about this, Betty. I just have to."

DANNY UNLOCKED the door and edged inside reluc-tantly, his heart pounding. It had been several days since Rosa's death, but this was the first time he'd been able to bring himself to visit her apartment.

He closed the door and breathed in the familiar scents, surprised that the experience wasn't as upset-ting as he'd expected. The whole apartment bore the stamp of Rosa's hardworking, thrifty life. A red-checked dish towel rested neatly over the oven door, and the table was set for breakfast with a single plate, a couple of pots of jam and a wilted flower in a small vase.

It was almost as if Rosa was hovering nearby, watching him and smiling. Danny remembered the way she'd looked that last evening in the hospital, the sweetness and peace on her face. He smiled, warmed by the memory. Danny couldn't help believing that somewhere in the broad, starry universe, her gentle spirit still flourished.

"I shoulda come here right away," he murmured aloud, padding softly into the living room where Rosa's old television set rested on a small plastic table draped with an embroidered scarf.

He looked at the plant pots and bits of furniture, wondering what to do with them. Rosa had told him that everything belonged to him. Still, except for a few keepsakes, Danny had no wish to take his aunt's belongings.

He could probably sell everything and make a few dollars, but he didn't want to do that, either. It seemed like profiting from her death, and he shrank from the idea. At last he decided to give everything away to Big Brothers and Big Sisters, and felt better immediately. He knew Rosa would have liked that idea.

Danny wandered into the tidy bedroom, with its sagging narrow bed and polished surfaces. There were crocheted doilies everywhere, and a doll in a ruffled dress sat on the pillow, staring at him with unblinking blue eyes.

Suddenly, he recalled Rosa's labored whisper on that last evening. Under the bed, she'd told him. There was something under the bed, and it was for him.

Danny knelt and lifted the bedspread, expecting a box stuffed with old photo albums and mementos. Instead, he found a battered suitcase made of cheap brown imitation leather, with a strap that wrapped around and fastened under the handle and a crescent-shaped mark in the corner.

He dragged the suitcase clear of the bed and struggled with the fastenings. Maybe Rosa had bought him some clothes and put them away. She did that occasionally, shyly offering Danny knitted cardigans, stiff dress pants and long-sleeved white shirts, things that he would never wear in a million years. But he always accepted them with thanks and pretended to like them, just so Rosa wouldn't be hurt.

But the suitcase, when he opened it, didn't contain clothes.

It was filled with money.

DANNY HAD NO IDEA how long he'd been crouching there on the linoleum floor, not even daring to breathe, staring at those neat stacks of bills. They were sorted according to denominations and secured with elastic bands. He saw bundles of ones, fives, tens, twenties, even a few fifties.

"God," he whispered at last, touching one of the stacks with a shaking forefinger. "God in heaven, Rosa, where did you *get* all this?"

But he knew where she'd gotten the money, and the knowledge burned in his throat like fire.

This was Rosa Clammer's life savings, painstakingly accumulated and set aside for him. All the years she'd been working, doing custom sewing and housecleaning, and then later when she started getting her pension checks, Rosa must have put some of the money away each month. She'd saved it and packed it carefully in the suitcase under her bed, because she didn't trust banks.

And she'd done it all for Danny, whom she loved...

Tears rolled down his cheeks, but they were healing and sweet. Once more he touched the stacks of bills almost reverently, marveling at his aunt's goodness and self-sacrifice.

When he made a quick count, he was almost overwhelmed again. The money in the suitcase totaled more than forty thousand dollars.

Danny closed and fastened the suitcase, then stood erect and wiped his eyes with a trembling hand, trying to think. His whole life had changed in the few minutes he'd been inside his aunt's bedroom.

His mind raced, considering the possibilities. He could buy a cab of his own and start pocketing his income instead of giving it all away at the end of the week. He could move to a better place, put some money in the bank, start building and saving. Best of all, he could ask Lynnette to go out on a real date, and take her to dinner at a nice restaurant.

TRAVELING ACROSS TOWN on the bus, reality began to sink in again. Danny hunched on one of the seats at the rear and looked around furtively, conscious of the suitcase resting against his legs. In his emotional state, he began to fear everybody sitting nearby. He had the nightmarish sensation that the suitcase had somehow become transparent, so that anybody who looked at it could see the bills inside.

Every time a group of passengers pulled the bell rope and got off, Danny watched them with dread, half expecting one of them to head for the nearest telephone and call the police. He began to sweat, shifting around nervously on the hard vinyl seat.

What would he do if the police stopped him? How could he possibly explain a suitcase full of money?

Danny groaned aloud, struck by a new thought. There had been a series of armed robberies in the city in recent weeks. Mostly it was convenience stores and video outlets that had been hit, late at night. Each time, young thieves in stocking masks had made off with all the money in the till.

They'd taken fives and tens and twenties, maybe a few fifties... Danny shivered, recalling his own brief life of crime. He hadn't been involved in planning the break-in that sent him to jail. He'd been bullied into driving the getaway car. But if the police stopped him now, he was dead. His criminal record made them suspicious of him and there was no way he could account for all this money in his possession.

Rosa hadn't left a will, and nobody who'd known her would ever suspect that she had more than a few dollars stashed in a coffee can. As for the nights of the robberies, Danny had no alibi; when he was finished driving cab, he went home and spent the long summer evenings either wandering in the park or sitting alone in his little apartment, watching television.

Nobody would ever believe his story. He was headed straight back to prison, and all because of his aunt's love and generosity.

He drew a deep breath and forced himself to think rationally. More than anything in the world, he hated the idea of having further dealings with the police. Soon the bus would reach his stop opposite the park. Then he'd hurry along the leafy trails to his apartment building. He'd be safe inside, away from all the curious and hostile eyes.

What would he do with the money after he got it home? He could hardly take it to a bank and make a huge deposit, all at once. But it wasn't a good idea to keep the money under his bed the way Rosa had, either. Especially not in the building he lived in. Maybe he'd open accounts at several banks, small enough not to be conspicuous, and then try to amalgamate the funds after one of the banks got to know and trust him. But it would have to be done very slowly and carefully....

While he was concentrating, the bus stopped near the park and Danny looked out, grateful for the shady evening stillness. He gripped the suitcase and clattered down through the back doors onto the sidewalk, trying to look casual as he walked away.

He set off through the park toward his building, distracting himself by thinking about Lynnette. Her English teacher, the one who'd had that race with the surfer kid, usually came running along the trail about this time of the evening, her golden retriever galloping in front of her.

Danny peered into the distance, wondering if he'd missed her tonight. Suddenly, he froze in his tracks.

Two young men in black leather jackets were approaching beyond a dense mass of shrubbery, talking together in low tones. Danny stood and watched them, gripping the suitcase in shaking hands.

He knew those guys. In fact, these days he spent a lot of his time trying to avoid them. They were small-time hoodlums, a couple of petty crooks who'd once seemed glamorous to him, but now only spelled danger. His probation officer didn't want him to talk with guys like these, and Danny hadn't the slightest wish to disobey her instructions.

But what was he going to do? In a few seconds they'd be around the bushes, in full view, and then they'd be on him. There was no escape. And they could very possibly demand to have a look at the contents of his suitcase. They certainly wouldn't hesitate to beat him up and steal the case if they suspected it contained anything of value.

Danny made a decision. He tossed the suitcase deep into the bushes nearby, wiped his hands on his jeans and advanced down the path, trying to look casual.

"Hey, look who's here," one of the thugs said with a meaningful grin. "Don't see you around no more, Danny boy. What's up with you?"

Danny shrugged. "Not much," he said. "I'm driving cab most days, keeping busy, that's all."

"You got any action?"

Danny shook his head. "I'm on parole, man. I was inside for two years. I'm not going back."

The other two grinned at each other, then turned and fell in step on each side of him, moving him toward his apartment building. Danny licked his lips nervously, trying not to glance back at the bushes where the suitcase was.

"Poor Danny boy, he's so scared," one of them commented to the other in a squeaky falsetto. "Can't take the heat no more?"

"Hey, forget it, man," his partner said abruptly. "We got things to do. We got no time for this little mama's boy."

Danny looked up hopefully but they continued to muscle him along the path.

Eventually, the two men tired of their bullying. They stopped and conferred briefly over his head, then punched him a couple of times and left, hurrying off through the trees.

Danny stood watching them, his breath coming in ragged gasps as he waited for them to disappear. Not until they climbed into a car parked by the curb and roared off down the street did he feel confident enough to head back along the path toward the bushes.

But just as he began to move in that direction, a big yellow dog came plunging through a grove of slim birch trees, almost knocking him down. Danny stood and waited for the blond woman to emerge from the trees. A moment later she was there, running easily along the path, her tall body glistening with sweat in the fading daylight.

She was so beautiful, Danny thought with detached admiration. And Lynnette really liked the woman. Lynnette was making a second attempt at the tenth-grade English course, but this time she understood it better.

"It's fun, the way she teaches it," Lynnette had told him a few days earlier. "She makes it real interesting."

Suddenly, for the second time in a few minutes, Danny stood transfixed with horror.

The big dog had paused near the bushes and was straining toward them, whining and scratching at the ground. The woman stopped running and looked down at her dog.

"What is it, Buster?" Danny heard her say. "What's wrong?"

Danny wanted to scream, wave his hands, do something to distract them. But he couldn't make a sound. He could only stand rigidly, the way he did in those nightmares where disaster was bearing down and he couldn't move his feet.

The schoolteacher dropped to her knees and crawled into the bushes behind her dog. In mounting panic, Danny ducked behind the screen of birches and waited for them to reappear. When they came out, the dog was leaping around in a frenzy of excitement and the tall blonde was dragging the suitcase behind her.

No! Danny wanted to shout. Don't touch that suitcase! It's mine, dammit! You can't take that money. You got no right...

But he didn't say anything, just crouched there in the trees, and watched.

The woman looked around at the deserted park, her face puckered with concern. Then she dropped to her knees, laid the suitcase out on the grass near the path and studied the bindings. At last, after another worried glance around the park, she began to unlatch the straps and buckles.

Danny watched grimly as she opened the suitcase. Even from this distance he could see the way her back tensed under the damp T-shirt and her head jerked erect.

She touched the stacks of money, then closed the suitcase hastily and rocked on her heels while the dog pressed close to her, sniffing at the imitation leather.

At last she got to her feet and began to walk quickly toward the parking lot, carrying the suitcase.

Danny crept out from his screen of leaves. Shell-shocked and numb, he watched until she was out of sight, her golden head and the noisy barking of her dog swallowed up in the gathering dusk.

CHAPTER FIVE

SUSAN DROVE HOME through the darkening streets in an old gray sweatshirt and warm-up pants, her thoughts whirling. As if sensing her agitation, Buster strained upward from the back seat to lick her ear with sloppy affection.

"Thanks, pal," she muttered dryly, reaching up to scrub away the dampness. "I needed that."

She couldn't get her mind off the suitcase with its neat stacks of money. It was just like a scene in a movie, the kind of thing an ordinary person never expected to encounter. But the suitcase was real, resting quietly in her trunk, giving no clue as to its owners or the dark deeds that had caused it to land in a mass of shrubbery in a deserted park.

Not entirely deserted, Susan reminded herself.

She'd seen somebody walking on the path not long before Buster found the suitcase. She frowned, trying to think who it had been, then relaxed when she managed to recover the image.

The thin, dark-haired boy with his wispy mustache, that's who it was. Lynnette's admirer, who'd stood shyly watching the girl that day when Susan had her race with Jason Caine. He must live somewhere nearby, because Susan often saw him wandering in the park during the evening.

But that boy couldn't possibly have anything to do with the suitcase full of money. His clothes were always shabby and his manner cautious and apologetic, as if he had no desire to draw attention to himself. He certainly didn't look the type to be involved in drug dealings or organized crime.

Because, of course, that's what this was all about. Susan hadn't taken the time to look carefully, but she knew there had to be quite a lot of money in the suitcase. It was probably the payoff for a drug deal, hastily jettisoned by the criminals when they saw somebody approaching.

She wondered how long the suitcase had been in the bushes. There was no way of telling, but it seemed strange that the owners hadn't come back immediately to recover their loot. Maybe the people who'd abandoned the suitcase had already been arrested or moved on to some other city, and the money would never be reclaimed.

Susan felt a surge of dark excitement. If the money wasn't going to be claimed, she could keep it and nobody would ever know.

For the briefest of moments, she allowed herself to dream about keeping the money and not telling anybody. Maybe there would even be enough to help buy her mortgage down to a reasonable level, so she wouldn't need tenants to help make ends meet. She could make some confident plans for the future, probably start a regular savings program.

At the very least, she could give some help to her parents...

But, of course, none of that was possible. Susan could daydream, but she knew the money wasn't hers. She had to turn it over to the police, she knew that.

She sighed, parked her car in the old garage and turned Buster loose in the backyard. Then she let herself into the kitchen where Mike and Emma sat at the table, reading together from one of Emma's books.

"I got new clothes!" Emma shouted by way of greeting when she saw Susan in the doorway. She slid from her chair and ran across the room to give Susan a hug. "Susan, wait till you see! A red T-shirt with Zofar the Horrible, and new running shoes with purple on them, and a... and some new..."

"Zofar the Horrible?" Susan asked, lifting Emma in her arms and looking at Mike.

He shook his head sadly. "Little girls just aren't what they used to be. How was your day?"

She smiled at him, then tensed when she remembered her conversation with Betty in the mall, and the dreadful suspicions that had haunted her ever since.

For a little while, that suitcase full of money had driven everything else out of her mind. But now, looking at him, it all came flooding back.

"Well, Susan," Mike began cheerfully. He paused to hug Emma who had briefly vanished into the hall, then reappeared dragging a couple of shopping bags. "Have you decided what you're going to do?"

Susan was at the fridge, about to reach for an apple. She paused and looked at him in alarm. "What?"

"I mean, does this look like the right thing to do? Are you willing to take a chance on it?"

She stared at him blankly. The glow of the antique lamp above the table highlighted his dark hair and the blunt planes of his face.

"You're holding the fridge door open," he told her gently. "You're wasting electricity and setting a bad example for Emma. I was asking about the college professor, and whether he looks like a better prospect than the last one."

Susan closed the door with a thump and turned away to pour herself a cup of coffee, her hands shaking.

"Oh, him," she said. "Actually, he seems . . . he seems really nice. I liked him. He's probably going to call me tonight or tomorrow."

"I see." Mike gave her an inscrutable glance, then leaned forward to help Emma who was struggling into her new shoes. She already had on a red T-shirt backward over her pyjamas, and was obviously planning to model her entire new wardrobe for Susan.

Susan sipped the coffee and watched them, moved by the tenderness of Mike's callused hands and the warmth in his eyes as he smiled at his daughter.

There was no mistaking the look of gentle pride on the man's face. No matter what their story might be, there was no doubt that Mike loved his little girl, and took wonderful care of her.

And Emma adored her father . . .

Susan shook off her troubled thoughts and forced herself to admire the child's new clothes.

"You must have spent an awful lot," she said to Mike when Emma finally trotted upstairs with her book and her shopping bags.

He shrugged. "It's expensive, all right. You can't buy just anything. Children have definite ideas and trying to get them what they want and still stick to a budget isn't easy."

"I know. I'd hate to be the one to disappoint Emma when she's got her mind set on something."

The next few moments passed in silence. Susan toyed with the handle of her mug, while Mike stared down at the cover of Emma's book.

"Daddy!" Emma shouted from upstairs. "I'm in bed, and you promised one more story. You promised you'd read the 'Sleepy Mouse' if I went straight to bed."

Mike got to his feet and smiled at Susan, looking so boyish and appealing that she caught her breath and stared at him, wide-eyed.

"I hate the 'Sleepy Mouse,'" he confided in a husky whisper, leaning toward her. "He's such a little goody-goody."

Susan stood frozen, breathless, so close to him that she could smell his after-shave and see the firm muscles in his jaw. She was conscious of his maleness, his strength, the muscles in his arms and the intensity of his gaze, and she felt herself drawn almost irresistibly, pulled toward him...

Then he was gone. Susan could hear him running lightly up the steps, two at a time. She stood by the counter, shaken, gazing unseeingly through the window at the darkened backyard.

After a while she pulled herself together, went to the foot of the stairs and called, "Mike!"

The low rumble of his reading voice stopped abruptly. "Yeah?" he asked. "What is it?"

"I have to go out for a while. There's something I forgot while I was shopping. I'll be back in a half hour or so."

"All right," he said. "Don't forget to lock the door. Are you taking Buster?"

"No, I don't think so. Mike . . ."

"Yeah?"

"If Peter calls, tell him I'll be back soon. Take his number, all right?"

"Who's Peter?"

"The *college professor*," Susan called impatiently. "The dating service was going to give him my message right away, so he might call tonight."

"If I have to keep being your social secretary," Mike said, appearing suddenly in Emma's doorway and looking down at her with mock sternness, "I'm going to charge an hourly wage."

Susan glared back, glad to have their relationship restored to its usual teasing lightness. She was still shaken by her reaction to him in the kitchen, when for a moment she'd had to fight the desire to touch him.

"THREE MONTHS," Sergeant Walters told her. The policeman sat behind his desk and frowned at the statement she'd just filled out, in which she described how she'd happened to find the money. "Now, this kid you passed on the trail, you're sure he's got nothing to do with it?"

Susan fidgeted, feeling self-conscious in her tattered sweat suit. "Of course I can't know for sure, but I'd be very surprised if he were involved. I see him in the park almost every night when I'm running. He's always walking by himself, and he certainly doesn't seem like the type to be doing anything criminal. What do you mean, three months?''

''Nobody else around? No cars parked at the curb, people sitting on benches, nothing like that?''

''Not that I can recall,'' Susan murmured. ''What did you mean when you said—''

''Hey, Curt,'' Walters asked, looking over his shoulder at another policeman, who was wearing plastic gloves and examining the suitcase and its contents. ''What you got? Anything?''

''I doubt it. Pretty tough to get prints off this textured vinyl stuff.'' The young policeman frowned at the surface of the case. ''And the handle looks all wet and chewed-up.''

''My dog,'' Susan explained. ''He found the suitcase in the bushes, and I guess he chewed on it quite a bit before I stopped him. He really likes to chew on things,'' she added.

''You touched the suitcase?'' the second policemen asked her.

''Several times. I opened it in the park, and carried it to my car, and then brought it here...''

The officers exchanged a glance. ''Any prints we find, likely gonna be hers,'' the sergeant muttered sadly. ''How about on the bills, Curt?'' he asked.

''It's tough. Practically impossible. Old bills like these, they've been handled by so many people, the lab never has much luck trying to lift individual prints off them.''

''How much is there, Curt?'' his partner asked.

The other man approached the desk, stripping off his gloves.

"Fifty-three thousand, two hundred and sixty-eight."

"Fifty-three *thousand?*" Susan whispered, staring at the young policeman. *"Dollars?"*

"Yeah," he said dryly. "Dollars."

"Now, like I told you, Miss..." The sergeant gave her an inquiring glance.

"Adamson. Susan Adamson."

"Right. Well, Miss Adamson, the waiting period is three months. We'll call you if anything comes up."

"What happens after three months?"

"If the money's still unclaimed, its yours."

"Mine?" she asked, dazed.

"Finders keepers," the policeman told her laconically. "If the original owner doesn't come forward, who's got a better claim than you?"

"But I thought... wouldn't the government..."

He waved his hand in a dismissive gesture. "The government can't keep everything they get their hands on, even though they'd like to. Now, with a lot of money like this, I'm not sure of your tax position, but you'd have to—"

"Three months," she murmured. She looked up at the sergeant behind his desk. "What do you think?" she asked, meeting his eyes directly. "What are the chances it won't be claimed?"

"Not a hope in hell," Curt said cheerfully.

Susan's spirits plummeted.

"See," the sergeant added, sitting on the corner of the desk and giving Susan an engaging smile, "this money, it's likely the payoff from a drug deal, something like that, right? Not much chance it's all legal and aboveboard."

"I know."

"And what likely happened, they had to dump the suitcase in a hurry because they were in some kind of danger, right?"

Susan nodded.

"So they don't walk away and leave over fifty thousand dollars just lying there. You can bet they saw you pick it up, and they're already planning to get it back. They probably put a tail on you when you left the park and then followed you down here, so they know where the money is."

"Put a tail on me?" she asked in horror. "You mean, followed me to my *house?* They know where I live?"

She thought about her quiet house, with Buster drowsing in the backyard and Emma sleeping upstairs, warm and cozy in her pink pajamas, clutching her stuffed kangaroo...

The sergeant looked at her with sympathy. "No need to worry, Miss Adamson. The minute you brought that suitcase down here, they lost interest in you. It's the money they want, not you."

"But I don't understand," she said. "How can they possibly claim the money? If they're...criminals, how can they come to the police station and just ask for it?"

"Oh, they'll think of something. See, we got no idea where this money came from. It doesn't match anything we're looking for, no current reports of stolen money. They know that, see? So they'll come up with some story, how somebody won the lottery and decided to give it to their parents, or took their life savings out of the bank to make a down payment on a house, something like that. And then they'll send somebody's old grandmother or pregnant teenage daughter down here to identify the suitcase, somebody who's squeaky clean, and we'll have to give it up."

"I see," Susan said. "They have the advantage because they know what the suitcase looks like, and how much money is in it. So as long as the person who claims the money is convincing enough, you'll have no right to deny them."

"Absolutely."

"And you're sure this is going to happen?"

"Just about a hundred percent. I wouldn't book any trips to Hawaii on the strength of getting that money, Miss Adamson."

"I hadn't intended to," Susan said. "But," she added with a wistful smile, "I would have liked to pay off some of my mortgage."

"Wouldn't we all?" The sergeant grinned, then looked down at her statement. "Is there anybody really close to you, Miss Adamson? People you confide in?"

"Well, there are my parents, they live in Victoria, and I have a girlfriend who teaches in an elementary school over in Burnaby..."

"Any boyfriends?"

Susan thought about the dating service. "A few," she said. "Nothing serious at the moment."

"You live alone?"

"Sort of. It's my house, but I have a tenant who lives upstairs. A young man with a three-year-old daughter."

"Did you tell him about the money before you came down here?"

Susan shook her head. "No, I didn't. We're not all that close," she added.

The sergeant nodded. "We'd prefer it if you didn't tell anybody about this money for the time being," he said. "Not even your family or friends."

"Why? You can't possibly think one of them might make a false claim!"

"Probably not. But it's an exciting story, Miss Adamson, and they might just drop it in conversation where somebody could overhear who *would* be willing to make a false claim of ownership. And we don't want that happening, do we?"

"I guess not."

"So you'll keep it a secret for a while? I know it's a lot to ask, when somebody's just found a suitcase full of money."

"Look, Sergeant, I don't want to tell anybody about it," Susan said abruptly. "The whole thing seems sleazy, somehow. And scary, too," she added.

The younger police officer looked at her with sympathy. "Nothing to be scared of, Miss Adamson. Like the sergeant told you, it's the cash they want, not you. We'll call you when it's been claimed."

"All right. But until you call, I'm going to try really hard not to think about it."

The sergeant got to his feet and gave her a courteous smile. "Constable Liepert will let you know right away if anything comes up, Miss Adamson. Thanks for being such a good citizen."

THE WEEKS PASSED with disconcerting swiftness as the calendar slipped into October. The mornings were chilled with golden frost, as clear and sweet as wine. By late afternoon, the shadows lay long and still on the grass where Emma and Buster romped happily in piles of dry leaves.

Susan went out several times with Peter Keeler, the second man she'd met through the video dating service, and found his company pleasant and undemanding. Mike spent his weekends repairing loose shingles on the mossy old roof and putting a cozy layer of new insulation in Buster's doghouse. Susan watched his strong brown hands, his quiet helpfulness around the house, and tried not to think about the future.

One Friday evening the three of them were sitting at the dinner table, eating a pie made from apples given to them by Mrs. Clark, the elderly widow who lived next door.

"Delicious," Mike said with a contented sigh, pushing his empty plate away and reaching for his coffee. "I didn't know you could bake pies, Susan. That pastry's terrific."

"It's my grandmother's recipe." Susan smiled at him. "It's a family secret."

"What's a grandmother?" Emma asked. She was finishing her pie, frowning with concentration as she tried to balance a dollop of ice cream on a forkful of pastry and fruit.

Susan glanced at Mike, then turned to the little girl. "You must have a grandma, sweetie," she said with forced casualness. "Your daddy's parents and your mummy's parents, those are your grandparents. Don't you ever see them?"

"No," Mike said briefly. "She doesn't. Emma, don't take such a big mouthful."

His tone was cold and dismissive, but Susan persisted. "Why not? Do they live on the other side of the country, or what?"

"Is a grandmother the same thing as a granny?" Emma asked in her clear voice.

Susan paused, unnerved by the way Mike looked on in watchful silence. "Yes," she said at last. "The very same thing."

"I wish I had a granny," Emma said wistfully. "They do nice things in all the stories. And Tommy's granny bakes him special cookies with faces."

"I'll make you some cookies with faces," Mike told her. "Tomorrow, all right? After I've done the upstairs windows, we'll make gingerbread men."

Emma brightened. "And use raisins for their eyes, and candy for buttons?"

"If you want."

"Will they have ears?"

Mike used a napkin to wipe crumbs from the little girl's face. "I'm not sure about ears. We'll have to give it some thought."

Emma climbed down from her chair and Mike watched her run off through the kitchen door. Susan looked on nervously, wondering how to pursue the topic. It was difficult to believe that all four of Emma's grandparents were dead. After all, they probably wouldn't have been much older than Susan's parents, who were both in their early sixties.

Her thoughts turned back to Betty's suggestion that Susan might be harboring a kidnapper. Was Mike deliberately keeping Emma away from her grandparents? Somehow, in spite of her best intentions, she'd never managed to broach the subject.

Mike looked at her with interest. "Is Betty still going out with the antique dealer?"

Susan got up and turned away on the pretext of pouring more coffee. "Yes, she is."

"Hasn't anybody warned her of the consequences?"

"What consequences?" Susan asked. "I haven't met him yet, but he sounds like a really nice person. Betty's crazy about him."

"So I gather. But if they become a couple, they're going to be Betty and Barney, you know. Has she thought of that?"

"Betty and Barney? Of course, the Flintstones."

He smiled again, his eyes crinkling with humor.

Susan put aside her dark suspicions for a moment and laughed with him. "Betty and Barney Rubble," she murmured. "Oh, that's funny. I'll have to tell her. I wonder if it's occurred to her."

"Maybe it has, and that's why she's started calling him Barnaby." Mike gave her a teasing glance. "So, Wilma," he said innocently, "what's happening in *your* cave these days?"

"If you mean Peter," Susan began with dignity, "we're getting along very well, thank you. In fact, we're going to—"

The phone rang, startling her. Each time it rang, she expected it to be a call from the police saying that the suitcase had been claimed and taken away. At first, Susan had dreaded this call, which would end all her dreams of unexpected wealth. But as the weeks passed without any news, she almost began to hope for the call.

At least it would stop the suspense, now almost unbearable. Especially when she couldn't talk to anybody about it, not even Betty.

"Hello?" she said, snatching up the phone on the kitchen counter. She heard the voice on the other end and relaxed. "Oh, hello, Peter. How are you?"

While Susan was on the phone, Emma wandered back into the kitchen and leaned against her father's chair, pulling a small red wagon that Mike had built for her. Inside the wagon were a couple of books, Gerald the kangaroo and Emma's new white running shoes.

"Daddy, you promised you'd teach me to tie my shoes," she said.

Susan watched, briefly distracted from her call, while Mike lifted the little girl onto his knee and took one of the shoes in his hand.

"Peter?" she said. "I'm sorry, I missed that. What did you say?"

She listened, nodding. "All right," she said at last. "I'll be waiting. Thanks, Peter. See you tomorrow."

She hung up and turned reluctantly to meet Mike's quizzical glance.

"What's up?" he asked, while Emma tugged at his ear and tried to get his attention.

"Peter and I are going over to the Island tomorrow." Susan began to gather the dishes and stack them in the dishwasher. "We're going to catch the early ferry."

"Wow." He pursed his lips and gave a low whistle. "Taking him home to meet the folks, are you? This *must* be serious."

Susan flushed. "I'm *not* taking him to meet my parents," she said. "He's doing some research in Victoria and I haven't seen my parents for a while, so we thought it would be a nice idea to spend the day together, that's all. I'll visit with Mom and Dad while he's over at the university."

"You won't introduce him to your parents? You'll leave him sitting outside in the car when he comes to pick you up?"

"Of course I'll introduce him," she said, exasperated. "I'm merely pointing out that having Peter meet my parents is not the purpose of the trip, that's all."

"I see." Mike's tone implied that he didn't believe her, and it annoyed her even further. Fortunately, Emma bounced on his knee and waved one of her shoes, demanding his attention.

"Daddy! You *promised*."

"All right, all right. You have to try hard to develop some patience, sweetheart," he told her, kissing her cheek. "Life requires a lot of patience. Now, these are the laces. The first thing we do is tie a simple knot, like this."

"It's called a granny knot," Susan contributed and was puzzled by Mike's frown. Then she realized that he obviously didn't want any more discussion about grannies. She subsided, a little intimidated by his expression.

"And then," he went on, addressing Emma who was watching him attentively, "we make two bunnies, like this, see?'' He folded the laces into twin loops.

"Bunnies," Emma echoed, fascinated. "Can I hold the bunnies?''

"Not yet. You have to keep watching closely. Now, one bunny runs around the other like this.'' One of the loops circled the other. "But now he's scared and he wants to hide. Poor bunny, he needs a hole to hide in.''

Susan paused with a stack of dishes in her hands and watched, as absorbed as Emma.

"So he peeks in here . . .'' Mike eased his thumb out of the way.

"There!'' Emma shouted. "There's a hole for the bunny!''

"My goodness. So there is,'' Mike said with a smile. "Now, this bunny pops into the hole. Then you pull on both their ears, and there you are. A nice neat bow.''

Emma looked at the shoe, then laughed and wriggled around to kiss her father's cheek.

He held her, smiling at Susan over the little girl's head.

All at once, Susan felt her heart melting. The moment was so cozy and sweet, this ageless circle of man, woman and child drawn safely together in the lamplight while darkness gathered beyond their windows.

Her smile faded as she met his gaze, standing for a long moment with the dishes forgotten in her hands.

Emma broke the spell. "Daddy, show me again! I can't make the bunnies.'' She struggled with the laces, her face puckered in concentration.

Mike demonstrated patiently, and Susan continued to tidy the kitchen, her heart still beating noisily. These unsettling moments were beginning to happen more often, and she didn't know what to do about them. She only knew that with each passing day, she grew more disturbed by the mystery of Mike and his daughter, and less able to question him about it.

As she wiped the counter and put away the last of the dishes, Mike wound up his shoe-tying lesson and sent Emma away with her wagon of toys, promising to come upstairs soon. The child left the room, then ran back to give Susan a kiss.

Susan knelt and hugged her, loving the feel of Emma's warm little body in denim overalls, the clean fragrance of her hair and skin.

"Good night, darling," she murmured. "Sweet dreams."

"I love you," Emma whispered, her breath warm on Susan's cheek. "I love you best of anyone except for Daddy."

Susan gave Emma another hug, then got to her feet, watching with a misty smile and a lump in her throat as Emma went down the hall.

When she turned around, Mike was standing next to her at the counter, reaching over her head to get the coffee can.

"My turn to make the coffee for breakfast," he said lightly, his arm still extended.

But his expression was far from casual as he looked at her, and Susan suddenly realized that he was much too near for comfort. She felt an urgent need to move away, put some distance between them, but movement was suddenly impossible. Instead, she stood frozen at the counter, looking into his face.

He had such high, blunt cheekbones, such a powerful jaw and finely shaped mouth . . .

He lowered his arms slowly and reached for her, grasping her elbows and drawing her close, his eyes dark with emotion.

"Mike," she whispered.

But she couldn't make any protest, couldn't do anything at all but sway toward him, drawn by the intensity of his face and the blue depths of those eyes. His arms closed around her and she shivered with pleasure.

His body felt hard. She felt as if she were being enclosed in a grip of steel. Yet his embrace was gentle, and when his mouth found hers, his lips were surprisingly cool and soft.

Susan returned his kiss with a hunger that embarrassed her. She hadn't realized until this moment just how many times she'd thought about being in his arms, nestling close to him, smelling the warmth of his skin and feeling the strength of his arms around her.

Shameless, panting, she pressed against him and strained her body into his, closer and closer, while his arms tightened around her and his lips moved on hers, open-mouthed with passion . . .

Abruptly she pulled away, her breasts heaving, and turned aside to rub her arms nervously.

He stood in silence, looking at her. "Susan?" he asked.

"Sorry," she whispered, giving him a quick glance and biting her lips to keep them from trembling. "Sorry. I . . . don't know what got into me. That should never have happened."

"You don't have to apologize."

"I guess," Susan murmured, trying to keep her voice light, "these things can be expected when two people live in the same house and get so familiar with each other. But we have to be careful, Mike. We can't let it happen again."

"You're right," he agreed in that same quiet tone. "We can't let it happen again."

"Because," Susan went on, forcing herself to meet his eyes, "this kind of thing could really complicate life, and we don't want that, right? I mean, it's best if we don't..."

"Yes," he said when her voice faltered. "It's best if we don't. Good night, Susan. If I don't see you before you leave in the morning, have a nice day in Victoria."

"I will," she whispered.

She stood by the counter, twisting a dish towel absently in her hands while he strode out of the kitchen without looking back.

CROUCHED IN the hydrangea bushes outside the big kitchen window, Danny watched their embrace in wistful silence. Buster pressed close to him, whining urgently. Danny shared a little more of the black licorice from his pocket, having discovered some time ago that Buster loved this treat.

"They're kissing," Danny told the dog in a muffled whisper. "They really love each other, don't they? It must be so nice, living with a woman who loves you like that."

He looked on enviously as the tall man went upstairs to tend to their little kid. The woman stood by the counter watching him go, her golden hair shining in the light.

The day after he'd lost the money, Danny had followed the schoolteacher in his cab when she left the park after her evening run. The next night, he'd returned to her house and slipped in through the back alley. He'd launched a brief campaign to win Buster's trust, then had settled in and begun to familiarize himself with every detail of the family's routine.

The only thing he couldn't understand was the relationship between the woman and the big guy in the station wagon who stopped by the house periodically to take her out.

Eventually he'd decided that the graying man must be her brother, because the dark-haired guy she lived with was often home when the other man visited and they all greeted one another with courtesy. It wasn't as if she was sneaking around or anything.

Danny would have been bitterly disappointed to find that she was the cheating type. He thought the blond woman and the dark-haired man belonged together. They were both so attractive that they appealed to his romantic nature. And the way the guy looked at her sometimes when she was busy and unaware of his scrutiny, with an expression of such naked adoration...it was enough to make Danny, hidden outside in the bushes, feel a lump in his throat.

He longed to ask Lynnette if she knew any details about her teacher's home life, but he was afraid to express an interest in the family, in case something happened. Sometimes he even had to take himself in hand and struggle to remember the purpose of all this spying. It wasn't to invade their privacy and peek at their private moments together.

He wasn't that kind of person, Danny thought with dignity.

All he wanted was to find out where they'd hidden the money. He knew it still had to be somewhere in the house, because nothing in their life-style had changed at all since the night she picked up the suitcase. They hadn't bought anything new, or even hired a baby-sitter and gone out to dinner together. They must be waiting until some time had passed and nobody was likely to ask questions before they started spending Danny's money.

He'd convinced himself of this because it was un-thinkable to consider anything else. Danny knew he would go out of his mind if he thought the suitcase wasn't inside that house with all of Rosa's careful savings intact. He thought about it so often that if he closed his eyes, he could actually see the cheap brown case hidden inside a closet or under a bed.

All he wanted was to figure out where it was. As soon as he did that, he was going inside to get it.

He shivered in the darkness and put an arm around Buster, who pressed close to him and licked his face.

Danny was terrified by the thought of breaking into their house. If something went wrong and he was caught, he would go to jail for at least five years.

"I'd rather die," Danny whispered to the big dog, his voice breaking. "God, I'd rather die."

Buster whined softly in response and nuzzled at Danny's pocket. Absently, Danny fed the dog an-other stick of licorice, thinking about his plan.

Once he knew where the suitcase was, he'd wait until they were both at work, and then he'd do the job. He'd be in and out of the house in a few minutes, and nobody would ever know.

"Except for you," Danny whispered to Buster. "And you won't tell, will you, boy? You're my friend. You won't tell."

Buster licked Danny's face eagerly. Danny smiled and got to his feet. Glancing over his shoulder, moving low and fast, he slipped through the yard and let himself out the back. Buster ran up and down by the gate, barking a couple of times in disappointment.

Danny reached over the fence to fondle the dog's ears and whisper a few soothing words, then turned and disappeared down the alley, as dark and quiet as a shadow.

CHAPTER SIX

SUSAN PAUSED by the kitchen window and watched the early sunlight filter through the brilliantly colored leaves of the red maple in the backyard. Buster nosed in the bushes, a fuzzy golden shape in the muted light of morning. The whole autumn world looked serene and peaceful.

She shivered, thinking about Mike's kiss the night before. How could she possibly have let it happen? What was she thinking of?

So many things were slipping beyond her control these days. In addition to her worries about Mike and Emma, Susan spent many hours obsessing about the suitcase and the difference the money would make to her life if she were actually allowed to claim it.

She turned away from the window and began to set the table for breakfast.

It was possible that Mike wouldn't come down for breakfast at all. Maybe he was as embarrassed as she was, and he'd stay tactfully out of sight until after she'd left with Peter.

Susan glanced hopefully at her watch. Less than an hour till her date was supposed to arrive. Of course, Peter wasn't all that punctual, but surely it was too early for him to get absorbed in some project and forget about the time...

Her heart sank when she heard footsteps clattering down the stairs. She looked up at the doorway as she struggled to compose herself.

But it was only Emma, dressed in her new red T-shirt, running shoes and a tiny pair of blue jeans with patches on the knees. The little girl carried a wooden box painted to look like a house, with a handle on top.

"Hi, Susan," she said, pausing by the table and struggling to lift the heavy box.

"Hi, sweetie. How are you this morning?"

Susan set the dollhouse on the table for her, then watched as Emma scrambled onto a chair and leaned forward to open the hinged box and expose the inside of the house.

Automatically, Susan bent to kiss the child's round cheek and rested her face for a moment against the shining cap of brown hair. Emma always smelled so good, like warm soap and sunshine.

"Is Daddy coming down for breakfast?" Susan asked with forced casualness, turning away to pop some bread in the toaster.

Emma shook her head, setting her mop of hair swinging. "He's working at his desk. He's writing something. He said to tell you he'd come down for breakfast later, and that you should wear your jacket today if it doesn't get any warmer."

"Okay," Susan said with relief. "Tell your daddy I'll take my jacket."

Emma beamed, obviously pleased with herself for relaying the message correctly, then poked at a small plastic bed in the dollhouse.

"See?" She turned around on the chair to look at Susan. "I put their bed in the living room."

"Why?" Susan asked. Emma was always able to divert her, no matter how troubled she felt.

"So the kids can watch cartoons before they go to sleep."

"Wouldn't it be better just to have a TV in their bedroom?"

Emma frowned, considering, then shook her head decisively. "The teddy bears wouldn't like it."

"I see." Susan carried a pot of jam to the table and paused to hug the little girl again. "You're a sweetheart, Emma Murphy," she whispered. "Did anybody ever tell you that?"

"Daddy tells me that all the time," Emma said placidly, arranging miniature chairs around a table and setting doll figures on them. "Now they're having their breakfast, too. They're having toast and jam, just like us."

Susan looked at the row of thimble-size people. "Think how tiny those pieces of toast must be," she said. "Like specks of dust."

Emma held up her fingers and measured an infinitesimal space between them. "Like this," she said, frowning in concentration. "*Very* small."

"Very, very small," Susan agreed solemnly. "Have some toast, darling. Look, I buttered it for you and cut it into triangles, just the way you like."

"Okay." Emma rested her chin in her hands and stared at the dollhouse. "How can you ride on a fairy?" she asked.

"Ride on what?"

"When you go away with Peter today," Emma said, "Daddy says you're riding on a fairy. Is she magic? Do you have to get really small to ride on her, like the toast?"

Susan looked at the child, bewildered for a moment, then laughed.

"It's a *ferry*, Emma," she said, almost wishing Mike would come down and share the joke. "It's a different thing altogether. Not like Tinkerbell, with wings and a magic wand. A ferry is a great big ship, big enough to carry lots and lots of people and their cars."

"Cars?" Emma said skeptically. "On a *boat?*"

Susan nodded. "And there's even a place where you can eat, and stores, and everything."

Emma thought this over, then turned back to her dollhouse. "The kids are in the bed watching TV," she reported. "And the mommy and daddy are up here in the bedroom."

"What are they doing?" Susan gave the girl a side-long glance.

"They're looking after the baby. He needs his diaper changed, like Steven at day care. See? The mommy and daddy take really good care of him."

Susan peered at the tiny doll figures as Emma moved them around inside the house. There really was a baby with a bald head and bright yellow bib, his whole body no larger than the tip of Susan's finger. She watched the two parent figures hovering nearby as Emma's small hands placed the baby carefully in the plastic crib.

Susan glanced at the hallway and listened, but there was no sign of Mike. She leaned close to Emma, lowering her voice.

"Do you remember anything about your mommy, Emma?" she whispered. "Do your remember your mommy taking care of you?"

Emma shook her head and lifted the crib, moving it out to the kitchen. "He needs some baby food," she announced. "He's hungry." She set the baby in a little white plastic high chair and shoved it closer to the table, then brought the two parents in and placed them nearby.

Susan hesitated, feeling guilty. It seemed so treacherous, pumping a child for information, but she had to know.

"Did you ever live with your mommy, like the baby does?" she urged. "Do you remember her at all?"

Emma looked at her in surprise. "I always just lived with Daddy. My mommy's in heaven."

"And you don't remember her? You don't remember living with her?"

"I only lived with Daddy. Sometimes we lived in a place that had a radio thing people talked in from downstairs. It made a funny noise."

"An intercom," Susan said after a moment's thought.

"Then we lived in the dirty place that had bugs, and then we lived here. But this is nicest of all." Emma climbed down from her chair and lifted the dollhouse carefully in her arms. "I want to show Buster the little people."

"Can't you eat one more piece of toast?"

Emma shook her head and started toward the door. Susan watched as the child took her jacket from a hook and went outside, where she was greeted joyously by Buster who galloped around her, wagging his tail.

Not much information from that little fishing expedition, Susan thought ruefully. In fact, she didn't know anything more about Mike and Emma's past.

She started to clear the table, wondering how she would manage without Emma in her life. The little girl had only lived with her for a month or so, but already the prospect of life without her seemed impossibly bleak.

Susan shook her head, gathered herself together and hurried to tidy the kitchen so she could get ready for her date with Peter.

HE ARRIVED shortly after nine o'clock, almost on time, and came up the walk with his firm, rather heavy tread, wearing faded brown corduroys and a warm cardigan over a turtleneck.

Peter Keeler was a broad, handsome man with thick graying hair and a placid expression that seldom changed. Susan liked his air of calm, his confidence and quiet intelligence. It seemed to her that Peter moved in a tranquil world without emotional highs or lows—unlike her own.

But the professor had a lighter side, too. Susan enjoyed the faculty parties and college functions she attended with him; she enjoyed moving in the company of gracious well-read people whose conversation was always interesting.

She greeted him at the door with a smile. "Hello, Peter. I'm almost ready. I'll just check on Emma, and then we can go."

He looked in obvious admiration at her flowered skirt and casual pink T-shirt. "You're as pretty as a picture," he said with the awkward gallantry that Susan always found rather touching.

"Thank you, Peter," she said. "You look very nice, too."

She paused by the closet to get her jacket, then went back through the kitchen to look at Emma. The child was still playing on the terrace with Buster and her dollhouse. Peter waited near the kitchen doorway, apparently lost in thought.

"You should see her playing with her little dollhouse." Susan smiled fondly at the scene on the terrace. "She's so cute, Peter."

He nodded without interest and Susan turned away. Peter had no affinity for small children. Whenever he encountered Emma, he looked at her with cautious astonishment, as if she were a visitor from another planet.

"Well," Susan said at last, gathering up her things, "I guess we'd better go, if we want to catch the early ferry."

She grinned briefly, thinking of Emma's concerns about riding on a fairy. But there was no point in trying to share the joke with Peter, whose sense of humor was far too obscure to appreciate a child's interpretation of words.

"Mike?" Susan called, pausing by the foot of the stairs.

"Yeah?"

Even the sound of his voice made her feel tense. She moved a little closer to Peter who stood next to her, waiting near the front door.

"Peter and I are leaving now. Emma's out on the terrace with Buster."

"Okay," he said. "I'll come down right away. Hi, Peter."

"Hello, Mike," Peter called up the stairs. "Enjoy your weekend."

"Let's go," Susan whispered, anxious to be out of the house before Mike could appear on the landing. She took Peter's arm and hurried outside into the warm autumn morning, determined to put Mike out of her mind and enjoy the day.

THE FERRY RIDE from the lower mainland to Vancouver Island took about an hour and a half, winding through the misty green islands in the Strait of Georgia. Often when Susan made the crossing, especially in the autumn, the islands were obscured by masses of damp fog rising from the ocean. But on this October morning, the air was crystal clear, and the water glittered with sunlight.

She sat on the upper deck on one of the life-jacket lockers, looking out over the water. Because the day had been so mild when they steamed away from Vancouver, she'd left her jacket in Peter's station wagon, down on the cargo deck. She wore only her T-shirt and cotton skirt, and the breeze off the water felt fresh and cool in spite of the sunshine.

But Susan was hardly aware of the temperature. Despite her resolve, her mind whirled with images she was unable to vanquish. Over the tranquil vistas of

land and sky and water, she saw other pictures—stacks
of money, Emma's cherubic face and laughing eyes,
Mike's arms holding her and his mouth on hers . . .

She shivered and wrapped her arms around her
knees, gazing at the distant horizon with a brooding
look.

"Getting chilly?" Peter inquired, coming up beside her and settling on the locker.

Susan turned to smile at him.

While she watched, he took a pair of heavy glasses
from his cardigan pocket, fitted them in place and began to read a loosely bound stack of papers he'd
brought with him, sipping from a foam cup full of
coffee.

"Is the coffee hot?" she asked.

"Not very. Are you sure you don't want a cup?"

"Not unless it's really hot. I can't stand lukewarm
coffee."

Peter lowered his glasses and peered at her over the
frames. "Are you sure you're not chilly?"

"I'm all right," Susan said. "The sun's warm."

He nodded and went back to his reading. In spite of
herself, Susan thought how differently Mike would
have behaved under the same circumstances. If Mike
suspected she might be getting cold out here on the
deck, he would insist on going down immediately to
fetch her jacket from the car. Or he would force his
sweater on her, or even command her to go inside, and
refuse to accept any protest.

But, of course, Mike was a really arrogant and
overbearing man. Peter was much more disposed to
take people at face value. If Susan said she was comfortable, he accepted her judgment.

In fact, Mike Murphy and Peter Keeler were about as different as two men could be. Peter readily admitted that he couldn't change a light bulb without help, while Mike seemed able to fix anything from faulty truck engines to broken toys. Mike was changeable and disturbing, full of teasing remarks and abrupt silences. Peter was solid and calm, unruffled in the face of changing circumstances.

Susan sometimes wondered how her professor had managed to rouse himself from his academic preoccupations long enough to go to the dating service, make a video and launch his search for a suitable woman to share his life.

But, as Peter told her seriously, everybody got lonely at times. Even scholars.

He seemed to enjoy her company in his quiet way, and found her physically attractive, as well. By now, they'd progressed to a chaste exchange of kisses at the end of each date. Susan admitted to Betty, when pressed, that she didn't find Peter's kisses wildly exciting, but she wasn't uncomfortable with them, either.

Not at all like Mike in *that* way, she thought. Mike's kiss had been so warm and passionate, taking her breath away, keeping her awake for hours as she tossed and turned . . .

Resolutely, Susan pushed the memory aside and returned to her examination of the two men and their differences.

Most significant of all, Mike's past was dark and shrouded in mystery, while Peter's life was an open book. He was forty-one, a graduate of Simon Fraser University where he now taught political science. He told Susan on their first date that he'd been married in his twenties to another teacher at the same college who'd been offered a full professorship at McGill in Montreal.

"So she took it?" Susan had asked.

"Of course," he'd said. "It's a marvelous position. Exactly what she wanted."

"And you didn't go with her?"

"I had tenure," he'd replied, as if that explained everything.

"Oh."

"We're still very good friends," he'd said. "She's remarried and has two sons, and she named one of them after me."

Remembering, Susan marveled again at such a calm and sensible approach to life. She had another traitorous image of Mike and what his reaction would be if his wife told him she was leaving him to accept a better job on the other side of the country.

Abruptly, she shook her head to dispel the memory of her tenant's vivid blue eyes, his strong face and unruly dark hair.

Emma looked a lot like her father. But her eyes were brown, so her mother's had probably been dark, as well. Susan thought of the poor young woman dying in that tragic winter crash on the Montana prairie.

She frowned, recalling Betty's suspicions and her own breakfast conversation with Emma.

It didn't mean anything, really, that Emma had no recollection of her mother. Betty claimed that small children's memories often didn't extend back for more than a few months. If Mike had kidnapped his child more than a year ago, Emma likely wouldn't remember any other home.

So it was still possible that Mike was lying about his past. This very morning, Emma's mother could be sitting somewhere, alone, yearning for her little girl...

Susan bit her lip and stared at the vacation homes dotting the hillside of one of the islands.

She was growing increasingly tormented by the whole situation. Part of her longed to confront Mike and demand an honest answer. But another, more cowardly part shied away from this course of action.

For one thing, their relationship would never be the same afterward. Even if Mike had some perfectly logical explanation for the mysteries of his life, and the strange isolation that he and Emma lived in, even then, the accusation would hang between them, spoiling the easygoing relationship they'd managed to build.

Worse, what if he *was* a kidnapper, and confessed as much when she confronted him? Reluctantly, Susan forced herself to examine this possibility.

As Betty said, kidnapping anyone, even your own biological child, was a criminal act. Would Susan feel compelled to turn him in to the authorities if she knew the truth? How could she, knowing how much Emma loved her father and depended on him?

The little girl didn't even remember any other parent...

She sighed and moved uneasily on the hard surface of the locker. Beside her, Peter flipped through the pages to the end, made a couple of notes in the margin and returned to his place, holding the loosely bound papers to keep them from flapping in the wind.

"Look!" Susan said, pointing over the deck railing. "Look, Peter, there's a seal! And another one, see? Right over there."

He lowered his glasses to peer in the direction she indicated, nodded without much interest, then went back to his reading.

Susan sighed again and returned to her gloomy thoughts.

The biggest problem of all was the wayward, irrational attraction she felt to Mike Murphy. It was purely sexual, nothing more. Mike was clearly aware of it, too, recognizing just as Susan did that it threatened to destroy the delicate balance they'd worked so hard to establish. But now, after that disastrous kiss had sounded a warning to both of them, they were going to have to be even more careful . . .

Susan nestled close to the man beside her and slipped her arm under his.

Peter looked down at her, briefly distracted from his reading, and gave her a vague smile. Susan smiled back and rested her cheek on his shoulder. He freed his arm to gave her a fatherly pat, then grabbed at his papers as the wind whipped them.

"I think I'll go inside to finish this," he said. "Coming, Susan?"

"In a minute." She watched as he got to his feet and pocketed his glasses.

He paused by the locker, gripping his papers under his arm, his hair lifting and blowing in the wind. "Do you want anything? I'm getting some toast in the cafeteria."

Susan shook her head. "No thanks, Peter. I'll come in after a little while, all right? I love watching the Island getting closer."

"All right," he said, moving across the deck toward the door, once again peering down at the document he carried. Susan watched him go inside, then turned back to the ocean vista beyond the ferry. She began to feel really cold, shivering with a deep chill that stabbed through her light clothes, but she was reluctant to leave the deck. She hugged her arms and stared at the misty blue horizon, her hair whipping in the wind.

THE FOLLOWING WEDNESDAY morning, Mike hung up the kitchen phone and turned to look at Emma, who sat on the floor near the counter holding Gerald in her arms. She had an old toothbrush which she plied vigorously across the kangaroo's smiling mouth.

"And up and down," she muttered. "And back and forth and all around. Gerald, stop wiggling. You *need* to have your teeth brushed, so you don't get cavities."

Mike smiled down at her and nudged her gently with his foot. "Almost ready, sweetheart?"

"In a minute." Emma scrambled to her feet. "I just have to put Gerald to bed. Kiss, Daddy."

She held the kangaroo up to be kissed. Gerald was wearing a pair of blue cotton pajamas designed to fit a large doll. The fabric strained across his ample hindquarters and hung loose and floppy on his narrow shoulders and upper limbs.

Mike leaned down obediently to kiss the kangaroo. These days, Gerald had a schedule like a shift worker.

He was lovingly tucked into bed every morning when Emma went to day care, then roused for hours of boisterous play in the late afternoon.

Mike watched his daughter race off down the hall. It had been weeks since Emma last took her kangaroo to day care. She was so happy and confident in her new home, bubbly and full of laughter, learning new things every day. It warmed Mike's heart to see her like this.

But his smile faded as he looked at Susan's closed door. A lot of Emma's happiness was in the hands of the woman behind that door, and Mike had no idea what Susan was thinking anymore.

He poured himself another cup of coffee, wishing for the thousandth time that he'd kept himself under control last Friday night and fought off that overpowering urge to kiss her. Ever since, Susan had been uncomfortably quiet and edgy even though they'd both tried hard to ignore his lapse and pretend nothing unusual had happened.

The truth was, something *had* happened that night, something that terrified Mike and threatened to upset all his careful controls. No matter how he struggled to put it out of his mind, he couldn't forget the way she'd felt in his arms. Her body was so strong, supple and sweetly rounded, womanly and exciting. Her lips were as warm and sweet as honey...

Mike shuddered and drew himself erect, his hands tensing on the coffee mug. He had to stop thinking about her this way. If he didn't, something catastrophic was going to happen between them, and ultimately Emma would be hurt.

Protecting Emma was such a deeply instinctive part of Mike's soul that he never questioned it. His whole life was dedicated to his little girl and the effort to surround her with safety.

But Mike knew, as well, that Susan was getting suspicious. He recalled their uneasy conversation about grandparents, and his jaw tightened. It wasn't the first time she'd dropped little hints like that.

Mike frowned, sipping his coffee. Maybe he should just tell her the truth, let her know the whole story and make her own decision. But everything in him rebelled at the idea. It had been so long since he'd talked to anybody about his life. There had been just Mike and Emma, all alone together. When he thought of sharing the truth with another person, even Susan, casting himself on her mercy and waiting for her to pass judgment on him . . .

Mike shook his head. He couldn't do it, not even to protect the happiness and security they'd found here. He'd rather take his daughter and move on, find another place to live where they would be left alone.

They'd certainly done it before. They could do it again if they had to.

FIFTEEN MINUTES LATER, Mike began to feel concerned. Susan had not yet made an appearance, and he'd heard her coughing late into the night.

"Susan?" he called.

There was no response. Mike eased the door open and slipped inside, looking around guiltily as if he were an intruder.

Susan lay in the bed, looking miserable. Her golden hair straggled limply, her nose was red and there were dark shadows around her eyes.

Mike moved over to stand beside the bed. He smiled tenderly as she woke and looked up at him. Suddenly, he felt the same kind of overwhelming, protective love that he felt for Emma when she was sick.

But he kept his voice carefully light and teasing. "Well, I'll be damned. I was right," he said.

"About what?" she asked, her voice thick and hoarse.

"I thought you probably wore a high-necked cotton nightgown, and I was right."

She blinked in confusion, and Mike began to feel concerned. She must be really sick. Normally, she'd be outraged that he was speculating about her night wear.

But she just heaved herself up on one elbow, winced and began to cough. "What time is it?"

"It's past eight. Emma and I are leaving in a few minutes."

Her eyes widened and she struggled to sit up. "It's past *eight?* I have to..."

Mike moved closer to the bed, gripped her shoulders and pushed her gently down against the pillows. "You don't have to do anything. I just wanted to know if I should call the school and tell them you won't be coming in today."

Sick as she was, Susan tensed when she heard this and wrestled feebly in his grasp.

"Look, do you want me to call?" Mike asked patiently. "It's getting late."

She nodded in defeat.

"Okay. I'll be right back."

He went out to the kitchen, dialed the school and reported that Susan wouldn't be coming in to work, then returned to her room where she waited in her nest of pillows, looking anxious.

"The school secretary agreed with me," Mike told her calmly. "Especially when I said you were awake and coughing most of the night. She said they all thought you shouldn't have been at work yesterday, either, but you were too stubborn to go home."

Susan coughed into a wad of tissues, then looked at him miserably. "Did she know who you were?" she asked, her voice somewhat more recognizable, though still thick and hoarse.

"I didn't say. I just told her you were staying in bed all day."

"Oh, great," Susan muttered, sneezing. "Just great. Now they all think I'm sleeping with someone."

Mike grinned. "Anybody who's seen you lately would know that your virtue is perfectly safe."

She settled back on the pillows with a weary sigh. "Do I look awful?"

"Terrible," he said cheerfully. "Look, I'll bring you some aspirin and hot lemon tea before we leave, and then I want you to go back to sleep. Don't get up at all. I'll come home at noon to check on things and make some lunch for you."

"You don't have to..."

"My world-famous chicken soup," he said firmly. "The same as I make for Emma when she's sick. It'll fix you right up."

"Is Emma all right?"

Mike sat on the edge of the bed and smoothed her hair back from her hot forehead. "She's fine. She's upstairs right now putting Gerald to bed and getting ready to leave."

Susan smiled, her lips cracked and dry. "I miss her."

"Should I call her? She can stand in your doorway so you can see her."

Susan shook her head. "Better keep her away. I'll be up soon. Thanks, Mike," she added.

He waved his hand in a dismissive gesture. "No problem. Now, everything's looked after, okay? Buster's fed and watered, the paperboy's been paid, the answering machine's on ... not a single thing for you to do. Just go back to sleep and get well soon."

Susan nestled gratefully among the pillows, closing her eyes.

Mike looked down at her and forced himself to speak. "Oh, by the way, Peter called last night."

Her eyes fluttered open and focused. "He did?"

"Yeah. You were already in bed, and I told him you weren't feeling well. He says he hopes you're better soon."

"Nice," she muttered, smiling to herself.

Nice, Mike thought bitterly.

It was nice of him, all right. Her damn absent-minded professor took her on the ferry and then sat inside reading while she was out on the windy deck catching pneumonia, and he didn't even bother to fetch her jacket, or offer his own sweater to keep her warm....

"Did he say anything else?" she asked.

"Just to let him know when you're feeling better," Mike said without expression. "He said to call him, and maybe on the weekend you could get together and do something."

She nodded and closed her eyes again, reaching blindly for the tissues on the bedside table. Mike moved them closer to her, feeling another hot flood of anger.

He'd hardly believed his ears the night before when he talked to Peter Keeler and the man had said, with such offhand casualness, that Susan could call him when she felt better.

If a woman like Susan were *his* girlfriend and he learned that she was sick, nothing in the world would keep Mike away. He'd be over there as soon as he could, seeing if there was anything he could do for her, making sure she was properly cared for. But the professor had sounded almost frightened by the news of her illness, as if there were something repulsive about a woman who was coughing and running a fever.

Mike leaned over her tenderly, adjusting the blankets and smoothing the pillow behind her head, stroking her hair with a gentle hand.

"Sleep tight," he whispered, aching to kiss her. At last, he turned and tiptoed out of the room, closing the door softly behind him.

CHAPTER SEVEN

LATER THE SAME MORNING, Danny parked his cab on a side street and got out, checking his watch. It was just past ten o'clock, exactly on schedule.

He took a deep breath and started down the sidewalk, standing aside courteously as a young woman passed him. She had two children with her, one of them pedaling furiously on a tricycle and a smaller one in a baby stroller.

The older child's voice drifted back to him on the autumn breeze, high-pitched and full of excitement. He looked about the same age as the little kid who lived in the house, Danny thought. Maybe three or four years old. He'd felt as though he knew the little girl after the long hours he'd spent hiding in the alley and watching the house.

Emma, that was her name.

Danny was both amused and a little frightened by her boundless energy. She ran around all the time, often playing outside until the autumn twilight gathered and the first stars came out. At last her father would coax her inside and she'd obey reluctantly, trailing her stuffed kangaroo, while Buster followed, then sat at the door and barked dispiritedly when she'd gone.

Danny grinned, thinking about Buster.

If he were *really* a thief, he'd steal their dog. He loved the big golden retriever, and felt a strong affinity with him. They were two of a kind, Danny and Buster. They both tried hard to look tough, but underneath they were softhearted and timid.

Danny frowned and plunged his hands into his jacket pockets, kicking through the drifts of leaves as he headed into the alley behind the house.

This was no time to think about being timid, because today was *the* day.

He was going inside that house, and nothing was going to stop him. He'd planned the job down to the last detail, and now he was going to do it.

Danny repeated the words over and over in his mind. *Nothing's going to stop me. Nothing's going to stop me....*

Finally, he reached the back gate, hesitated and looked furtively up and down the alley a couple of times, then opened the latch and slipped inside. Buster was there as soon as he entered the yard. The big dog nuzzled Danny's legs and licked his fingers, looking hopefully at his pocket.

"Hi, big fella," Danny whispered. He edged back into the shelter of the bushes, smiling as Buster crowded in beside him, his tail wagging excitedly. "Hi, Buster. How are you this morning? Look, here's your licorice."

He fed the dog a few sticks of black licorice, then squatted with his arm around Buster's neck and wished desperately that he could just stay here all day, playing with the dog, throwing sticks and rolling on the grass the way Emma did . . .

But Danny wasn't a kid anymore. He was a grown man, and he had a man's work to do. He owed it to Rosa to get her money back.

The thought of his aunt gave him courage. Danny settled on his heels and studied the house through narrowed eyes.

By now, he had a pretty clear idea of the inside layout. The kitchen faced the backyard, and the room on the lower floor at the front was their bedroom. Danny had often seen the woman go in there after her evening run. If the light was on before she pulled the drapes, he could see a dresser and closet doors behind her, and a quilt tossed over a bentwood rocker.

At first he'd been puzzled to observe an upstairs light on late at night, too, but had finally decided that it was some kind of study or den. The little kid slept upstairs, and the guy seemed to stay awake for a long time in the evening after the woman went to bed. Maybe he worked up there, doing drafting or something.

Danny spent quite a lot of time speculating about their family life. He was surprised and touched to see how much time the man spent with the little girl. The guy looked like a pretty tough dude, but he was warm and gentle with his daughter. In fact, he was almost always the one who watched her while she played, and called her in at night for her bath.

Danny had never had a father, or much of a mother, either, except for Rosa. He felt wistful sometimes when he thought about the child's life in this quiet street, living with two parents who loved her, playing in a big leafy yard with a dog like Buster. If he ever had kids, he'd want them to grow up like this...

He put the thoughts firmly out of his mind, gathered himself together and slipped across the yard toward the back wall of the house. Buster followed, loping happily at his feet.

Danny dropped onto his stomach and eased a basement window out of its frame, having watched the dark-haired man do the same thing on the weekend. The guy was repairing all his storm windows, sealing them with new putty and securing them for winter, but he hadn't finished this one yet.

Danny set the window carefully on the grass and patted Buster who licked his face and nosed curiously at the window frame. Finally, trying not to think too much about what he was doing, Danny turned and wriggled backward through the window, dropping lightly onto the basement floor.

Inside, he clenched his hands to keep them from shaking, stood up and looked around. It was such a different feeling, actually being inside the house instead of crouching outside and looking at it.

No wonder it was different, Danny thought grimly. Looking wasn't illegal. Being inside was worth five years of his life if he got caught.

But he wasn't going to get caught. He glanced up at Buster's quizzical face framed in the open window, then took several deep breaths and began to creep up the old wooden stairs.

The basement door opened into the kitchen. Though he knew he was alone in the house, Danny eased it aside with caution, grateful that the man who lived here was the type who kept hinges oiled. The door swung open soundlessly and he stepped into the room, briefly distracted by the pretty curtains, the bright wallpaper and neat banks of cupboards, the loaves of freshly baked bread on the counter.

Suddenly, Danny was overwhelmed by the awful reality of where he was. Only the memory of Rosa's years of loving sacrifice gave him the courage to continue.

He had long since decided that the suitcase was probably hidden upstairs somewhere. If he owned this house, that's where he would hide the money, in an unused bedroom or maybe even in the attic. Anyway, he had all day to look, because nobody ever came home for lunch. They both stayed and worked at their jobs until at least four o'clock in the afternoon.

Danny tiptoed through the kitchen and started down the hall. Suddenly, he heard a sound and froze in alarm. He ducked into a paneled alcove just off the living room and flattened himself against the inside wall, then relaxed.

It was only the mailman, clattering up the steps to drop a pile of letters through a slot in the door. The mailman fished a thick catalog from his bag, tried unsuccessfully to fit it into the slot and finally dropped it outside on the veranda floorboards, then descended the steps and vanished.

Danny exhaled silently and was about to step out of the alcove when he heard another noise from somewhere much nearer. He plastered himself against the wall again, almost fainting with terror while footsteps approached down the hall next to his hiding place. Out of the corner of his eye, he saw the schoolteacher pass so close to him that he could have reached out and touched her.

She wore furry slippers and a pink bathrobe over a long nightgown, and her hair was rumpled and untidy.

But Danny couldn't take time to think about her, or even wonder what she was doing here at ten o'clock on a Wednesday morning. He watched her pass the alcove, his heart thumping so loudly, he was afraid she might hear.

She bent to pick up the scattered letters, then opened the front door to get the catalog. While she was outside, Danny edged his way from the alcove, faded back down the hallway and hurried through the silent kitchen. He slipped behind the basement door and pulled it with agonizing slowness until it latched softly, then tiptoed down the stairs.

Each one of them seemed to creak loudly, though he hadn't noticed the noise when he'd climbed them a few minutes ago. In his overwrought state, even the rustle of his clothes and the sound of his breathing were exaggerated, echoing through the quiet house like gunshots.

He lifted an old apple crate into position beneath the empty window, reached to grasp the sill and pulled himself up, his body scraping on the rough concrete wall of the basement. Hindered by Buster, who whined and licked his face happily, Danny wriggled out through the narrow window and sprawled on the grass, almost fainting with relief to be back in the light and warmth of the autumn day.

Hastily, he fitted the window in place, turned the little wing nuts that fastened the frame and sat on his heels looking around. Then, screwing up his courage one last time, he scrambled to his feet and ran across the shady yard, slipped through the gate and pelted down the alley, dimly conscious of Buster's mournful howls echoing behind him.

Not until he was two or three blocks away, almost back at his cab, did Danny stop to draw breath.

He paused next to a tall hedge of lilacs, gasping, his body gripped with raw spasms of terror and delayed shock. His stomach began to heave. He leaned into the massed shrubbery, afraid he was going to be sick, but finally he managed to pull himself together, then turned and wandered down the quiet street to his cab.

SUSAN STOOD in the kitchen, riffling through a pile of letters.

Bills, bank statements, a letter from the teachers' pension association ...

She lifted her head suddenly, startled by a sound from the backyard followed by a noisy storm of barking. Setting the mail on the table, she crossed the kitchen and opened the door to look out.

She felt a sudden chill, a prickly sort of fear, although she could see nothing disturbing. She had the distinct feeling that someone or something had recently been in the yard. She shivered a little and hugged her arms, then took a deep breath and tried to shrug off her fear.

Buster was at the back gate, his front paws clattering at the upper rails as he jumped up and down in a frantic effort to get out. He peered at something down the alley, barking noisily.

Susan, who knew her dog well, recognized the bark as his take-me-with-you pleading. She smiled. Most likely a group of neighborhood children had passed through the alley, bound on some adventure, and Buster was begging to be included. That was the presence she'd sensed, she told herself, just a group of kids off on some morning adventure.

"Poor baby." She watched as Buster wandered back toward her, his tail drooping dispiritedly. "Wouldn't they let you play?"

Suddenly, he caught sight of a squirrel and was off again, leaping at the base of the tree and barking wildly. Relieved of her foreboding, Susan watched him a moment longer, enjoying the feeling of the sun on her face, and the faintly wicked sensation of being home all by herself on a workday morning.

Playing hooky was fun, she decided, padding back into the house. As long as you weren't sick, she added grimly, as a fresh spasm of coughing racked her body and made her throat burn.

Mike had left a thermos on the counter, with a note propped beside it. It read:

Susan,
Drink this if you need something to soothe your throat. You can add more honey if it's not sweet enough. It's been around since Hippocrates, so it must be good.

She took a mug from one of the hooks and poured a cup from the Thermos, bending to sniff the heady concoction of lemon, cinnamon, honey and some other, less identifiable fragrances. She sipped the spicy brew and found that it was, indeed, soothing to her raw throat.

What a strange, contradictory man he was, Susan thought, running her fingers over the writing on the note. His handwriting was just like him, blunt and strong and capable. There was something else about his writing.... He was so literate. He wrote with such an easy, confident flourish. The man was a mystery, all right, one she would try to figure out once she was feeling a little better.

Susan went back to paging through the day's mail. Her hand froze, and she stared in alarm at a letter addressed in an unfamiliar hand to Mr. Michael Murphy.

Susan picked up the letter slowly, as if it were a living thing that might bite her.

Mike had never received a personal letter while he'd been living in Susan's house. The envelope was stained and tattered, and bore evidence of being forwarded at least five or six times. But the stationery was good quality, cream-colored and heavy, and the handwriting on the envelope was fluid and graceful.

Susan's hands began to shake as she peered at the envelope. It was a woman's handwriting. For a long time, Susan stood and looked at the letter, trying to decide what to do. If only she didn't feel so weak and sick, if only her brief surge of energy hadn't faded. If only she could think clearly...

On impulse, she crossed the room, consulted a list of numbers on a small bulletin board near the phone and dialed.

"Could I speak to Betty Morrell, please?" she asked.

She listened while the secretary told her politely that Miss Morrell was in class at the moment.

"Actually, I think Betty's class has library period on Wednesday mornings. I was hoping she might be free to talk with me for a minute. Could you tell her it's Susan, please, and that it's kind of an emergency?"

After a long pause, Betty's voice came on the line, sounding breathless and frightened. "Susie? What emergency, for God's sake? I was so worried, I almost broke my neck running through a second-grade obstacle course in the hallway."

"Well, it's sort of an emergency," Susan said apologetically.

"Hey, you sound awful! Where are you?"

"Home," Susan said. "I didn't go to work today. Look, Betty, there's a—"

"Poor kid, are you really feeling terrible? When I called last night, Mike told me you were too sick to go to your rock-climbing class, and he was thinking of keeping you home from school if you didn't feel better this morning."

"Keeping me home from school," Susan echoed. "What am I, one of your first-graders?"

"Hey," Betty said mildly, "don't knock it. I wish somebody at my house had enough concern to keep *me* home from school when I'm sick."

"I thought you didn't like him."

"I never said that. I have some nasty suspicions about the guy, but I can't deny that he's appealing in a lot of ways," Betty said. "Look, are you upsetting my entire day's routine just to chat about your tenant's little quirks, or what? I have to get back down to the library before my kids wipe out poor Mrs. Tibbing."

"Betty...there's a letter," Susan said hesitantly. "The mailman just brought a letter."

"He frequently does," Betty said dryly. "What *kind* of letter, sweetie?"

"It's a letter for Mike. It's been forwarded all over the country, from Ontario to Alberta to British Columbia, and I can't make out the return address. But I think it's a...a woman's handwriting."

Betty gave a low whistle. "A light dawns," she said. "This is an *ethical* dilemma, right?"

"He's coming home at noon," Susan said. "He's coming to check on me and make me lunch. I've got about..." She glanced at the clock. "About half an hour."

"To steam or not to steam," Betty said cheerfully. "This is the question?"

Susan made a face. "You always put things so...bluntly," she murmured. "Couldn't you be a little more tactful?"

Betty chuckled. "And call it what? Research? Investigative analysis?"

"Betty, I've never snooped into somebody else's mail in my whole life. I wouldn't even have considered it, except that—"

"Except that this is different," Betty said firmly. "The man's living in your house. He might well be a wanted criminal. And other people are involved, too, you know. I think you have some obligation to learn the truth about this guy, and since you seem completely incapable of coming right out and *asking* him, like any normal person..."

"It's not that easy," Susan said. "This whole situation is getting so complicated."

"Complicated? In what way?" Betty asked, suddenly alert.

But Susan's head was beginning to pound again, and she had no desire to pursue this aspect of the conversation.

"Never mind," she said wearily. "I'm sorry to bother you at work, Betts. I'll figure something out, okay?"

"Are you going to open it?"

"I don't know. Probably not. I'd really like to, but it just feels so . . . corrupt, somehow."

"You've always had such a tender conscience," Betty said. "Not like me. Hey, are you going to your needlework class tomorrow night?"

"Not unless I feel a lot better. I don't know if I'll even be in good enough shape to go to work."

"Take some antihistamine tablets and go back to bed," Betty advised.

"Good idea. By the way, how's Barney?"

"Barnaby," her friend corrected. "Ever since Mike pointed out that Flintstones thing, I can't stand calling him Barney. When I do, I feel like we're both wearing fur suits and have bones in our hair."

Susan laughed hoarsely, cheered as always by Betty's conversation. "You'd look very cute in furry clothes," she said. "Both of you."

"Yeah, right. Hey, did I tell you we're taking lessons in ballroom dancing? We start this weekend with the fox-trot."

"No kidding?"

"No kidding. It's something we've both always wanted to do, and we're good enough friends by now that if we walk all over each other's feet, its not going to matter."

"You're so lucky," Susan said wistfully, thinking about Betty's warm, uncomplicated relationship with her new boyfriend.

"I know." Betty's voice was serious for once. "I can't believe how lucky I am. Susie, I think this might be it."

"You mean . . ."

"This noise you hear is me knocking on wood," Betty said, almost shyly. "But yeah, I think it's serious. He just might be the man I've been looking for. I think it could be permanent."

"Oh, Betty, I'm so glad."

"How's Peter? Are you two still getting along?"

"Anybody could get along with Peter. He's really easygoing."

"But?"

"No buts," Susan said. "He's a very nice man. He's intelligent and courteous and well read, and I enjoy going out with him."

"So everything's fine?"

"Sure. Except for my rotten cold, that is. And this damned letter on my kitchen table."

"I keep feeling like there's something you're not telling me. Something else is bothering you, Susie. I can always tell."

Susan hesitated, almost overcome by the urge to tell Betty about the suitcase full of money. She'd resisted until now, certain that the suitcase would be claimed and vanish from her life. If that happened, as the police had assured her it would, then there was no need

for the people closest to her to know anything about
it.

But as time passed and the money went unclaimed,
Susan vacillated between a desire to ignore the whole
thing, and a growing need to talk about the possibility of actually claiming over fifty thousand dollars. It
would make so many changes in her life.

"Susie?"

"Nothing." Susan gathered herself together and
stared out the window at the falling leaves. "I have to
let you go, Betty. Think of that poor librarian."

"Oh, God, Mrs Tibbing! Yeah, I'd better rescue
her. I'll call tomorrow and see how you are, okay?
Maybe I'll drop by, if Mike doesn't have you in quar-
antine by then."

"I'd love that. Goodbye, Betty."

"Bye, kid. Don't forget, my advice is to steam that
letter open. I would if I were you."

"I know you would. You're not a big coward like
me. See you later, Betty."

Susan hung up and stared at the envelope. Should
she open it? And if she did, was she prepared to deal
with the information it might contain?

MIKE PARKED his truck by the curb and hurried up the
front walk. He let himself in the door, struck at once
by the silence. Mike seldom came home for lunch, and
he and Susan were almost never alone in the house.
Emma was always somewhere nearby, chattering in the
kitchen, playing in her room upstairs or romping
through the yard with Buster.

But today, Mike had chosen not to disrupt his daughter's routine by bringing her home from day care while he made lunch for Susan.

When he tiptoed down the hall, he found Susan at the kitchen table sipping a cup of his homemade cough medicine as she leafed through a catalog. She was dressed in her navy track suit, with her hair brushed and even some lipstick on, looking a great deal better than when he'd left her this morning.

"Why are you up?" he asked brusquely, stepping into the bathroom to wash his hands. "You were supposed to stay in bed all day. That's why I came home to fix you lunch."

"I couldn't sleep any longer. I took some antihistamine and drank about three cups of this medicine you left, and I feel a lot better."

"At least you sound better." He came back into the kitchen and opened the fridge to get out his jar of chicken soup. "Your voice is much clearer."

When she didn't respond, Mike glanced at her with concern. "What's that you're looking at?"

"A catalog of Christmas gifts. Look, you can buy Emma her very own backyard carousel for just fifteen thousand dollars."

"Emma's got Buster. He's a lot more fun than a carousel."

Instantly he regretted his casual words. From the beginning, he'd tried to avoid comments like that, any indication that he and Emma were settling in and starting to take this place for granted.

"Oh," Susan said, "I almost forgot. There's a letter for you."

Mike's hands tensed on the jar. "For me?"

"It's somewhere in here..." Susan leafed through a pile of mail. "Here. It looks pretty well-traveled, doesn't it?"

Mike glanced at the familiar handwriting on the envelope and his heart sank. But he remained carefully expressionless, turning away without speaking to pour the soup into a casserole dish. He adjusted the controls on the microwave and got a couple of bowls from the cupboard.

"Aren't you going to open it?" Susan asked.

"Maybe later. I want to make sure you get some hot soup first. Can you eat a couple of slices of toast, too?"

She shook her head. "My throat's still pretty tender. I think just the soup will be fine."

He nodded and set out the bowls, searching for something to get his mind off the letter which still lay in full view on the table.

"We're working outside today," he told Susan. "Pouring the concrete footings for the equipment room and lockers."

"It's a nice day to work outside." She began to leaf through the catalog again.

There was something constrained and awkward about her, something besides the fact that she wasn't feeling well...

Of course, he thought. It was that letter. He'd seen how she kept glancing at it. She was worried about the letter, and there wasn't a thing he could do to set her mind at ease.

"How was your morning?" he asked nonchalantly as he ladled hot soup into her bowl. "Pretty quiet?"

"Really quiet. Except that Buster went crazy around ten-thirty, and barked for a long time."

"Why?"

She shrugged. "I don't know. Something in the back alley. But you know," she added, looking troubled and uncertain, "I had the strangest feeling."

"What feeling?"

"I don't know." She picked up her spoon and stirred the rich broth. "Like maybe there was somebody around."

"A prowler, you mean?"

"I don't know. What prowler hangs around a house on a sunny morning? But when I looked out in the yard, I just felt . . ."

She waved her hand in a gesture of dismissal and took a mouthful of soup, then looked up in surprise. "Mike, this is really delicious. What's in it?"

"Odds and ends," he said. "Chicken feet, calf brains, good stuff like that."

Susan gave him a wry smile, then returned to her soup. They ate in silence, the quiet broken by a few racking coughs from Susan.

"Back to bed," he said firmly when she finished her soup. "Come on. Have a nap this afternoon, and I'll take care of the dishes."

She went without protest, causing him even more concern. After the door to her room closed, he spent a few minutes cleaning up the sunny kitchen, then made a quick tour of the house, checking the windows and the basement, still mildly troubled by Susan's feeling that somebody had been near the house. But everything was in order, neat and secure.

Finally, Mike took the letter from the table and climbed the stairs to his room. He sat on the bed looking at the envelope, wishing he could just throw it away without reading it. But something compelled him to open the letter and scan the closely written pages.

He sat for long time looking at the papers in his hand. Then he ripped them to pieces, working methodically, tearing and cross-tearing until a pile of scraps littered the flowered bedspread. Mike gathered the scraps and dropped them into the wastebasket, watching the little blizzard of paper with a bleak expression. At last he sank onto the bed again and sat without moving, his face buried in his hands.

SUSAN LAY UNDER her warm quilt, trying to sleep. She heard Mike leave the house, and the hum of his truck engine as he drove away. The clock on her dresser ticked the hour away with little jerky movements of the minute hand, and the air was still and heavy. Finally, she got up, stepped into her fuzzy bedroom slippers and padded upstairs.

She paused in the upper hallway and looked into Emma's room. Mike kept the place neat but it still bore the stamp of the little girl's vigorous personality.

Emma insisted on arranging all her toys in a certain fashion before she was content to leave in the morning. A group of dolls and stuffed animals sat around the child-size table, having a tea party, while others were involved in a rodeo in the corner. Susan, who had been invited upstairs a number of times to watch the rodeo, was well-acquainted by now with the complicated arrangement of fences, ropes, corrals and animals.

Emma's imagination was an awesome thing. Susan was continually fascinated by the world that Mike's daughter created around herself, a colorful, vibrant place where anything could happen. She felt a familiar desolation, thinking how barren her life would be when Mike and Emma left.

But Emma wasn't her child, and Mike was only her tenant. She had her own life to live. Betty had been right to caution that this kind of emotional involvement was dangerous and upsetting.

She moved down the hall, thinking that she hadn't been inside the other bedroom since Mike moved in. Susan paused in the doorway, feeling breathless and a little frightened. His masculine presence had subtly altered the room, even though he seemed to have almost no personal possessions except for a few books arranged on the dresser. Susan bent to look at the titles. They were mostly scholarly novels, and a few well-worn books of essays. One of them was a treatise on ethics that she vaguely recalled from her senior-year philosophy class.

She straightened, frowning. The man was so baffling, so enigmatic...

Susan held her breath. Deliberately quashing the feeling of guilt over what she was about to do, she eased open one of the desk drawers, wondering where he might file a letter. But all the drawer contained were some neatly folded maps, a small pocket calculator, a bundle of gas receipts, a slide rule and some plans, on graph paper, of a playground set he was designing for

Emma. Susan lifted the plans, marveling at their precision, and saw another paper underneath.

She picked it up and looked at it in openmouthed astonishment. It was a charcoal sketch of a woman and a child sitting together in a rocking chair, reading from a big storybook.

The child was Emma, and the woman was herself.

Susan looked at her own features, so carefully, generously rendered, and felt tears stinging her eyes. She was not only astounded by his skill, but deeply moved by the feeling in the little sketch. The picture looked so tender and warm. She thought of Mike sitting up here at his desk late at night, drawing their images from memory....

Suddenly, she felt very uncomfortable about what she was doing. She replaced his papers hastily, closed the drawer and turned to leave. She was almost out the door when she saw the scraps of paper in the wastebasket. Her hand froze on the door frame as she looked down at the basket.

A few moments passed, but they seemed like an hour. At last, almost reluctantly, Susan knelt on the floor and searched through the torn bits of notepaper, picking them up and trying to decipher the graceful handwriting.

She laid the pieces out on the hardwood floor, frowning with concentration, fitting them together like a jigsaw puzzle. Isolated words sprang into view, then some partial sentences. Susan stared at them in horror.

"...don't know where you are, or if this will ever reach you, but..."

"...and the police couldn't find you. For God's sake, have pity and..."

"...if not for us, then for Emma. She has a right to..."

"...please, Michael. Please. My heart is breaking, and the doctor says..."

Susan gathered the papers, and dropped them into the wastebasket. She rocked on her heels and stared unseeingly at the blanket chest in the hallway.

Finally, she got to her feet slowly and wandered into Emma's room, sinking onto the bed and taking Gerald in her arms. The stuffed kangaroo smiled at her blandly. Susan hugged him like a baby.

She was in deep water here, and she knew it. Susan thought about the evening Mike and his daughter had first appeared on her veranda along with Gerald. If only she'd been strong enough to resist the little girl's charm, none of this would have happened. She'd have some ordinary, comfortable tenant, probably another female teacher with a quiet social life who caused no worry at all.

Instead, she had this enchanting child who made her heart ache with love, and a man with blue eyes and strong hands and kisses that took her breath away...a mysterious stranger who made chicken soup and tenderly bandaged cuts on knees, who repaired windows and read Aldous Huxley and drew sketches with a fine artistic hand...

And, Susan reminded herself firmly, a man who'd lied to her about his past, who was running from the police and using her house as a hiding place.

She got to her feet, tucked Gerald back under the covers and walked downstairs, her face set with resolve.

She'd wait another couple of weeks, until Halloween was over. Then whether the suitcase had been claimed or not, she would give Mike a month's notice. She couldn't bear the responsibility of trying to decide what to do about Mike and his daughter. Emma adored Mike, whether or not he had legal custody of her. But there was also the mother's anguish to be considered, and Susan wanted no part of the legal wrangling and the inevitable misery.

She pushed away the unwelcome image of the man and his daughter, wandering through the cold rainy streets of Vancouver on Christmas Eve, looking for a place to live. Mike earned good money, though he never seemed to spend a penny on anything except Emma's needs. But he would certainly be able to find another place to live. It wasn't Susan's responsibility to provide them with a home in which to spend Christmas. If Mike wanted so badly to have his child all to himself, he could make a home for her somewhere else.

Susan knew she couldn't turn him in to the police. But she wouldn't keep on sheltering him, either. It was too much to ask of anyone.

Her head started to throb, and she felt a deep, almost unbearable weariness. She wandered though the kitchen and crawled gratefully into the cozy, dark comfort of her bed.

CHAPTER EIGHT

THE WEEK DRAGGED ON, then the weekend. On Monday, Susan felt well enough to go back to work. But she was exhausted before the last class of the morning, and grateful to learn that her substitute had left an essay assignment that kept the tenth-grade English students occupied for most of the hour.

Susan slipped a throat lozenge into her mouth, closed the record book she was using to compile examination results and got up to walk around her desk.

"Okay," she said. "Let's spend the last few minutes talking about Emily Dickinson. You were supposed to read the biography, weren't you?"

Several heads nodded agreement.

"Good. What do you know about her?"

Lynnette waved her hand eagerly.

Susan smiled at the girl. Lynnette had changed her wardrobe considerably since the start of the term. She now wore jeans and plaid shirts like most of the other girls.

Since the opening days of school, Susan had learned quite a lot about Lynnette. The girl lived with an alcoholic mother and a mostly absent father, and provided almost all the care for a houseful of small brothers and sisters. In the light of her wretched home situation, Lynnette's innocent sultriness had a kind of gallantry that appealed to Susan.

The girl seemed shy and reluctant to make friends at school, though Susan still occasionally saw her in the company of the young man who'd been in the park the day Susan had found the suitcase. She frowned, trying not to think about all that money, and returned her thoughts to her class.

"Lynnette?" she asked, her voice still faintly hoarse. "Can you tell me something about Emily Dickinson?"

"She was a poet," Lynnette said triumphantly, then looked hurt when the other students laughed and groaned.

"Hey, shut up!" Jason Caine turned in his seat to glare at his classmates. "You guys got any better answers, you blockheads?"

Susan approved of his defense of Lynnette, but not his method. She wavered, trying to decide whether or not to rebuke him. He settled in his desk, folded his hands and gave her his most winsome smile.

"Sorry, Miss Adamson," he said humbly. "I guess I'm still a little cranky."

Susan nodded. "How long has it been now, Jason?"

"Three weeks, five days." Jason consulted his watch. "And two hours," he added.

"That's terrific, Jason. You haven't had a cigarette for almost a month?"

Jason nodded, looking cherubic. "I got it beat, Miss Adamson. When you're not sick anymore, I'll be ready to challenge you to another two-miler."

"No way, Jason. If you've really quit smoking, I don't stand a chance against you."

Jason beamed. Susan smiled back at him, then remembered the topic under discussion. "Well then, Jason. What can you tell me about Emily Dickinson?"

"She was a virgin," Jason said promptly. He grinned as the other students burst into delighted guffaws.

Susan suppressed a chuckle, and was relieved when the buzzer rang to signal the end of the period. She gathered up her books and handbag and made her way through the noisy corridors toward the staff lounge, stopping off briefly at the office to pick up her messages.

"Fire drill in fourth period," she read aloud, balancing the load of books in one arm. "Staff meeting on Wednesday, teacher-student volleyball game at noon on Friday, pep rally, track team meeting . . ."

She looked up as one of the school secretaries tore a strip from a yellow message pad and handed it across the counter.

"Gloria, I feel as if I've been gone for a month." Susan took the message. "Now what?"

"Relax," Gloria said. She was a shapely redhead who looked like a movie star, wore tight sweaters and short skirts and caused a great deal of warm speculation amongst the high school boys. "It's just a call from your friend Betty."

"Oh, good," Susan said. "I thought maybe they dumped three more extracurricular assignments on me while I was away."

"That'll teach you to get sick." Sheila, one of Gloria's assistants and a good friend of Susan's, came through the office carrying a stack of freshly printed examination booklets. "What does Betty want?"

Susan read the phone message. "She's coming over to my place for a visit tonight after supper. I haven't seen her since last week."

Sheila and Gloria exchanged a glance while Susan headed toward the door. "Well, are you going to ask her?" Gloria said. "Or should I?"

"Ask me what?" Susan paused by the door, making way for a committee of twelfth-grade girls heading for the principal's office.

The secretaries exchanged another significant look.

"About the guy," Sheila said at last. "We want to know who the guy is."

"What guy?" Susan looked at them in bewilderment, wondering if they were talking about Peter. "The man I'm dating, you mean?"

"Dating!" Gloria said with a meaningful grin. "Get that, Sheila? The woman calls it *dating*."

"Well, that's one word for it," Sheila agreed solemnly.

Susan felt increasingly puzzled. "I haven't got the faintest idea what you two are talking about."

"The *guy*," Gloria insisted. "We want to know who this guy is that you're living with. The one who calls in and says you've been coughing all night, so he's not going to wake you up."

"Oh," Susan said, relieved. "That's not a guy. That's just Mike."

"It's just Mike," Gloria told her assistant.

"I see." Sheila nodded. "*Just* Mike."

"Oh, for goodness' sake!" Susan said. "He's my tenant. He has a little girl about four years old, and they rent the upstairs suite in my house. It's nothing interesting, girls. Sorry."

"What does he look like?" Sheila dropped the pile of exam booklets on a table by the door. "He sounds so yummy on the phone."

"Yummy?" Susan asked.

"All deep-voiced and masculine, like a real heart-throb. Does he look that way, too?"

"See for yourself." Susan gestured at a group of construction workers outside the window. Some of the men were sitting on benches in the school courtyard, having their lunch and lounging in the sunlight.

Gloria and Sheila both pressed close to the window. "He's one of those guys?" Gloria asked. "Which one, Susie?"

"In the faded blue shirt," Susan said. "With the dark hair."

"Oh, my *God!*" Sheila turned to look at Susan. "He's gorgeous! Even better than he sounds."

"Do you think so?" Susan looked at Mike, who was sitting on the bench with booted feet extended, his untidy dark hair gleaming in the sunlight.

"Is he taken?" Gloria asked, still staring out the window. "Why don't you bring him in here sometime and introduce us, Susie?"

"No chance, girls." Susan turned to leave. "Mike doesn't date. He's got a little girl, and he spends all his free time with her."

"For *that,*" Sheila breathed, pressing her forehead against the glass, "I could even learn to love children. I really could."

"You're crazy, both of you," Susan said fondly, closing the door behind her as she left.

But her smile faded as she headed down the hall to the staff room. For some reason, she didn't really like to think about Mike going on a date with one of the school's attractive young secretaries.

"HI, GUYS," Betty said, appearing in the kitchen doorway just as they finished their evening meal. "Long time no see. Emma Murphy, I want the *biggest* hug you've got."

Emma launched herself at Betty while Mike and Susan looked on, smiling.

"Hi, Mike." Betty disengaged herself gently from Emma's embrace and pulled a chair up to the table. "How's the construction business?"

"Building rapidly," Mike said dryly.

He got up and began to clear the table with his usual quiet efficiency. Emma helped, balancing the dinner plates carefully as she took them to her father at the counter.

Betty turned to Susan. "So, how are you feeling, kid? Back to normal?"

"Almost."

"Did you go for your run tonight?"

"No, she didn't," Mike said from the counter. "She won't be well enough to go running again until sometime next week."

Betty raised an eyebrow at Susan, who pulled a face and rolled her eyes.

"How about rock climbing?" Betty cast a teasing glance in Mike's direction. "Are you allowing her to go to her class tomorrow night?"

"I guess so." Mike rinsed plates at the sink. "But only if she promises not to exert herself."

"Don't listen to him. We're learning to belay in harness this week," Susan told Betty, "and I have no intention of sitting and watching while everyone else has all the fun."

Emma came and leaned against Betty's chair. "Susan was really sick," she reported. "Daddy was worried."

Betty's face softened. "We were all worried, sweetie," she murmured, stroking Emma's shining hair. "But Susan's feeling better now."

"All better," Emma agreed.

Betty turned to her friend. "Hey, Susie, since you didn't have your run before supper, let's go out for a walk. Is that okay, Mike?" she asked with mock concern. "It's nice and warm tonight, and we'll walk really, really slow."

"Is Buster going with you?" Emma asked, looking worried.

"Why, sweetie?" Susan looked down at the little girl. "Don't you want him to?"

"I need him," Emma said. "We're playing a game after supper. He's going to be a big scary bear."

"Okay, we'll leave him at home. I'm sure he'd hate to miss your game."

"Emma, stay here and help me with the dishes, honey," Mike said. "Susan and Betty will be back soon. Make sure you take your jacket, Susan," he added.

"Yes, sir!" Susan said and went to get her jacket from the porch. She and Betty walked outside into the crisp autumn evening, pleasantly scented with wood smoke and damp leaves.

"You *like* it," Betty said firmly. "Admit that you like it."

"What? Autumn?"

"No, you idiot, I'm talking about Mike. You pretend to be annoyed, but you really like the way he fusses over you and looks after you."

Susan shrugged. "In a way. I guess it's kind of...comforting." She looked down at her feet, suddenly overcome with emotion.

"Susie?" Betty asked. "What is it?"

Susan hesitated, staring sadly at a window decorated with cutouts of Halloween pumpkins and witches. "Remember last Wednesday morning?" she said at last. "I called you at school and said Mike got a letter?"

"I know. I haven't really talked to you since. Mike wasn't allowing visitors. Did you steam the letter open like I told you to?"

"I couldn't."

"You're so moral. What a drag."

"So shoot me for not being any good at this underhand kind of stuff," Susan said.

"Did he tell you what was in the letter?"

Susan shook her head and kicked through a drift of leaves. "After he went back to work, I found it in his wastebasket. He'd shredded it and thrown it away."

"So you played jigsaw?"

Susan nodded.

"Good girl. And?"

"And you were right," Susan told her with a sigh. "I couldn't make out the whole thing," she added. "I just felt so awful, skulking around his room and snooping into his things. But I saw enough.''

"Like what?"

"There were a few lines about Emma, and the police looking for him, and how Mike should be thinking about Emma instead of himself."

"Oh, damn," Betty muttered. "What else?"

"In the letter," Susan said, "the woman who wrote the letter...Emma's mother...she said..." Susan's voice faltered. "She said her heart was breaking. She talked about being in a doctor's care."

"Oh, *hell*," Betty said fervently.

Susan paused under a streetlight and looked at her friend. "What am I supposed to do, Betts? What would you do if you were me?"

For once, Betty didn't have a quick reply. She turned and began walking again, hands plunged deep into her jacket pockets, while Susan fell slowly into step beside her.

"I guess," Betty said finally, "it's really hard to talk to him about it, right?"

"It's impossible. Like you said a long time ago, when does a person bring up the subject, and how? And if it happens not to be true, or there's some kind of circumstance that explains what he's done, how would our relationship ever survive the suspicion?"

"But if it *is* true..."

"That's the worst part of all," Susan said in despair. "I'm afraid to ask Mike about this because I honestly can't deal with the possibility that it's true. Then I'd be forced to do something about it, and I don't want to."

"Susie, you have to think about that poor woman, too," Betty began gently. "Imagine how she must be suffering."

"But I don't *know* her! I know Mike and Emma, and I keep thinking how much they'd both suffer if they were separated. I can't get it out of my mind."

"Kind of like the old story where Solomon has to decide which mother the baby belongs to, right?"

"Exactly. And I'm not wise enough to make a decision like that. I know," Susan went on, "that Mike's probably doing a terrible thing. If he really did steal Emma from her mother and run away, then he's breaking the law and causing someone unforgivable pain. But he loves Emma, and she's never known any other parent. She'd be devastated if somebody came and took her away from Mike."

Betty listened without comment, waiting for Susan to continue.

"Doesn't it seem kind of strange?" Susan asked after a moment's silence.

"What?"

"That the post office was able to find Mike when the police can't. I mean, if the police are really looking for him, wouldn't they be able to find his address, too? That letter came right to my house, Betty. It was forwarded to him at my address."

Betty shrugged. "That doesn't mean anything. The police are flooded with work. They can't spend all their time following up a three-year-old report on some missing kid. They usually need help from ordinary citizens to catch the bad guys. Even though that letter got sent to you, the police aren't going to know Mike's actually living in your house unless you come forward and tell them.''

"I can't," Susan said. "I just can't. I don't want to take that responsibility."

"So who should make the decision?"

"I don't know! Somebody else," Susan said. "Judges, child welfare agents...people like that. It shouldn't have to be me."

Betty reached out and squeezed her arm. "You know, you're absolutely right, kid," she murmured. "It shouldn't have to be you. Come on, now, let's turn around and start back before Mike has fits."

"There's something else," Susan confessed as they crossed the street and began walking toward home.

"What is it?"

"Somebody's watching my house."

"What?" Betty stopped under a streetlight. "Watching your house? How do you know?"

"I just know. I get a creepy feeling sometimes, when I go outside to check on Buster, or hang sheets on the clothesline or weed the flower beds. Like somebody's watching me."

Betty shivered. "You're scaring me, Susie."

"It's worst when I come home from school. Lots of times, I feel as if somebody's been there while I was gone."

"Inside the house?" Betty asked in horror.

"No, not inside. Just...watching."

"So, why don't you tell the police?"

"Tell them what? That I have this creepy feeling? You're the one who keeps saying how busy the police are. You think they've got time to check out my creepy feelings?"

"Have you told Mike?"

"I've mentioned it. But I don't want him to go into his overprotective mode, so I play it down."

Betty nodded.

"But," Susan added, "just the same, I notice that Mike has been checking the doors and windows a lot more carefully these days."

"So, what do you think?" Betty asked.

"I think it may have something to do with Emma."

"Emma?"

"I think maybe her mother's hired a private investigator, and he's found our house. After all, the post office found it, so why couldn't someone else? And he's watching and waiting for a chance to grab her and take her back."

Betty shook her head. "You're crazy," she said. "You're absolutely crazy, Susie. I've never heard anything so ridiculous in all my life."

"You think so?" Susan looked at her friend. "I've been dying to hear you say that, Betty. Tell me I'm just nuts, and I should put the whole thing out of my mind."

"You're just nuts, and you should put the whole thing out of your mind," Betty said. "Now, forget the creepy-crawly feelings, and tell me what you're going to do about Mike. You can't talk to him, and you don't want to turn him in, so are you just going to let him go on living in your house?"

"I can't do that, either. It feels ... so wrong, somehow." Susan took a deep breath. "I've decided to ask him to leave. Then at least he won't be *my* problem anymore."

"When?"

"Next week. Right after Halloween. Emma's so excited about Halloween, Betty. This is the first year she's really been old enough to understand about costumes and trick-or-treating, and she talks about it all the time. I don't have the heart to deliver an eviction notice right now."

"What a softie," Betty said tenderly. "So, as soon as Halloween is over, you're turning them out into the big cold world, where somebody else has to decide about their fate?"

"That's right."

"And then what happens?"

"What do you mean?" Susan asked.

But of course she knew what would happen. She'd be miserable. Buster would be miserable and the house would be empty without Emma's toys or Mike's tools, with no childish chatter and warm laughter, no strong hands fixing things, no sociable breakfasts and late-evening snacks....

"What happens to you?" Betty repeated. "I thought without Mike's rent, you couldn't make the mortgage payments."

Susan drew a deep breath and lowered herself onto a bench next to the bus stop. "Betty, sit down."

"Now what?"

Susan glanced around, then leaned forward earnestly. "If I tell you something, will you promise not to repeat it to anybody?" she whispered. "Not to a soul? Not even Connie or Barney?"

"Barnaby," Betty corrected automatically, then winced when Susan punched her shoulder. "Yeah, yeah, I promise. I super-solemnly double-swear," she announced when Susan looked unconvinced. "Cross my heart and hope to die," she added, tracing a cross on the front of her plaid duffel coat. "You know I've always been good at keeping secrets."

"I know. You're like a sealed tomb." Susan paused, gripping her hands between her knees and staring at the pale crescent moon drifting above the trees. "Betty, I . . . I found a suitcase full of money."

Betty laughed. "Excuse me," she said. "I've developed early senility from too much time spent with six-year-olds. I thought you just said you found a suitcase full of money."

"I did. One night in the park, when I was running. Actually, Buster found it. The police asked me not to tell anybody but I can't stand it anymore, so you have to remember you can't say a word to anyone."

Betty stared at her. "You're not kidding," she breathed. "Are you?"

"I'm not kidding." Susan glanced nervously into the dark masses of shrubbery along the sidewalk.

"A suitcase full of *money*?" Betty asked in disbelief. "Where was it?"

"In the bushes. Buster smelled it and started whining, and I crawled in and dragged it out. When I opened it and saw what was inside, I took it right down to the police station."

"When did all this happen?"

"About six weeks ago. Just after Mike and Emma came to live with me."

"Six weeks! And all that time, you haven't said a word about it?"

"The police asked me not to. They said they didn't want to risk having somebody come forward with a false claim, identify the money and take it home."

"That makes sense," Betty said. "Is it quite a lot of money, Susie?"

"Over fifty thousand dollars."

"Fifty thous—" Betty began.

Susan clapped a hand over her friend's mouth. "Not so loud!" she said, looking around at the bushes again.

Betty fell silent, still wide-eyed with shock. "So what happens to all this money?"

"If it's not claimed in another six weeks, it's mine."

"I don't believe it," Betty said. "You're making the whole thing up."

Susan shook her head. "Apparently, that's the law. They hold it for three months, and then it belongs to the finder."

"Susie, you must be going out of your mind! No wonder you got sick, with all this going on."

"It feels so good to tell somebody," Susan said with a sigh. "At first I didn't even want to think about it, because the police were so certain the suitcase would be claimed right away. But last time I went down here, Constable Liepert said that since nobody's come forward after all these weeks, there's a good chance I'll be getting the money."

"When?" Betty whispered.

"Early December. In fact, I'm giving you a new muffler for Christmas."

"A scarf?" Betty asked in confusion.

"No, you dummy!" Susan hugged her. "A muffler for your car. And I can pay for Dad's new wheelchair, and buy my mortgage down so I can handle the payments..."

"And then you won't need a tenant."

"That's right."

Betty shook her head, still looking dazed. "You know," she said at last, "I really should take up running. I had no idea it was so profitable."

Susan laughed. "Come on," she said. "We'd better start back now, or Mike's going to be upset."

They walked home slowly through the deepening twilight, crunching leaves underfoot.

"Susie..."

"What?"

"Do you think there could be some kind of connection between the money and whoever's watching your house? Like maybe this creepy feeling you've been having isn't related to Emma at all?"

"No. I don't think so. The police said that whoever owns the money would have lost interest in me as soon as I turned it over to the police. Besides," she added firmly, "people like that wouldn't spend weeks just hanging around and watching. If they thought I had their money, they'd do something about it right away."

"I guess you're right. I just can't get over it," Betty muttered. "I just can't get over it. All this stuff's been going on in your life, and I didn't know anything about it. Fifty thousand dollars, for God's sake!"

"Let's not talk about it anymore, okay?" Susan said, feeling anxious again. "Let's not talk about Mike, or the money, or anything. Let's just think about fun stuff."

"Like what?"

"Halloween, for instance. What are you and Barnaby doing?"

"I'm taking him to my staff party. We're dressing up as Donald and Daisy Duck. We've got these cute little matching sailor suits, and big yellow bills..."

Susan laughed. "I hope I get a chance to see you."

"What are you and Peter doing?"

"We're going to a faculty party."

"Wow," Betty said, looking impressed. "Your life is really changing, isn't it, Susie? Dealing with huge sums of money, hanging out with classy people, harboring criminals upstairs in your antique bathtub..."

Susan shook her friend's arm indignantly. They smiled at each other for a moment, then turned and walked on in companionable silence.

DANNY CROUCHED in the dense shrubbery near the garage, watching as the two women came up the walk. Buster whined and ran to greet them, his tail rotating like a windmill. Danny held his breath, hoping the dog wouldn't return to the fence and give away his hiding place. When he'd slipped in through the alley, he didn't expect everybody to be outside after supper like this.

But even Emma was in the front yard, bundled in a jacket and knitted hat, industriously piling leaves with her little rake while Mike worked next to her. Every time Buster approached, she shouted with mock terror and ran away, giggling delightedly when the dog chased her.

Danny grinned from his hiding place. Again he thought how much fun it must be for a little kid, having this nice family and a dog like Buster to play with. His smile faded and he settled back on his heels against the sheltered wall of the garage, feeling a wave of loneliness.

He'd finally gotten up the courage to kiss Lynnette Campbell, and now he couldn't get her out of his mind. His dreams were filled with images of her big dark eyes and delicate skin, her shy smile and gentle laughter, and the way she looked up to him as if he were a strong, capable man.

Danny adored her. Even her name was music to his ears.

"Lynnette," he whispered softly in the darkness. "Lynnette."

He closed his eyes, imagining again how it would feel to take her out on a date to a really nice restaurant. But to do that he'd need some money, and he hardly had enough cash to buy food for himself. He would have to save for weeks just to take her to a movie.

Danny opened his eyes and glared at the scene before him. Actually, he had thousands of dollars, but it was hidden somewhere inside that house and he couldn't get at it. The unfairness of it drove him wild with frustration.

Lately, too, he was haunted by fears that maybe they'd put the money into the bank or something. But he couldn't bear to think such thoughts, so he dismissed them whenever they popped into his mind. If they'd banked the money, he told himself, there would be some sign of it. The guy would have bought a new truck instead of working so hard on those rusty old fenders. The woman would have quit her job so the kid wouldn't need to go to day care. Something would have changed if they had access to all that money.

He'd been really worried last week after his attempted break-in, when she stayed home from her job for a long time and quit going out for her evening run. But she'd been sick or something. Their life was back to normal now.

They were still waiting, Danny told himself firmly. They were lying low, holding on to the money, and as long as they kept waiting he still had a chance.

The smaller woman laughed at Emma and Buster, then moved over to talk with Mike. She had dark hair and looked a little like Lynnette, Danny thought.

"So, Mike," he heard her ask. "What are you doing for Halloween?"

Mike leaned on his rake. "Doing?" he asked.

She waved her hand casually. "Susie and Peter are going to a faculty party in full costume. Barnaby and I are dressing up as Donald and Daisy Duck. What are you going to be?"

Mike shrugged and returned to his raking. "I thought I'd go out trick-or-treating disguised as Emma's father."

"I'm going to be a policeman!" Emma shouted. "With a gun and everything."

"A gun?" The woman looked down at Emma. "Where did you get a gun?"

"At day care. She traded two of her dolls for it," Susan said. "We really don't approve, Betty. It looks quite real. Mike and I don't like the idea of toy guns."

Emma's face clouded, and her lower lip jutted ominously. "It's *my* gun. I'm keeping it. I need it so I can be a policeman."

"Just till after Halloween," Mike said. "Then we're giving it back. You know we talked about it, Emma."

The four in the front yard were distracted by Buster, who treed a neighbor's cat and then stood barking furiously at it.

Nobody noticed as Danny seized the opportunity to slip out through the back and disappear down the darkened alley.

CHAPTER NINE

"SUSAN!" Emma shouted. "Come look at me. I'm all ready."

Susan glanced at herself in her dresser mirror. It was Halloween night, and she was getting ready for her date with Peter. She touched her hair, dabbed on some lipstick and went into the kitchen where Emma stood bouncing by the table.

The little girl wore dark pants, a long-sleeved blue shirt and a miniature yachting cap. Mike had pinned a row of official-looking badges and chevrons to her "uniform," and painted a fierce black mustache on her face.

"Freeze!" she shouted, drawing a gun from the holster around her waist. Emma's gun was a wicked-looking semiautomatic pistol, made of plastic but very realistic.

"Emma, darling," Susan said, stroking the jaunty cap, "Daddy doesn't want you pointing the gun at people."

"Okay," the child replied. "What are you, Susan?"

"I'm a football player." Susan turned around to display her costume. "Do you like it?"

"It's neat. Daddy's downstairs finding a sack for me." Emma changed the subject. "Then we're going out trick-or-treating for a *long* time, and I'm going to fill my sack right to the top. I'm going to get lots and lots of candy, and eat every bit of it.''

Susan turned away to hide her smile. ''Daddy might have something to say about that.''

The doorbell rang, and Emma ran off to answer it. She loved greeting the other small trick-or-treaters, and distributing miniature chocolate bars from the table in the front hall.

''Emma,'' Mike called from the top of the basement stairs. ''All I could find was . . .''

He came into the kitchen with an old cotton flour sack in his hands, and stared at Susan.

''What the hell?'' he muttered.

She tensed, feeling defensive. ''Well, I'm hardly the type to dress up as Cinderella or Tinkerbell,'' she said. ''Am I?''

Mike recovered his equilibrium and regarded her with warm approval. ''Tinkerbell never looked so good.''

Susan had borrowed the uniform from the high school equipment room. Tight silver pants fitted snugly over her hips, and her shoulders bulged with heavy pads under a powder blue jersey with the number 38 lettered in silver on the front and back.

''Turn around,'' Mike said, coming over to stand by the table. ''Let me look at you.''

''Oh, Mike, I don't . . .''

''Come on, turn around. Everybody else gets to see you. Why not me?''

Reluctantly, she turned to display the uniform, her cheeks warming uncomfortably when he gave a low whistle of admiration. "If football players looked like that," he said, "even I could become a sports fan."

"Bang!" Emma shouted, racing into the room with her gun drawn. "Bang, bang! All the bad guys are running away. I scared them."

Mike and Susan exchanged an eloquent look. "Tonight's the end of your career as a policeman, Emma," Mike told his daughter firmly. "We agreed, you know. Right after Halloween, that gun goes back to Matthew at day care."

Emma cast him a rebellious glance, then caught sight of the sack in his hands and began to caper around the table. "Come on, Daddy!" she urged. "Hurry, let's go trick-or-treating before the other kids get all the stuff!"

The doorbell rang and she ran off down the hall again, her round cheeks flushed with excitement.

"She's going to get sick," Mike said gloomily, watching the doorway after she disappeared. "She's already tired and overheated, and she hasn't even left the house."

"All kids love Halloween. It's so exciting. Don't you remember, Mike? Didn't you get excited when you were a little kid, dressing up in a costume and being outside after dark?"

"I guess so," he said briefly, his face clouding. "So, is Peter dressing up tonight?"

"I hope so. I told him he had to find some kind of outfit to wear and he said he would, but he didn't sound very enthusiastic about it."

"You're going to feel pretty dumb wandering around in that football uniform if Peter's not wearing a costume, aren't you?"

"He'll have a costume," Susan said. "He promised."

Mike nodded, looking unconvinced. "Is there a helmet?" he asked.

"Helmet?"

"With your costume. Did you borrow a helmet, too?"

"Of course. I thought it would be better than a mask."

Mike gave her a teasing smile. "Well, you'd better wear it, then. In fact, don't take it off all night. Especially while you and Peter are dancing."

Susan understood what he was implying and felt the color deepen in her cheeks. She looked at his tall, muscular body in jeans and T-shirt, the sparkling blue of his eyes, the hard planes of his face, and felt almost weak with desire.

All at once she pictured herself at the faculty costume party, dancing with Mike instead of Peter. The image was so vivid that she could feel his arms around her, his face close to hers, his strong hand firmly pressing into the small of her back.

This, she realized suddenly, was the whole purpose of dancing. It allowed you, in front of everyone, to be shamelessly physical with a man who might otherwise be denied to you. While you were dancing, your bodies could press intimately together, your hands join, your cheeks touch, and nobody minded. It didn't mean anything, and yet in a way it meant everything in the world to dance with a man ...

As Susan imagined the dance, her longing to be in Mike's arms was suddenly so fierce that she felt shaky, almost sick. It really was time to get Mike out of her life, before something happened that both of them would regret.

Next week, she told herself firmly. Right after Halloween she would ask him to leave, and try not to think about the hollowness of life without Emma, without Mike...

"Will you be able to manage without us?" he asked.

Susan's eyes widened in shock.

"When we leave to go trick-or-treating," Mike said, obviously startled by her expression. "Can you answer the door and get ready at the same time?"

She turned away. "I'm almost ready now," she said. "And Peter won't be here till sometime after seven. The trick-or-treaters will be mostly finished by then."

"Okay." Mike waved to her as Emma came running back and grabbed his hand, dragging him toward the door. He took his worn leather jacket from the front closet, shrugged into it and knelt to help Emma put on her small duffel coat.

"Daddy!" she protested as he buttoned the coat up to her chin. "Nobody can see my badges."

Patiently, Mike undid the buttons and transferred some of the bright metal badges to her coat, pinning them carefully in place. Susan leaned in the hallway and watched, fascinated by the confident grace of his fingers as he worked on the tiny clasps.

She loved watching Mike do things with his hands...

He hugged Emma, holding her close for a moment, then got to his feet. "Okay, we're all set. Give Susan a kiss and we'll go, honey."

Emma held her face up obediently to be kissed. "G'bye, Susan," she whispered. "Don't smear my mustache."

"I wouldn't think of it," Susan promised.

She kissed the little girl's neck just below her ear, nuzzling and tickling. Emma wriggled in her arms and laughed in delight. Then she pulled away, ran down the veranda stairs and set off into the darkness with Mike, swinging her treat bag jauntily from one hand.

Susan stood in the doorway and watched until they were swallowed up in the leafy stillness of the autumn night. Even after they were gone from sight, she could still hear their voices, Emma's high-pitched excited chatter and Mike's quiet responses, fading gradually into silence.

When she finally turned to go back inside the house, her cheeks were wet with tears.

SUSAN HOVERED near the buffet table with her football helmet under one arm and a handful of nacho chips in her other hand, looking for the guacamole.

"Hi," a warm voice said at her elbow. "I certainly wouldn't mind being tackled by *you.*"

She sighed, already tired of this joke, and turned to see a dashing Zorro in cape and sombrero, with a sexy smile and flashing dark eyes behind his mask. "You don't have to bother saving me, Zorro," she said. "I'm not a damsel in distress."

"You look as if you could probably look after yourself," Zorro agreed. "But you're far too pretty to be alone."

"I'm not alone. I'm with Peter." Susan gestured at an earnest group of men in the corner, embroiled in an intense political discussion. Peter stood in their midst, hands in his pockets, wearing his customary tweed jacket and corduroy slacks.

"Good old Peter," Zorro said with grin. "Forgot this was a costume party, did he?"

"Peter has a lot on his mind," Susan said loyally. "He's working on another article for *Poli-Sci International,* and grading his midterm papers, and—"

"We're all grading midterm papers," Zorro said calmly, turning to examine the buffet table. "What's your name?"

"Susan Adamson."

"Well, hello, Susan. Do you happen to know where the guacamole is?"

"I was just looking for it. The bowl was right here a minute ago. Somebody must have snitched it."

"The mystery of the missing guacamole. Hey, this sounds like a job for Zorro. Wanna be my sidekick?"

Susan smiled. "Do you teach at the college, too? When you're not rescuing damsels in distress and hunting for stolen chip dip, I mean?"

Zorro nodded, tipping his sombrero with a courtly flourish. "Steven Albright," he said. "Chemistry and physics. Where did Peter manage to find a ravishing creature like you?"

"You wouldn't believe me if I told you."

Zorro gave her a smoldering glance. "I probably wouldn't. If I'd known where to look, I would have been there first."

Susan turned away, nibbling absently on one of the chips in her hand.

"Aha!" Zorro exclaimed suddenly, diving across the table and retrieving a crystal bowl. "Here it is. Allow me."

He set the bowl in front of Susan and bowed, sweeping his cape aside to reveal a black silk shirt and trim black leather pants.

''Zorro triumphs again,'' she said cheerfully, dragging one of her chips through the bowl and savoring the rich flavor.

He examined her with warm interest, then drew his sword and used the tip to trace a small Z on one of her padded shoulders.

Susan met his eyes behind the dark mask, both amused and a little dismayed at the irony of the position she found herself in.

She'd spent most of her adult life searching for a confident professional man who combined sophistication with good looks. Except for Jerry, her former fiancé, such men had been few and far between. Nowadays, though, it seemed she was practically tripping over them.

There was Graham McBride, her very first date from the video service, who still called occasionally. And Peter, looking handsome and casual as he argued Marxist theory with a group of other professors. The flirtatious rogue at her side was probably a nice, mild-mannered intellectual when he was out of costume. And each of these men, in his own way, was precisely what she'd been looking for all these years.

So why wasn't she interested? Why did she feel this sense of detachment, almost boredom?

The exclusive party, the clever costumes and witty chatter and sophisticated company would have brought her great pleasure a few months ago. She would have enjoyed being here, surrounded by the kind of men she'd always dreamed of meeting, conducting a casual flirtation with somebody like Steven Albright.

But tonight she found herself glancing frequently at her watch, wondering when she could catch Peter's eye and suggest that it was time to think about leaving.

MIKE WANDERED through the crisp autumn evening, hands plunged deep in his jacket pockets, watching Emma. The little girl was panting with excitement, running from house to house while he waited outside in the shadows.

"Daddy," she shouted, running up to him with her sack dragging. She could hardly catch her breath and leaned against him, scarlet with excitement. "I got a popcorn ball! Look, Daddy! And that other lady was giving out little candy bags tied with ribbons, see?"

Mike grimaced as he looked into the sack. It was soiled and dusty, laden with sugary treats. "I think you've got enough, haven't you?"

"Just a few more," Emma pleaded. "Just one more street."

Mike sighed. "One more. Then we're starting to walk back home, okay? You've been out long enough."

But Emma wasn't listening to him. She was already gone, racing off down the street with a gang of little robots, aliens and Space Invaders. Mike watched her small running figure, wondering how it was possible to love one person so much that your whole being was absorbed by her.

Although, he thought as they finally turned around and scuffed through the leaves toward home, he had to admit that his focus was beginning to expand these days. For years, he'd thought of nobody but Emma. All his efforts and dreams had been centered around the task of providing her with a safe, loving home. But now there was another claim on his emotions.

Involuntarily he pictured Susan, with her quiet face and gentle smile, her sweet husky laugh and the warmth she showed whenever she and Emma were together. Unable to stop himself, Mike let his thoughts dwell on her hungrily, recalling every detail of her face. She had one front tooth that was slightly crooked, giving her smile a winsome, lopsided look that he found irresistible.

And her body...

Mike swallowed hard, remembering the way she'd looked in those tight football pants. It had taken all his self-control not to fall on her like a wolf, right there in the kitchen, and begin ripping her clothes off. He clenched his hands briefly into fists, wondering how much a man could bear of this kind of frustration.

Living under the same roof with a woman he desired so intensely, having breakfast together, talking for hours and sharing a newspaper in easy companionship, then watching her go off on dates with another man...

"I'm so tired, Daddy," Emma said plaintively, interrupting his thoughts.

Mike scooped her into his arms and carried her and her sack of treats down the alley. The back lane was usually deserted, but tonight a smattering of noisy ghosts and goblins were using it. In the distance, a man walked toward them through the shadows, hands in his pockets.

Mike peered down the alley at the man, unable to see his face clearly or determine his age. Probably another father, or maybe an older brother returning home after supervising trick-or-treaters, Mike thought.

As they drew near the house, Emma began to wriggle in his arms. "I want down, Daddy. I want to let Buster out so he can see my candy."

Mike set her down on the graveled lane and watched as she trotted off to open the back gate. Buster hurtled outside, sniffed at her joyously, then lifted his head with sudden alertness and bounded toward the man who was about to pass them.

Mike looked on with astonishment as Buster leaped happily on the stranger's legs, barking and wagging his tail.

The man fended him off nervously and hurried along the fence. He glanced up furtively as he went by, with Buster still bounding along next to him. Mike had a blurred impression of a young man with a pale frightened face, a wispy mustache and thin shoulders under a shabby denim jacket.

"Buster!" he called sharply. "Come here."

Buster trotted back reluctantly with his tail drooping, while the stranger vanished into the shadows beyond the neighbor's hedge.

"Some watchdog!" Mike said, looking at Buster's lolling tongue and happy pink grin. "You'd give a stranger the keys to the house if you knew where to find them, wouldn't you?"

"You can have some licorice, Buster," Emma said soothingly, rummaging through her bag. "Buster really likes licorice," she told her father.

Mike nodded grimly. "I'll just bet he does. Come on, Officer Murphy. It's about time for your night shift to end."

She began to droop again and he lifted her effortlessly, carrying her inside the empty house and upstairs to her room.

For a while, Emma's bedtime routine occupied him so that he had no chance to think of anything else. He ran a bath for her and helped her scrub the mustache from her face, then lifted her slippery little body from the tub and dried her tenderly, concerned that she still seemed hot and flushed.

"You have to settle down now," he said softly, wrapping her in a big soft towel and carrying her to her room. "Settle down, sweetheart. It's all over. Halloween's all over, and it's time to go to sleep with Gerald in your nice cozy bed."

"I want some more candy," she murmured sleepily against his shoulder. "I want to eat my other popcorn ball."

"No you don't. You've already eaten far too much candy. I'm putting the rest away, and tomorrow we'll decide what to do with it."

Emma didn't argue—a strong indication of how tired she was. She fell asleep halfway through the story of the Sleepy Mouse, well before her favorite part where Sleepy's mother makes him a warm new cover for his bed out of leaves and rose petals.

Mike closed the book and looked down at her flushed face on the pillow. The little girl's skin was as soft and fresh as the flower petals in the story, and her long dark eyelashes cast a dense fan of shadow on her cheeks.

Mike moved around the room quietly and picked up the scattered clothes, folding them neatly on the ruffled chair. Then he put the police hat and holster in the toy chest. The gun fell out of the holster and Mike bent to pick it up. He paused for a moment with the toy weapon in his hands and looked down at it with a shudder of revulsion.

"God!" he whispered, grimacing in distaste and tossing the gun into a drawer. Involuntarily, he wiped his hands on his jeans and wandered into the darkened hallway, then down the stairs to the kitchen.

He made himself a mug of cocoa and gazed absently at the crescent moon above the treetops, wreathed in lacy bits of cloud that glowed bright silver at the edges. The night was silent and beautiful, but somehow Mike felt uneasy—nothing he could put his finger on—a tinge of menace, of lurking danger to his home and family.

He recalled Susan's mentioning, more than once, a feeling that somebody was watching the house. He frowned and looked closely at the yard. All the little trick-or-treaters had been tucked into bed by now, and whatever Halloween high jinks might be happening in the city, they were far from here. Buster slumbered peacefully in his doghouse, which was bathed with moonlight. Even the birds and squirrels were silent.

For some reason, he kept thinking of that young man in the ragged denim jacket, slipping furtively along the back alley, and Buster's excited reaction when he saw the stranger approaching.

Mike frowned and gripped the edge of the curtain in his fingers, trying to recall the man's face. But after a moment he shook his head and turned away. He hadn't managed to get a really clear look at the stranger, but he'd seen enough to set his mind at rest. That young man, he realized instinctively, was too timid and frightened to be a threat to anyone.

"HEY, MISS ADAMSON," Jason said the next day in English class. "Did you go trick-or-treating?"

Susan looked up from the pile of essays she was marking. "I went to a college faculty party," she said calmly. "Have you finished reading the story, Jason?"

"Yeah." He leaned back in his desk, beaming at her. Most of her other students were still absorbed in their textbooks, but a few looked up to see what was happening.

"Come up here and I'll find something for you to do. Back to work, everybody."

In addition to his ebullient personality, Jason possessed a razor-keen mind and usually finished his class assignments far ahead of the others, leaving him free to seek other distractions. Susan was well aware of this, and kept a supply of special assignments on hand especially for Jason, interesting challenges and puzzles that he enjoyed.

"I've got a puzzle for you here," Susan said, rummaging in a side drawer of her desk. "You have to read all the clues and figure out which man owns the zebra."

"Hey, great," Jason said with obvious pleasure, taking the printed sheet.

"This one's a real challenge," Susan warned. "My tenant and I spent about two hours the other night trying to solve it."

"Did you get it?"

"Mike finally worked out the answer. He's a very bright man."

Jason stood by her desk, smiling at her. "Did you see the postings? I made the shortlist for the track team."

"I know. Mrs. Smith told me she was really pleased with you."

"Thanks, Miss Adamson." He paused on the way back to his desk, a lanky figure in his torn jeans and sloppy plaid shirt. "Hey, and thanks for putting in a good word for me."

"Don't thank me, Jason. You did it all on your own."

"I really want another race with you, Miss Adamson. You gotta give me a second chance."

She shook her head. "I'd need to train hard for about three months. Mrs. Smith told me how fast you're running."

Jason grinned happily and was about to speak, when the intercom crackled overhead. "Miss Adamson? Are you there?"

"Yes, I am," Susan said into the speaker. "What is it?"

"Can you come to the main office for a minute, please?"

Susan got to her feet and looked at the students. "If you finish the story before I get back," she said, "you can go on with the assignment I gave you yesterday. No horseplay, okay? And Jason, I want to know who owns that zebra."

She left, hurrying through the silent halls to the office.

Gloria and Sheila glanced up when she entered, looking tense.

"What?" Susan asked in alarm. She paused just inside the door and looked from one to the other. "What is it? Not my parents? My father—"

"Not your parents," Gloria said.

"Then what is it? What's the matter?"

"Now, don't get all upset," Gloria said soothingly, coming around the counter to stand next to her. "Carla called us from over at the day care, that's all. She wonders if you know exactly where Mike's working today."

"*Emma?*" Susan whispered, feeling an icy chill of fear. "Has something happened to Emma?"

"She's just a little sick, that's all." Sheila came to join them and patted Susan's arm. "Nothing serious. Probably too much trick-or-treating last night," she added.

"But Carla thinks she should probably go home," Gloria chimed in. "And she's not sure how to get hold of Mike today."

"I think he said they'd be outside this afternoon, stringing some temporary wiring for the new lights. I'll go see, all right?"

"We can send one of the kids to find him, Susie."

"No, I'd like to go. If something's wrong with Emma, I want to be there."

"Okay. Is your class all right?"

Susan nodded, already heading out the door. "They have enough work to keep them busy, and I have a spare last period. Can you look in on them in a few minutes if I'm not back, Gloria?"

"Is that your class with Jason Caine?"

"Yes, it is."

"Good. I like Jason," the secretary said tranquilly. "We've finally reached an understanding, Jason and I. He doesn't make chauvinistic comments, and I don't give him detentions."

Susan gave her a strained smile and left the office, hurrying through the big front doors. A soft rain was falling, more of a heavy mist, and fog obscured the school grounds. She ran under the covered walkway to the new gym, where a crew of men in hard hats and raincoats worked on the outer walls.

"Is Mike Murphy around?" she asked, looking up at the scaffold.

One of the men gestured with a hammer. "In there." He pointed at a small mobile building parked near the new construction. "Coffee break."

Susan nodded and hurried through the swirling mist toward the trailer. She ducked inside and shook droplets from her hair. Three men lounged inside on wooden chairs, laughing comfortably and sipping coffee, their Thermos mugs on the floor beside them.

Susan paused awkwardly, conscious of their startled, admiring glances.

"Susan," Mike said in surprise, setting down his cup. "What are you doing out here?"

"The office called me down," she said. "Carla says that Emma's . . . she's not feeling well."

He got to his feet and automatically reached for his jacket. "Not feeling well?" he asked. "What do they mean? Has she had some kind of accident?"

"I don't know. I think she's just sick. Sheila suggested the culprit might be too much Halloween candy."

"Damn!" he muttered, shouldering his way out into the rain beside her. "You know, all week I've had a feeling..."

He fell abruptly silent, and the two of them hurried into the school and down the corridors to the day-care centre.

HOURS LATER, just after nine o'clock at night, Susan stood by the front door watching as the doctor shrugged into his coat and prepared to leave. It was raining heavily now, a dark, chilly autumn downpour that slashed on the pavement and swept piles of sodden leaves through the gutters and into the storm drains.

"Thanks, David," Susan murmured, shivering as she looked out. "It was really nice of you to come over on such a miserable night."

The doctor smiled. David Schwartz was a cheerful young man with a freckled boyish face and a casual manner that belied his years of experience. He supplied on-call medical services to the school staff and students. Everybody loved him.

Just the kind of man she was looking for, Susan had often thought in the past, except that Dr. Schwartz already had an attractive wife and four wickedly energetic young sons...

But tonight Susan's thoughts were far from any concerns about her own life. She glanced up the stairs in the direction of Emma's room, where Mike was sitting with his daughter. Then she looked back at the doctor.

"Did she catch it from me?" Susan asked, lowering her voice. "I tried really hard to stay away from her when I was sick a couple of weeks ago, but maybe I was still a little careless."

"You can't blame yourself," the doctor reassured her. "Kids can pick these things up anywhere. Day care, shopping malls, restaurants . . . even doctors' offices can be pretty fertile breeding grounds for germs."

"And Mike said she got so worn-out when she was trick-or-treating . . ."

The young doctor nodded. "We see a lot of sick little kids around Halloween. They're overexcited, overtired and so zonked out with sugar that there's no nutritional base to pull them through. Any nasty bug that's floating around has a good chance of infecting them."

"She looks so sick," Susan whispered. "I'm scared. Shouldn't she be in the hospital?"

"Mike doesn't want her in the hospital, and he's the boss. Emma's his child."

"But can we take proper care of her at home? What if she gets really feverish?"

"Mike knows what to do. Alcohol rubs, cold poultices and ice packs on the extremities, lots of fluids . . . apparently, he's done it all before."

"I still think the hospital would be . . ."

"Actually," Dr. Schwartz told her, "Mike has a point, you know. If he takes Emma to the hospital, she'll only be getting sporadic attention from a nighttime staff of people who are busy with dozens of sick kids. If she stays home, she'll have the entire, concentrated attention of two adults watching every single degree on the thermometer."

"But we're not professionals," Susan said. "We wouldn't know what to do if there's some kind of crisis."

"You know, Susan," he said gently, "I'm not so sure about that. Mike seems to have a lot of specialized medical knowledge." The doctor smiled briefly. "In fact, I have absolutely no qualms about leaving Emma in his hands, sick as she is. Good night, Susan," he added, strolling out onto the veranda. "Call me if things get really crazy."

"What would you consider 'really crazy,' David?"

The doctor considered. "Convulsions, irregular pupil size, a temperature above 106...any of those things."

Susan watched as the doctor splashed down the front walk and his car was swallowed up in the rainy darkness. Then she turned and hurried back up the stairs to Emma's room.

Mike sat by the bed, wearing a white T-shirt and ragged blue jogging pants. He had a basin of cold water on a nearby table, and he busied himself wringing the towels in the cold water and laying them over Emma's bare chest and shoulders.

Susan looked down at the girl. It was hard to see that jaunty, irrepressible spirit so dulled and listless. Emma was wearing only her pink flannel pajama bottoms, rolled up past her knees, and her little body was limp on the mat of towels that Mike had placed beneath her. The child's eyes were closed and she was flushed. She murmured occasionally, incoherent scraps of words and phrases.

Mike took a thermometer from Emma's armpit and held it to the light, frowning, then shook it and replaced it.

"How high now?" Susan asked.

Mike looked up at her, his face so drawn with anxiety that his cheekbones jutted harshly in the shadowed light. "A shade under 104."

"Oh, Mike..." Susan came around the bed and stood beside him. "That's a whole degree higher in just half an hour, isn't it? Don't you think we should—"

"Here, Susan," he said. "Take the rubbing alcohol bottle and swab her chest and neck. Use lots of liquid."

Obediently, Susan took the plastic bottle, soaked a facecloth and rubbed it tenderly over Emma's chest, moved by the feel of her ribs and breastbone, as delicate and fragile as a bird's.

"Oh, Mike, she's so hot," she whispered.

"Body temperature in children is more volatile than in adults," Mike said, measuring medicine into an eyedropper. "For you or me, a reading of 104 would mean that we're seriously ill. In a child, it's certainly significant but not quite as dangerous."

"But she seems really sick. I'm not sure that we can do this."

Mike set down the medicine bottle and looked at her directly. "You'll just have to trust me, Susan," he said. "Accept that I know what I'm doing and I'm capable of looking after her. All right?"

"How?" Susan asked, her fear making her reckless. "What are you, Mike? Are you some kind of doctor? Is that what you're running away from?"

Instantly, the familiar, shuttered look appeared on his face, and he turned away to wring out and replace the damp cloths.

Suddenly, Emma coughed, a deep racking cough that shook her with a harsh spasm. Mike leaned over to place his ear on her chest, listening closely while her body continued to heave.

"Mike!" Susan whispered, but he waved his hand to silence her.

"Her lungs are pretty congested," he announced, sitting up at last. "Susan, look through those medicines the doctor left and find the purple bottle, please."

"This one?"

He nodded, and looked at the thermometer again. "Measure out the largest dose marked on the dropper tube, but try to be really precise."

Susan obeyed, and then watched while Mike pried open Emma's clenched jaw and dribbled the medication through her lips.

"What's her temperature now?" she asked.

"Still climbing. Do you want to take over the damp cloths for a minute? I'm going downstairs to get more ice."

Susan nodded and took the chair he'd just left. There was no point in continuing to argue with him. For Emma's sake, they had to work together.

Susan began to wring out towels and put them on Emma's flushed body. Mike came back into the room with fresh ice water to replenish the basin, but Susan was hardly aware of him. She worked at his side as the hours passed, and didn't mention going to the hospital again.

But, she thought, as soon as Emma was feeling better, Mike Murphy was going to get a piece of her mind....

SUSAN WOKE UP and blinked, looking around in confusion. She had been dozing in a chair and Emma lay in the bed with Gerald in her arms, her face white and still. The poultices and rubbing cloths were gone, along with all traces of medicine, and the blankets were pulled neatly to the child's chin and turned down. Mike sat on the other side of the bed, watching his daughter in brooding stillness.

Susan looked at the little girl's face, so pale and silent, almost waxen. She felt a dreadful clutch of fear that almost sickened her.

"Mike," she whispered, reaching out a trembling finger to touch Emma's cheek.

"She's fine," Mike whispered. "Her fever broke about half an hour ago, but you were so tired I let you sleep while I tidied everything up."

Susan sagged with relief. "Oh, Mike, that's wonderful... What time is it?" She couldn't take her eyes from Emma's peaceful face, the gentle rise and fall of her chest under the blankets.

"Past midnight. Come on, Susan, it's time for bed. You have to work tomorrow."

She turned in her chair to look up at Mike. "How could she be so sick, and then a few hours later be all better?"

"She's not all better," Mike said, bending to adjust the blankets around Emma's face. "She'll be feeling rocky for the next few days, tired and full of aches and pains, probably coughing a lot, too. The fever was just an initial symptom."

"But it's the most dangerous part?"

He nodded. "By far. Fevers in children are pretty scary. They need to be watched closely."

"Scary!" Susan muttered, getting slowly to her feet. "Mike, I was terrified."

"So was I," he confessed, smiling at her.

"But you still didn't want her to be in the hospital overnight?"

"I knew we could take care of her at home," he said quietly, stroking Emma's cheek as she slept.

Susan went out into the hallway and waited for Mike to join her. "But how did you know that?" she persisted. "What if there had been a crisis, Mike? How could you be so sure of yourself?"

He didn't answer her, taking her elbow instead and moving her toward the stairs.

Susan resisted, turning to face him. "I want to know, Mike," she whispered. "I want to know who you are, you and Emma. Please tell me the truth."

"I've told you the truth," he said. "Everything I've told you is true."

"Oh, Mike..." She looked up at him in despair, then paused, mesmerized by the nearness of his face and body. Her weariness ebbed, replaced by a sudden flow of energy and tingling excitement.

Mike's face was deeply shadowed by the night-light in the hall, his eyes dark with emotion. He stood so close to her that Susan could feel the warmth of his skin and see the stubble of beard along his jawline. He gazed at her steadily, his face intent and still.

"Go to bed, Susan," he said softly. "Please, go to bed now."

But neither of them moved. They stood together, staring at each other, while the old house creaked and the autumn wind sighed around the eaves.

Then Susan moved into his arms and clung to him.

CHAPTER TEN

THE WORLD stopped turning, locked in stillness while they held each other. When his mouth found hers, Susan had the distant sense that ages were passing, galaxies colliding, universes unfolding around them, all in the space of a kiss.

She moved against him recklessly, blind with passion. The frustration and confusion of the past months raged within her, compounded by her terror over Emma and her relief at the girl's recovery. Her usual caution seemed to have vanished completely, burned up in a storm of desire.

"Susan," he said, his voice ragged and husky. "Please, sweetheart, don't do this to me. I can't stand it..."

She kissed him again and pulled him close to her, running her fingers through his tousled hair and straining against him.

"You feel so good," she whispered. "Just so good, Mike."

He tried to push her away. "We can't do this," he muttered urgently. "Susan, stop and think. If we do this, nothing will ever be the same afterward."

Dimly she recognized the wisdom of what he was saying but she didn't care anymore, didn't seem able to stop herself.

"What's the matter?" she murmured against his neck. "Don't you want me?"

He groaned and held her so tightly that her body ached at the strength of his embrace. Susan could feel the moment when his resolve broke and he began to respond, kissing her with rising passion and running his hands hungrily over her body.

He started to move down the hall, still holding her. Locked together, they stumbled into his room, kissing and murmuring incoherently.

"Is it all right?" Susan asked with her last glimmer of rational thought. "I mean, will Emma be..."

"With all the medication she took, she'll be sound asleep till morning," Mike whispered. But he took a moment to prop the door slightly ajar so they could hear if the child called out.

Then he turned to Susan, his face so taut with purpose that she trembled. He began to undress her slowly, never taking his eyes from her as he unbuttoned her shirt and tossed it aside, unfastened her bra and gazed at her naked breasts.

The rain had stopped, and outside the window the moon gleamed fitfully through banks of clouds. Susan stood quietly in the silver light, letting him kiss and caress her breasts, feeling a kind of shivering excitement and anticipation that she'd never known before. Mike unzipped her jeans and knelt to pull them down, then removed her socks as gently as if she were a child.

He looked at her in awe, running his hands over the curve of her hips, down the smooth muscular line of her thighs.

She reached out and tugged wordlessly at his T-shirt, watching while he pulled it over his head and stepped out of his jogging pants and socks. Susan gasped at the beauty of his powerful body, the mat of dark hair on his chest and the bulging strength of his arms and legs.

She moved into his arms again, thrilling at the burst of sweet fire as their skin touched. "Oh, Mike," she whispered. "I've never felt so..."

"What?" he asked, his lips moving against hers as he leaned down to turn down the bed covers. "How do you feel, darling?"

Susan tumbled with him into the bed and luxuriated in his embrace. "I feel so right," she said at last. "I feel as if this is exactly what I've been waiting for all my life."

"Oh, Susan..."

He lay next to her, running his hands over her breasts and down the length of her body. "You're so beautiful," he whispered. "The first time I ever saw you, I couldn't believe how lovely you were. All curves and sunshine."

She nestled in his arms, thinking about their first meeting, remembering his engaging grin and the startling blueness of his eyes as he'd stood on the front porch in his work clothes.

He drew her close and kissed her, holding her with such tenderness, she felt herself melting in his arms, growing soft and moist with desire. Then, somehow, her panties were gone along with his undershorts as their bodies entwined, warm and delicious in the silvered light.

Susan felt the bulging maleness of him, the hardness of muscle sheathed in warm skin, the strength of his fingers, the crisp hair on his chest as it brushed against her nipples, arousing her almost unbearably.

His hands moved on her body with more purpose, stroking rhythmically, caressing and fondling. Susan responded by running her fingers over his chest, then trailing them slowly down his hard flat belly. She paused to cup and fondle him, thrilled by his powerful maleness.

He groaned at her touch and arched above her, looking down at her in the moonlight. "Now?" he asked.

She nodded, breathless and drowning in passion. "Please, Mike."

He lowered himself toward her, slow and cautious as he eased inside her. She gasped with delight. Then he began to move within her, warm and strong, so sweet that she felt tears gathering in her eyes.

"Are you all right, Susan?" he murmured. "Am I hurting you?"

She shook her head urgently. "Don't stop, Mike. It . . . it feels so good."

Gradually, she lost awareness of the room, the house, the moonlight, everything in the world. She was lifted, carried beyond the silvery treetops and the clouds, among vibrating oceans of stars that shimmered with unearthly radiance in the blackness of the night.

"Oh, Mike," she said at last, when the heavens released her and she found herself back in the rumpled bed, still nestled in his arms as he trembled against her. "Oh, Mike, that was wonderful."

She stroked his hair tenderly, gazing over his shoulder at the ghostly play of light and shadow on the ceiling. Mike kissed her cheek and cuddled her warmly in his arms, sighing with contentment.

"You know what?" he whispered in her ear. "I've dreamed about this for at least a million hours. Pounding nails, stringing wire, pouring concrete, and thinking about making love to you."

"What a relief," Susan told him with a smile. "Now that you've finally done it, you can stop thinking about it."

"Are you kidding?" He nuzzled hungrily against her neck and shoulder. "I'm ready to start all over again."

"I thought you were tired."

"Tired?" He leaned up on his elbow to look down at her, raising an eyebrow. "What man could be tired with a woman like you in his bed?"

Susan laughed and kissed him. Before long, their embrace turned to passion again.

DANNY PAUSED outside a jewelry store in a downtown mall, and gazed wistfully at the window display. He played a game in his mind, thinking about the stacks of bills in the suitcase and trying to decide what he'd buy Lynnette for Christmas if he had all that money.

They weren't engaged or anything, and when they went to the movies, she usually insisted on paying her own way. Danny hadn't actually bought her anything but popcorn. So it wouldn't be right to buy a really lavish gift, even though he would give her the moon and stars if he could.

Besides, Lyn was so shy, she'd be embarrassed by something costly and extravagant.

Maybe that little lizard pin, with its gold body studded with colored gems. Danny smiled at the bright piece of costume jewelry, thinking how nice it would look on the lapel of Lyn's black winter coat. She'd really love a pin like that. She'd open the wrapping paper, take the lid off the box and exclaim with delight. Then she'd look up at him . . .

Danny's heart melted with love when he thought about her big dark eyes, her soft voice and the way she held his arm timidly when they crossed the street. There was something so fragile about her under the tough facade. He was almost afraid to touch her.

If only he had the money, he thought sadly, everything would be different. He'd feel big and confident then, able to look after her and protect her from anything bad. People kept saying money wasn't important, but they were crazy. Money gave you the power to hold the world at bay, to look after the people you loved and keep them safe.

Rosa had known that. She'd worked and struggled all her life to surround Danny with that kind of safety. And now it was gone, vanished into the hands of a couple who owned a big house and had high-paying jobs, and didn't need the cash at all. They would probably lie low for the winter, Danny thought bitterly, and then use the money in the spring to add a sun room to their house, or go on a trip to Europe, or some other wasteful thing.

All Rosa's money would be gone in one burst of extravagance. Enough money for him to marry Lynnette in a few years and look after her in comfort . . .

As a rule, Danny tried really hard not to hate the good-looking couple who had his money. After all, it wasn't their fault, he kept telling himself, trying to be fair. Anyone would have done the same thing if they found a suitcase full of money abandoned in the park. They'd take it home, hide it, then start spending it when they figured they were safe.

Still, it was so bitterly frustrating to watch them all the time, observe their comings and goings and the comfortable routine of their lives. Not only did they have everything Danny wanted out of life, *his* money was hidden somewhere inside their house where he couldn't get at it.

But soon, all that was going to change. Danny had almost recovered from the sickening horror of the morning he'd practically stumbled over the woman inside her own house.

He knew he had to try again, but this time it would be different. He wasn't going to make a mistake like that again. And if, despite his best plans, something went wrong, he wasn't going to run away. He intended to be prepared.

Danny was buying a gun.

He hunched his shoulders and looked around furtively, then hurried into a store and edged toward the rear, easing his way past shelves bristling with weapons. He considered a rack of sawed-off shotguns that looked really threatening, but were too bulky to hide under his jacket. Next, he examined a display of little silver derringers that caught his eye with their dainty brightness. He hefted one absently and decided it was too small to be effective.

At last he settled on a businesslike handgun, a semiautomatic pistol with a brown textured handle and a gleaming blue-black muzzle.

"It's a nice display, isn't it?" a voice asked at his elbow. "A really wonderful selection."

Danny turned, startled to see a clerk standing down the aisle from him, a thin young man in a candy-striped blazer with his arms full of skinny, plastic dolls.

"Not many stores carry a selection like this anymore," the clerk went on, stroking the handle of a military-style submachine gun.

"Nobody should," Danny said coldly. "It should be against the law to sell stuff like this to little kids."

"I beg your pardon?" the clerk asked.

Danny waved his hand at the banks of toy guns, thinking about his own troubled adolescence. "It's not funny, you know, letting kids play with guns that look this real. If I had kids, I wouldn't let them anywhere near this stuff."

"So what are you doing with that plastic handgun?" the clerk asked suspiciously.

Danny's stomach clenched. "I need it for...for this play I'm in," he mumbled. "I'm...playing a cop."

The clerk seemed satisfied, turning away to tend to his display of dolls, but Danny felt even sicker as he hurried to the checkout to pay for his gun.

Considering what he was planning to do next week, he didn't even like to think about cops.

SUSAN WOKE to the darkness of the November morning and stared blankly up at the ceiling, wondering why she felt so good. Then memories began to flood into her mind. Her eyes widened, and she rolled over to bury her face against the pillow.

She was pleasantly conscious of her body, eased and satisfied, luxuriating in the cozy warmth of her bed. But her mind wasn't nearly as peaceful. Memories crowded and collided, a welter of tastes and sensations and overpowering emotions.

She saw Emma's limp, fevered body, then her placid sleeping face after the fever broke, and felt again that blessed surge of love and relief. She remembered Mike's arms around her, the crushing strength of his embrace, and the sweetness of his mouth as they stumbled down the hallway to his room. And then his hands, his body, the tender fulfillment of their love-making...

At last Susan came to herself and scrambled hastily out of bed. She had to get ready for work. There was no sound or movement from upstairs. Mike had been sleeping deeply when she'd climbed out of his bed and tiptoed downstairs to her own room, sometime in the small hours of the morning. Susan shook her head, marveling at herself. She should be just as exhausted as Mike, but she wasn't. In fact, she felt absolutely wonderful, full of vibrant energy that made her want to sing and dance. She finished dressing in record time.

I guess I really needed that, she told herself with a wry smile, gulping her coffee.

She shivered as she recalled the exquisite feeling of their two bodies, joined and moving gently together, perfectly tuned to each other's needs...

Suddenly, she longed to creep upstairs and look in on him, just to watch him sleeping, feast her eyes on his finely sculpted features and his muscular bare chest with its mat of curly hair. But she resisted, knowing

Mike had called in the day before to report that he wouldn't be coming to work, and he really needed these few extra hours of sleep.

It was harder to resist the urge to write him a loving, tender note. There was so much emotion inside her, aching to be expressed, but she felt a little nervous about his reaction to their lovemaking. Probably better to talk face-to-face, she decided, and see how he really felt before she committed something to paper.

So she contented herself with a hastily scribbled note reminding him that she'd made arrangements to meet Betty after work for dinner and a movie, and that he should call her at school if there was any change in Emma's condition. After a moment's hesitation, she signed it, "Love, Susan," and propped it near his breakfast plate.

THAT EVENING, when Susan arrived at the restaurant, Betty was already seated at a table covered with a bright red gingham cloth, sipping a glass of Chianti.

"Hi, Susie." She flourished the wicker-covered bottle. "About time you got here. I was afraid I might have to drink this whole thing myself."

"I was late getting away from school," Susan explained, taking off her jacket and hanging it on an oak coat tree in the corner. "I had at least a million things to do today. It's always like that on Fridays."

Betty poured some wine into the other glass and raised her own, smiling as Susan sat down across from her. "Well, here's looking at you, kid," she said cheerfully. "And your prosperous future."

Susan took a gulp of the dry red wine, savoring its rich flavor.

"Wow," Betty said, her eyes widening. "Look at you. You're positively radiant. Being rich must really agree with you."

"Rich?" Susan asked in confusion. Her cheeks warmed under her friend's curious gaze, and she looked away quickly.

"The money in the *suitcase,*" Betty said with patient emphasis. "Have you forgotten that you recently found fifty-three thousand dollars? Has that trivial detail just escaped your notice?"

"Sort of," Susan confessed, taking another sip of wine and looking at the menu. "Have you ordered for both of us? Is the lasagna on special tonight?"

"Yes and yes. Plus garlic toast and salad with feta cheese. Susie, what's wrong with you? Is something the matter?"

"Why should anything be the matter?"

"Well, let me see," Betty said, her voice heavy with sarcasm. "Though obsessively punctual, you're almost half an hour late today. Your face is glowing like a supernova, and you seem to have overlooked the tiny little matter of fifty-three thousand dollars about to fall in your lap. And then you ask me why anything should be the matter?"

Susan shifted awkwardly in her chair. "I'm just . . . everything's fine," she said, and smiled in relief as the waiter arrived with a basket of garlic toast. "I love this stuff," she told Betty. "Don't you? Isn't it just the best . . ."

"Susan Elaine Adamson," Betty said sternly. "Look at me."

"Lots of places don't have real garlic toast, you know," Susan went on hastily, talking with her mouth full and waving her hand expansively. "They just toast regular bread and spread that garlic butter on it, and pretend it's—"

"Shut up and look at me," Betty commanded.

Susan stopped talking and met her friend's gaze reluctantly.

Betty studied her for a moment. Her eyes widened in amazement. "You *didn't,*" she breathed.

"Didn't what?" Susan said innocently, her cheeks warming.

"You *did.*" Betty leaned back in triumph. "I can always tell. You're almost thirty and you still blush like a schoolgirl."

"Thank you for pointing that out," Susan said with dignity. "Look, can we just—"

"So, what's Peter like in the sack?" Betty asked cheerfully, helping herself to garlic toast. "More lively than he looks, I hope."

"Peter?" Susan asked, then blushed even more furiously.

"Not Peter?" Betty looked at her in sudden alertness. "Then, who on earth . . . Oh, Susie," she whispered. "Tell me you didn't."

"This is a perfectly ridiculous conversation. Where's our salad?" Susan turned in her chair and looked toward the kitchen. "I'm starved."

"Not Mike," Betty said flatly. "Please, please, tell me you didn't go to bed with Mike."

"I didn't go to bed with Mike."

"You're lying."

"I know," Susan murmured with a fleeting grin. "But you asked me to say it."

"Susie, you must be crazy. How did you ever let it happen?"

"It just happened," Susan said. "Emma was really sick, and we were both up for hours, till past midnight, sponging her down and trying to get her fever under control..."

Betty leaned across the table, her concern obviously shifting for the moment, at least. "Is Emma all right?"

Susan nodded. "Mike seemed to know exactly what to do. He kept working on her, and her fever broke around midnight. It was like a miracle," she added with a fond smile, remembering. "One minute she was burning up, practically delirious, and then I dozed off for a little while and when I woke up, she was sleeping like an angel, almost completely back to normal."

"And she's fine today?"

"I didn't see her, but Mike called the office while I was in class this morning and left a message saying she was a lot better."

"Oh, good," Betty said. "I really love that little kid, you know."

"So do I."

"So," Betty asked after a brief silence, "how did we get from the sickroom to the bedroom? Don't tell me," she added dryly. "Let me guess. You and Mike accidentally fell into each other's arms. You were both so relieved and happy, you just couldn't keep your hands off each other."

"Actually, that's pretty much the way it happened."

Betty drained her wineglass and stared into the distance.

"Betty? What are you thinking about?"

Just then, the waiter brought their salads. Susan picked up her fork and began to probe at the mounds of feta cheese.

"Oh, Susie," Betty said at last, drawing herself together with an obvious effort and looking sadly at her friend. "Look, you don't even know this guy. You don't know anything about him. In fact, last time we talked about the situation, you were so nervous about him that you were planning to ask him to leave. And now, all of a sudden you're hopping into bed with him. What's going on?"

"I just . . . we were . . ." Susan faltered, then fell silent.

"You were overcome by a wild impulse," Betty said. "Right? You were carried away on an overwhelming tide of lust."

"I guess we were. But he was so wonderful," Susan whispered. "I mean, he was sweet, and really tender, and . . ."

"Did you at least use some kind of protection?"

"Not that's it's any of your business," Susan said. "But yes, we did. He's very considerate."

"Considerate! You don't even know whether or not the guy's a criminal," Betty said. "You don't know where he comes from, or who he really is, or whether he's telling you the truth about anything."

"He told me he hasn't lied to me about anything. He looked straight into my eyes and said that."

"Oh, *right,*" Betty scoffed. "And, of course, a tough cookie like you can spot a liar in a second. So how did he explain the letter?"

Susan looked down at her salad.

"My God. You've never asked him about that letter, have you?"

Susan shook her head.

"Well, you have to do it," Betty said. "You have to ask him about the letter and see what he says. If you don't, *I* will."

"Betty, if I catch you meddling in this, you'll be sorry. I'm warning you."

"Okay, okay," Betty said, patting Susan's hand. "No need to get all upset. Now, you mustn't let him know you actually saw the letter from Emma's mother. That's very important."

"Why?"

"Because you want to catch him in a lie, that's why, and get him to expose his true colors."

"You don't know anything about his true colors," Susan said.

"So that makes two of us."

Susan thought about her moonlit interlude with the man, the tenderness of his hands, the sweetness of his lovemaking, and realized that Betty was right. She'd been intimate with Mike, more spontaneous and uninhibited than she'd ever felt with anyone. But she really didn't know him at all.

"Look," Betty was saying, "what you do is casually bring up the matter of the letter, like it's something you just thought about. Don't let him know you saw it. Find some way to remind him of the day it arrived, and then ask him what was in it."

"And if he lies..."

"Turf him out," Betty said calmly.

"I don't know if I can."

"Why not? You were fully prepared to do it a couple of weeks ago."

"But that was before we..."

"Before you tumbled into the sack together," Betty said implacably. "And if you're going to allow *that* to compromise your principles, kiddo, you're letting yourself in for all kinds of misery."

"I know," Susan murmured.

"Promise me you'll ask him about the letter. Right away, before anything else happens."

"Betty..."

"Promise me."

"All right, I promise. I'll do it tonight." Susan looked down at the table, tracing the gingham pattern with her finger. "I feel so bad about Emma," she said in a low voice.

Betty's face softened. "I know. It's hell, isn't it?" she said in a gentler tone. "But Mike and Emma are a package deal, you know. Regardless of their status, or whether he's on the run with her or not, he's definitely her daddy. Emma goes where Mike goes."

"But she's so happy at my house. She loves the yard, and Buster, and her room, everything about the place."

"You can't devote yourself to giving Emma a warm secure home, Susie. That's Mike's job, not yours. What you've got to do is get them out of your house before you're trapped by emotion. And then you have to concentrate on getting on with your own life."

Susan's eyes burned with tears. "Betty, I can hardly imagine life without them."

"Oh, Susie." Betty sighed and reached over to touch her friend's arm. "Dammit," she muttered. "Why did Peter have to be so boring? If only he'd been a little more exciting, none of this would have happened."

"Peter's not boring," Susan said. "He's just not . . ." She faltered, looking down at her plate.

"Not the kind of guy you want to fall into bed with," Betty concluded.

Susan nodded unhappily.

"Maybe we should go back to the dating service and get them to start playing your video again. Your dream man's still out there somewhere. It's just a matter of finding him."

Susan looked absently at the waiter as he brought their steaming plates of lasagna, and tried not to think about the feeling of Mike's naked body pressing against hers.

CHAPTER ELEVEN

SUSAN AND BETTY went to the movie and lingered for a long time afterward over coffee and cheesecake. Even then, it wasn't late enough for Susan to go home. She didn't want to find Mike waiting up for her, and have to struggle through an awkward conversation about her working day and Emma's health. Not while her mind was in this kind of turmoil.

Better to come in when the house was all dark and Mike had gone to bed. Then she wouldn't have to face him....

She paused under a streetlight to wave goodbye to Betty, then hurried down the street to her own car. After a brief hesitation, she headed toward North Vancouver and stopped in at the police station on the way home.

Constable Liepert was on duty, working in his shirtsleeves behind an oak desk loaded with files, accident reports, requisition forms and other paperwork.

"Hi, Curt." Susan hesitated in the doorway. "Got a minute?"

"Susan!" The young policeman looked up, his eyes lighting with surprise and pleasure. "Hey, can I buy you a coffee?"

She shook her head. "No thanks. I was out with a girlfriend, and we drank about a gallon of coffee." She seated herself in a scarred wooden chair and grimaced at his desk. "Don't you ever get caught up?"

"Not a chance. Some days I get halfway to the bottom of the pile, but that's about the best I can manage."

"It's not like on television, is it?" Susan murmured. "Police work, I mean."

"Stakeouts and shoot-outs?" the constable asked with a grin. "Not this job. It's mostly just tons of paperwork and frustration."

Susan fingered the straps of her handbag. "Actually," she confessed, "I'm only here to waste your time again. Wondering if you've heard anything."

"About the money?"

"What else?"

"Not a word. It looks like you're going to be a lot richer, Susan. In just…" He opened a file drawer and took out a manila folder. "A little over a month." He looked up at her. "Time flies, right? It'll be three months in December."

"I know. I can't believe it's really going to happen."

"Got any plans on how to spend it? Oh, yeah." The policeman leaned back in the chair and laced his hands behind his head. "You were going to use it on your mortgage, right?"

"Mostly," Susan murmured, then gave him an apologetic smile. "I still don't like to talk about it," she said, gathering her handbag and preparing to get up. "I feel kind of…superstitious, you know?" she added. "Like if I talk about getting the money, something will keep it from happening."

Constable Liepert stood up and walked her to the door. "Well," he said cheerfully, "if you need any help spending it, give me a call. I'm a single guy, Susan, and I'd love to help you spend that money."

It wasn't the first time he'd relaxed his air of professional detachment. Susan realized that Constable Liepert was actually a very handsome and confident young man.

"Sorry, Curt," she told him.

"Hey, how come?" He held the office door open for her, pretending to be hurt. "You got something against cops?"

"Not at all," she said, responding to the teasing glint in his eye. "In fact, you're probably one of the nicest men I've met lately. But . . ."

"But what?" he asked with interest. "I'm not your type?"

Susan looked at him blankly for a moment, thinking about the bewildering procession of men who'd been moving through her life.

"I don't know what my type is," she said, trying to smile. "As soon as I find out, I'll let you know."

WHEN SHE DROVE into the garage, all the lights in the house were off, including Mike's. Susan sighed with relief and let herself quietly into the kitchen. She tiptoed to her room and got ready for bed, undressing and pulling on a warm flannel nightgown. But while she was brushing her teeth in the bathroom, she discovered her face looking back at her with cold accusation.

Coward, the mirrored face was saying. Sneaking into your own house like a criminal, not even going up to see how Emma is . . .

"Emma's fine," Susan murmured aloud. She began to brush her teeth vigorously, avoiding that cool mirrored face. "Mike called the school and said she was fine," she mumbled around her toothbrush.

And breaking your promise to Betty, the other Susan went on relentlessly. You promised you'd talk to Mike about the letter. You said you'd do it tonight.

"Mike's asleep," she whispered.

But Mike never fell asleep until after she was home and safely in bed . . .

She sighed again. Finally, with a reluctant grimace at the mirror, she scuffed into her slippers and tiptoed upstairs to Emma's room where the little girl lay in her bed in the soft glow of the night-light.

Emma slept deeply, holding Gerald in her arms. She looked peaceful in the shadowy glow, her chest rising and falling evenly. Susan stepped closer to the bed to look at the child, then smiled in delight.

Both Emma and Gerald wore neat white bandages around their throats, secured with tape.

"Gerald has a sore throat, too," a voice whispered behind her, making her jump.

She felt Mike's hands on her shoulders, his hard body pressing against her.

Despite herself, Susan relaxed against him, loving the feel of him. Every part of her responded to him with yearning, an utterly overpowering urge to nestle and cling.

"Does he?" she murmured as Mike's arms slipped around her and he kissed her neck. "Poor Gerald."

"Actually, he's a pretty good patient." Mike's mouth moved down to her shoulder, nuzzling hungrily. "As long as he gets to watch cartoon videos and have stories read to him all day."

"Gerald's a nice kangaroo," Susan whispered. She turned to face him and put her arms around him, all her good intentions disappearing. "But he can be a bit of a tyrant."

"Speaking of tyrants," Mike muttered, "part of me is starting to make some pretty lusty demands, too."

"Really? What part?" Susan pretended wide-eyed innocence, then burrowed shamelessly against him.

Mike laughed softly, his breath warm on her cheek. "If you can't tell by now," he said softly, "that nightgown must be made of steel."

She smiled and kissed him, then moved with him down the hall to his room, forgetting all about her promise to Betty.

QUITE A LOT of time passed before she was able to think about where she'd been and what she'd done earlier in the evening.

Or remember her own name, for that matter.

At last they lay together, quiet and satisfied. Mike held Susan with her back curled against his stomach, hands warmly cupping her breasts.

"I love this," he murmured contentedly. "I could sleep like this every night for the rest of my life. I feel as young as Emma."

"Mmm," Susan responded, smiling in the moonlight. She understood exactly what he meant. She loved the feeling she had with Mike, a sense of peace and safety and utter contentment.

Suddenly, her mind clouded with memories, like dark wings drifting across the face of the moon.

She frowned, thinking about Betty's accusations, and her advice. Susan was supposed to bring up the letter casually, as if the thought had somehow just occurred to her...

That was all right for someone like Betty, she thought. Betty was naturally creative and devious, but Susan couldn't find a way to be casual about something so important. Her mind worried and fretted over the problem, increasingly anxious.

"Was the movie good?" Mike asked.

"Pretty good. I couldn't keep my eyes off Mel Gibson."

"Yeah?" He clutched her with mock jealousy.

"I never noticed," Susan whispered, "how much he looks like you. It's just amazing."

Mike chuckled fondly and kissed her ear. "You're crazy, but it's a nice thought."

"I know." Susan turned to catch one of his kisses on her mouth, then snuggled back against him, gazing into the darkness with a brooding look. "I mean," she added, "I know that I'm crazy."

"How's Betty?"

"Oh, she's fine. She and Barnaby are probably getting engaged at Christmas."

"No kidding!" he marveled. "The first guy she ever dated from that video service, and she struck gold. What a lucky girl."

"He's lucky, too, you know. You should see her light up when she talks about him. I've never known anybody to have such a gentling influence on Betty."

"So how about you, sweetheart?" he asked, squeezing her breasts gently. "Are you going to acknowledge that old Peter's a washout, and go back to the dating service to keep on looking for your dream man?"

"I'm not telling," she said with dignity. "I have to keep a *few* secrets from you."

Susan felt her cheeks warm in the darkness, thinking how many secrets she was keeping from the man who held her so intimately. She'd never told him about the suitcase full of money, or how she'd been planning to ask him to leave, or that she'd read parts of the damning letter from Emma's mother...

"Hey, speaking of secrets," she said, struggling to keep her voice light and casual, "you know what? I just remembered that you never told me a thing about that letter."

"What letter?" His hands tensed against her breasts, then relaxed.

"Don't you remember?" Susan asked in that same carefully offhand tone. "Weeks ago when I was home from school with my cold, and you got a letter? I kept meaning to ask you about it, you know, and it just slipped my mind."

"It was nothing," he said.

"Nothing? How could it be nothing? I mean, it had to be from somebody, didn't it?"

"Nobody important."

"It was forwarded so many times. It must have traveled thousands of miles."

"I guess," he said in a noncommittal tone.

Susan hesitated, feeling increasingly tense. "You never get letters," she said at last. "I just kind of wondered who it was from. Was it from your parents?"

"My parents died when I was a teenager."

"Really? I don't think you've told me that before. You never talk about your childhood."

"There's not much to tell." After a brief silence, he went on, speaking with obvious difficulty. "I was an only child. I grew up in Ontario. My parents both died when I was fifteen. And that's pretty much the story of my childhood."

"Both of them? Was it an accident?"

"Their sailboat sank off the coast of Maine when they were on a holiday."

"Oh, Mike," Susan whispered. "I'm so sorry. That must have been awful for you, losing both your parents when you were so young."

He was silent.

"What did your father do?" Susan asked.

"He was a doctor."

She hesitated, unnerved by the cold, dismissive tone in his voice. But she couldn't stop now, not while he was actually talking about himself.

"Is that how you know so much about looking after sick kids?" she asked, trying to sound casual.

"I guess so."

"If you were only fifteen when they died, where did you go afterward?"

"Here and there. It was a pretty hard time for me," he said. "I had to hold down two jobs while I finished high school. That's when I learned to do construction work."

Susan frowned in the darkness. "But if your father was a doctor," she began cautiously, "there must have been enough...I mean, didn't he leave enough money to look after you?"

"Not after his debts were settled."

They were silent for a long time while Susan searched for a way to get back to the topic of the letter.

"The police and the Coast Guard weren't sure it was an accident," Mike said abruptly, startling her.

"What do you mean?" Susan asked, then stiffened with horror. "Their boat, you mean?"

"Yeah. It was a calm night, and there were no distress calls. His finances were in such a mess, they thought maybe he just took the easy way out. But it's hard to believe he'd take my mother with him."

"Oh, Mike," she whispered. "You can't know that. Nobody can ever know."

"I suppose not."

Susan stared at the branches swaying outside the window. "So that letter...it wasn't from anybody in your family?"

"Look, forget the letter, Susan," he said. "It was nothing. It was just a letter from somebody I used to know, a person who has nothing to do with my life anymore."

His tone indicated that he had no intention of discussing the matter any further. But Susan couldn't let it go. She wanted desperately for him to say something, anything, that would place his actions in a better light and take away this icy coldness in her heart.

"Did you answer it?" she asked finally, holding her breath.

"Of course not. I told you, it was from a person that I never want to talk to again."

"But if you—"

"That's enough, Susan. I'm not talking about it anymore."

"But I just—"

"Drop it, okay?"

She moved restlessly in the bed, stunned by the coldness of his response. She thought of Emma, lying cozily in her bedroom with Gerald in her arms, and the poor mother who yearned and ached for her missing child.

No matter what the woman had done, or what had happened between her and Mike, nobody deserved to be treated like that.

Briefly, Susan considered going down to the police station and telling them about Mike. She pictured herself walking into the office where Constable Liepert worked, and saying, "Look, Curt, there's a man living in my upstairs suite and I think he's kidnapped his own child. I think he's on the run."

It would be so easy to do, and yet it was utterly impossible for Susan. Not after Mike had made love to her so tenderly, and especially when she'd witnessed the deep, powerful bond that tied Mike to his daughter. All she could do was what she'd long ago decided, what Betty kept urging her to do.

The only possible course of action for Susan was to get them both out of her life, and separate herself from this awful situation.

Long after Mike had fallen asleep, Susan lay in his arms and looked at the darkened square of window, her eyes blurred with tears. Finally, she slipped out of bed and crept downstairs to her own room, feeling as cold and sad as the brooding winter night.

DANNY AND LYNNETTE walked hand in hand through masses of brightly colored booths filled with wooden toys and homemade Christmas ornaments. Lynnette paused by a display of chunky poodles made out of golf balls.

One ball formed the body, with another glued in place for the head and four balls for the legs. A white golf tee was attached upside down to form a perky tail, and the head was topped with a tiny knitted puff and floppy ears.

"Look, Danny," she said, enchanted. "Look, aren't they cute?"

Danny smiled, far more impressed by her childlike pleasure than by the little ornaments. "Do you want one, Lyn?"

She glanced at the price tag. "They're seven dollars," she said, turning away.

Danny calculated rapidly. "I can afford seven dollars," he said, although he would have preferred to slip away and buy the pair of turquoise earrings she'd admired earlier. He wanted to surprise her with the earrings for Christmas, but they were almost twenty dollars. He couldn't afford them and the little golf-ball dog, too.

"I don't want the dog, Danny," she said in her soft voice. "I just thought it would be a cute thing to give to Miss Adamson, that's all."

"Miss Adamson?" He tensed, and his palms felt clammy.

"My English teacher," Lynnette said casually, moving forward. "She's been so nice to me. Oh, look, here's a Christmas tree angel! Don't you just love craft fairs?"

She moved off toward the next booth, her eyes shining. Danny followed, battling one of the tides of frustration that washed over him so frequently these days.

Lynnette was clearly enjoying herself, but Danny knew well enough that she picked events like craft fairs and band concerts for their dates because they were inexpensive. She didn't want him to spend money on her when he had so little. Danny had never met a girl like her. Her consideration moved him almost unbearably.

"Hey, Lyn." He came up beside her and looked at her pretty face as she gazed at one of the frothy treetop decorations.

"Yes, Danny?" She turned to give him one of the shy smiles that always made his heart turn over. He took her hand and squeezed it, leading her off through the crowded aisles.

"What would you do if you had a whole bunch of money, Lyn? I mean, really lots."

"How much?" Lynnette paused to admire a cradle woven from basket reeds. She set the cradle swinging with her hand and looked down at it wistfully.

"Lots," he repeated. "Thousands of dollars. Like..." He gave her a sidelong glance. "Like, say... fifty thousand dollars."

She laughed. "That's crazy, Danny. Nobody has that much money."

"But what if they did?" he persisted. "What if *you* did, I mean. What would you buy?"

"Nothing," she said after a moment's thought. "If I had that much money, I'd put it in the bank and feel safe forever. I'd know that nothing could ever scare me anymore.''

"What are you scared of, Lyn?'' he asked, his heart thumping painfully.

"Dentist's bills for the kids, rent increases, all those unexpected things. Bills that you're afraid you can't pay, but you still have to. It would be so nice,'' she added with a sigh, "not to worry about those things. Just to know that whenever they came along, you'd have enough money to look after them.''

Danny paused by a booth filled with stained-glass mobiles, which were winking and glimmering in the light. They cast soft rainbows on her face, her delicate cheeks and gentle mouth.

"I love you, Lyn,'' he said huskily, putting his hands on her shoulders and drawing her closer to him.

She smiled at him and raised her face to be kissed. Danny bent and touched her lips with his, as thrilled as he'd been the very first time they kissed, behind the coffee machine near the cab-dispatching office. They clung together for a moment, oblivious to the throngs of people moving past them, and Danny's heart swelled with love until he thought his chest would explode.

But hours later, after he'd taken Lynnette home and ridden back across town on the bus to his own shabby apartment, he was still brooding about what she'd said.

He couldn't bear to think of Lynnette being frightened by the lack of money. She was so gentle and unselfish, such a good person. In a lot of ways, although she was young and beautiful, Lynnette reminded him of his aunt Rosa.

It was a shame the two women had never met. Rosa would have loved this girl so much, Danny thought.

He let himself into his apartment and looked around, depressed by the stained plaster on the walls, the sagging doors and cramped, squalid kitchen. He could never bring Lynnette to a place like this. She deserved beauty, luxury, all the best and nicest things money could buy.

Money...

Danny sank onto the old couch and buried his face in his hands. He thought about that dreadful night in the park in early autumn, when he'd dumped Rosa's suitcase in the bushes and the blond woman had come along and discovered it.

He should have confronted her right away. Danny realized it now. He should have told her the suitcase was his, and demanded that she give it to him. Now, with the new confidence that came from having somebody like Lyn in his life, he might be able to do that.

But he was so afraid of the police. What if he faced Lynnette's teacher and she reported him to the police. They would come to the apartment to question him for sure. Despite his newfound confidence, Danny knew he wouldn't have the courage to stand up to them. He shuddered, thinking about rough voices and handcuffs, metal bars and stone walls and doors with heavy locks.

Restlessly, he got up and wandered into the kitchen, opening a cracked drawer by the sink. He rummaged through a stack of ragged dish towels and brought out the gun, holding it up and hefting it lightly in his hand. It was only plastic, but it still gave Danny a feeling of security. He was going to feel a lot safer with this gun in his hand.

He stared at the black night outside the window, his young face grim with purpose.

Danny had decided to try again on Tuesday night, just a few days from now. He couldn't face the thought of another daytime break-in. Not after actually seeing the woman in the house like that. If something went wrong and he had to run again, he'd be far too visible. Better to do it after dark, when he could melt into the shadows and disappear.

And Tuesday night was the only possibility, because the house was always empty for at least a couple of hours. Danny had observed their routine so obsessively that he knew what happened every night of the week at the big house on Birch Drive.

The woman left first on Tuesdays, driving off alone in her car. Danny assumed she must be going to some kind of athletic, outdoor thing, because she wore jeans and hiking boots, and carried a lot of heavy gear in a big gym bag slung over her shoulder. Lynnette said she was the outdoors type, with a lot of active hobbies.

Soon afterward, the man and the little girl left together, driving away in his old truck and returning a couple of hours later, before the woman got back. From the child's excited chatter as she danced out to the truck with her father, Danny knew they were going to the movies, taking advantage of the cheaper rates on Tuesday nights.

In fact, this was another thing that made Danny feel hopeful about the money. If they'd already put it in the bank and started spending it, he reasoned, the guy wouldn't have to wait for the cheapest night to take his kid to the movies.

He pictured the suitcase full of money, thought about it lying in some deserted upstairs room, in the back of a closet or behind a wardrobe somewhere. He wasn't worried about finding it, because it was too big to hide. He'd go in right after the dark-haired guy left with his kid. Then he'd have at least two hours to search for the suitcase.

To keep his courage up, Danny let himself think about how he would feel afterward, when he was back here in his own apartment with the money safely hidden under *his* bed. He sighed, trying to imagine the relief. No more chilly hours spent huddled in the bushes, watching their house. No more obsessive brooding about the couple inside the house.

Best of all, no more nightmares about police and jail...

He hefted the toy gun in his hand again, sighted down the barrel and squeezed the trigger a couple of times. Finally, he hid the pistol under the dish towels and moved across the kitchen to make himself a cup of instant coffee.

SUSAN WOKE early on Saturday morning, feeling warm and rich with sexual fulfillment. She rolled over and nestled under the bedclothes, smiling drowsily. Then, with disconcerting abruptness, reality came flooding in.

She sat up, drawing the curtain aside to look out the window at the typical November day: dark and windy, with a steady rain that rustled drearily through the willow branches and pattered on the sidewalk. The wind gusted, tossing handfuls of rain against the glass.

Susan stared at the gloomy sky, then let the curtain drop. She got out of bed and moved quietly around the room, dressing in jeans and a warm sweater, pulling on an extra pair of fleecy socks. Finally, she paused by the door, wishing she could somehow magically be transported somewhere else so she wouldn't have to deal with the problems that waited out there in the kitchen...

At last, reluctantly, she opened the door, walked down the hallway and entered the kitchen, where Mike stood by the counter operating a hand mixer.

"Hi," she said.

He turned to smile at her, the hard planes of his face brightening. "Hi. Coffee's ready, and I'll have your breakfast in a minute."

"What are you doing?"

"Making some whipped cream. We're having strawberry crepes with whipped cream."

"Oh, my. That sounds festive." Susan's spirits plummeted even further.

"I thought we had a few things to celebrate." Mike gave her a meaningful smile as he brought a platter of crepes to the table, then produced an enamel bowl filled with sliced strawberries.

Susan kept her eyes lowered as she helped herself to some of the delicate crepes. "Where's Emma?"

"Cartoons," Mike said.

"But she loves whipped cream. Will she be coming down for breakfast?"

He shook his head. "Not while Zofar the Horrible is on. I promised I'd bring her up some breakfast on a little tray. It's a special treat because she's been sick."

"But she's feeling better this morning, isn't she?"

He nodded, pulling up a chair and seating himself opposite Susan. "She's still got a cough and a bit of a raspy throat, but she seems pretty normal otherwise. I won't be able to keep her in bed today."

Susan spread some strawberries on her crepes and added a mound of whipped cream. The meal looked delicious but when she took a mouthful, it tasted like dust.

I can't do this, she thought in despair. I just can't do it.

But she had no choice. She took a deep breath, put down her fork and looked at the man across the table. "Mike, we have to talk."

He raised his head, his eyes dark and watchful. "We do?" he asked, carrying his mug over to the coffeepot. "Here, I'll get you some more coffee."

"I think you know what we have to talk about it."

He turned away from the counter, his coffee cup full, and sat down again, meeting her eyes steadily. "I'm not sure. Why don't you tell me?"

"Mike, it has to stop. I can't go on like this."

"Sleeping together, you mean?"

Susan was silent, unable to look at him.

"If you think things are moving too fast," he said gently, "we can slow down, Susan. You can have all the space you need. Just say the word."

Susan shook her head in despair. "That's not what I'm talking about."

He stirred sugar into his coffee. "I see," he said quietly. "So, what are you talking about?"

"I think..." Susan's voice faltered. She drew a deep breath and forced herself to continue. "I think you're going to have to leave, Mike," she said. "In fact, I'm giving you a month's notice, as of today. You should be able to find another place to live before the middle of December, don't you think?"

"Another place to live?" He stared at her, his face hardening. "Susan, what are you talking about?"

"It's my house," she told him, trying to sound calm and reasonable although she was perilously close to tears. "If I decide I don't want to have a tenant living here, I have every right to—"

"Hi, Susan," Emma's husky voice interrupted.

The little girl stood in the doorway, wearing a yellow sweat suit with a leering Garfield on the front, and a pair of furry yellow slippers. She carried her kangaroo in her arms.

Susan looked at the child's round, sweet face. "Hi, honey," she whispered.

Emma's eyes widened. She edged closer to the two adults at the table, looking anxiously from one to the other. "What's the matter, Daddy? Why does Susan look so sad?"

Susan met his eyes for a moment, then looked away. "I'm not sad," she murmured unsteadily. "I'm just...I'm a little worried about Gerald. I didn't know he had a sore throat."

"It's a lot better now," Emma reported. "Daddy put a bandage on his throat and I gave him some special pills, and now he's not sick anymore."

"That's good. Come sit on my knee. It feels like ages since I've seen you."

Susan held out her arms and Emma ran to snuggle in her lap, still holding Gerald. Susan hugged the little girl, burying her face in Emma's soft hair. She tightened her grip, almost overwhelmed by love and sorrow.

"Do you want some breakfast?" Mike asked.

Emma looked with interest at the bowls of strawberries and whipped cream. "You said I could have my breakfast on a tray."

"I know. If you want to go back and finish watching your cartoons, I'll bring it up in a few minutes."

"I want lots and lots of whipped cream. *Tons* of it," Emma commanded.

"Tons of it," Mike agreed. "Now, go back upstairs for a while, okay, honey? I need to talk to Susan."

Emma slid from Susan's lap and edged around the table to take a strawberry from her father's plate. "Guess what?" she asked Susan, popping the strawberry into her mouth.

"What, dear?" Susan asked, barely trusting her voice.

"Daddy says if I'm all better on Tuesday night, we can go to the movies again. We're going to see *Dumbo the Elephant.*"

"I've always loved that story," Susan said. "I felt so sorry for Dumbo. I used to cry every time I heard it, and the other kids laughed at me."

"Is that why you're crying now?" Emma asked, looking intently at another of Mike's strawberries.

"Yes, I guess it is," Susan said with a lump in her throat. "Poor Dumbo, I always wanted so much for him to find a . . . a happy home."

Emma gazed up at her for a moment with wide, thoughtful eyes, then grabbed the strawberry and ran from the room.

Mike watched her run down the hall then turned to Susan.

"You want me to leave?" he asked in a low voice, leaning across the table to stare at her. "Why? What's wrong?"

"You know what's wrong." Susan got up to fill her coffee cup.

Mike moved around in his chair to look at her. "I don't have the slightest idea what you're talking about. Susan, I already told you, if this relationship is moving too fast, we can back off until you're comfortable. God knows, I don't want to rush you into something you're not ready for."

"It has nothing to do that," Susan said wearily.

"Is it Peter?" Mike asked. "Is he the guy you want, after all? I know you're attracted to those handsome professional types," he added, "but I always thought Peter was a little boring."

"He may not be the most exciting man, but at last Peter doesn't tell lies about everything," she said in a low voice. "Peter's as honest and open as any man can be. He's never lied to me."

"Neither have I," Mike said, looking directly at her.

Susan met his eyes. "Are you *sure* you want to say that, Mike?" she asked quietly. "You've never lied to me? About anything?"

"That's right." His face took on the hard, remote look she knew so well. "I've never lied to you."

She wavered, longing to believe him and give him another chance. But it was impossible. She'd seen that letter with her own eyes, the letter he dismissed as being "nothing," that he said had come from somebody who didn't matter to him at all . . .

Susan was on the verge of asking him about the letter when the phone rang. She reached for the receiver. "Hello?" she asked brusquely.

It was Peter, calling to make arrangements for a trip downtown to see the new art exhibition at the city gallery. He was on his way out of town to a seminar, and wouldn't be back until early in the week.

"Should we go to the gallery on Tuesday night?" he asked.

Susan sighed, painfully conscious of Mike's eyes resting on her as she spoke. "Peter, I have my rock-climbing class on Tuesday night. I've been going to that same class ever since we met."

"Wednesday, then?"

"All right," she said. They exchanged a few more remarks, then hung up.

Susan looked at the phone, wondering how her life had ever reached this point. Sleeping with one man, dating another, dealing with a huge sum of money, harboring criminals, turning little children out onto the street . . .

"What about Emma?" Mike asked, reading her mind as he often did.

"What about her?" Susan asked, carrying her coffee mug back to the table.

"If you throw me out, her whole life will be disrupted. Doesn't that bother you?"

"Of course it bothers me! It tears my heart out. But what can I do? Let you stay here forever, even if I don't want you, just because I can't bear to see Emma without a home?"

"Don't worry, Susan," he said coldly. "I won't stay here a second longer than I have to. I'll start looking for a place today."

"Mike," she began, stung by his tone. "I didn't mean—"

"Never mind." He got up and began to clear the table. "I get the message."

"But it's not what you think," she said. "It's just that I . . ."

"You don't want me," Mike said tonelessly. "So we both have to leave. Even Emma, who hasn't done anything wrong."

"Maybe *you* should give some thought to Emma's welfare," Susan said, angered by the unfairness of the situation.

"Emma's welfare is my chief concern in life. It always has been," he said quietly.

"Really? Well, if you care about her so much, why don't you—"

"Daddy!" Emma shouted from upstairs. "I want my breakfast!"

"Right away," he called back.

Susan watched as he prepared the tray, her eyes blurring with tears. Suddenly, Mike Murphy almost seemed like a stranger to her. It was hard to believe she'd ever held this man, kissed his mouth and thrilled to his embrace.

It was over. Mike was already gone from her life, and so was Emma.

CHAPTER TWELVE

DANNY CROUCHED in the shadows among the familiar, sheltering branches of juniper, hugging his arms to keep the cold away. It was Tuesday night, and rain had been falling intermittently ever since the weekend. Just now, mercifully, it seemed to have stopped for a while, but the wind was so cold that it cut through his thin jacket like a sword of ice.

Even Buster wasn't his usual ebullient self. The big dog had greeted Danny with automatic good cheer, taken his offering of licorice and then slunk gratefully back to the warmth of his doghouse, where Danny could see his eyes gleaming faintly in the darkness.

The back door opened and the woman came outside, bundled in a warm duffel coat and boots, carrying her gym bag. She passed Danny's hiding place on the way to the garage, looking tense and unhappy.

Danny noticed with surprise that the guy didn't come out with her. Usually, her husband stood in the back doorway while she left, and they exchanged some cheerful banter before she got into her car and drove off. Afterward, the man always lingered a while watching her vanishing taillights with a look of love and yearning that Danny only began to understood when he met Lynnette.

He felt exactly the same whenever Lyn left him and walked away, as if his whole world was going with her, and all his happiness . . .

But tonight there was nobody to say goodbye when the woman drove off, just the big old house standing silent and hushed in the winter chill.

Maybe they'd had a fight, Danny thought, remembering her grim expression. Maybe they were fighting about what to do with the money.

He shivered and slapped his hands against his chilled body, then tried to see the face of his watch. It shouldn't be long until the guy and the little kid left for the movies. Danny intended to witness all the departures, and know for certain that the house was empty before he ventured inside.

He wasn't taking any more chances.

Before long the man came out, wearing jeans and a denim jacket lined with sheepskin, his collar turned up against the cold. The little kid trotted at his side, bundled in a fur-trimmed snowsuit and red rubber boots with yellow ducks on the sides.

Danny grinned, so tickled by the boots that he forget where he was for a moment.

When he remembered, his hand tightened nervously on the gun in his pocket. He waited, tense and silent, while the man and the kid went to the back driveway, climbed into their truck and drove off. For fifteen minutes afterward, he forced himself to stay concealed in the chilly, dripping masses of juniper, making sure none of them were coming back for any reason.

Finally, he gathered himself together, emerged from the bushes and stretched his cramped muscles, then sprinted across the yard to the basement window.

It was a lot harder to get the window off this time, because the guy had finished repairing it and had fastened it properly from inside. Knowing this would be the case, Danny had brought a screwdriver and chisel to pry off the window. He would have to damage the frame a little but he wasn't concerned.

It didn't matter anymore if they knew about the break-in. After tonight, he'd never be coming back. He would have his money, and he'd never see them again.

"Suits me just fine," he muttered to Buster, who'd ventured from the warmth of his doghouse to lick Danny's ear and nuzzle at his jacket pocket.

At last Danny managed to remove the storm window. He set it on the ground along with the inner window, then wriggled through the opening and dropped to the basement floor. He hesitated for a moment in the clammy darkness, breathing deeply and waiting for his body to stop trembling. Then, operating from memory, he felt his way carefully toward the stairs.

He found the wooden railing and climbed slowly upward, easing the door open into the kitchen where a light had been left on. Even though Danny had seen everybody leave, he stood perfectly still for a while, one hand on the doorknob, listening for any unusual sounds. Satisfied, he edged his way along the carpeted lower hallway and started to go up the stairs. On the second floor, he discovered that the attic wasn't a loft-type with ladder, as he'd expected, but another whole floor with its own narrow staircase leading up to a closed door. Danny eyed that wooden door with a surge of hope.

He'd already planned to start at the top and work down. For one thing, he believed the suitcase was probably hidden on one of the upper floors. And even if it wasn't, he still preferred to start at the top of the house. That way, he'd be closer to the ground and less likely to be trapped if his search took a while and somebody happened to come home early.

But he didn't like to think about that possibility. It was far too terrifying. When he pictured somebody coming into the house and catching him, he felt sick to his stomach.

Once again, Danny fingered the gun in his pocket. Then, with infinite caution, he began climbing the steps toward the attic.

SUSAN CLUNG to the wall, gripping the rope tightly in her left hand as she reached for another hold. Her fingers ached, and her legs burned with effort. On the floor below, Wayne, her partner, worked the belaying rope, watching her every move.

"Transfer your weight, Susie," he called. "You're almost there. Reach up."

Susan obeyed, clutching the handhold and digging her fingers into its grooved top. She gasped with relief and sagged against the wall.

"Resting a minute," she called down as she gripped the handhold and pressed her cheek into the cool, pitted surface of the wall.

All around her, climbers swarmed like spiders over the interior of the huge facility. The walls were covered with people, wearing shorts, colorful T-shirts and light climbing boots, moving laterally across the rough surface with its complex masses of ropes and holds. High above, a few experienced climbers even ventured out onto the ceiling structures, practicing the techniques of belaying across horizontal overhangs and back onto vertical cliff faces.

Susan took a few deep breaths and called to her partner. "Moving up."

"Okay. Do it."

She started to climb again, straining upward for the next handhold. But she was damp with effort, and as she gripped the hold, her fingers slipped. She fell away from the vertical surface and her body swung out in a crazy arc in the climbing harness. Her partner belayed rapidly and she flew back in against the wall, slamming her head on one of the wooden holds. She gasped at the sharp burst of pain and floundered for a toehold, then clung to a metal projection, breathing hard.

"Susie?" Wayne said anxiously from the floor. "Are you okay? Wanna come down?"

"No! Just give me a minute, okay?"

She held on for a few seconds, waiting for the pain in her temple to subside, and began to edge grimly upward. Before long she was back in the rhythm of the climb, moving with fluid grace from hold to hold.

When you really got it right, she thought, it was like a dance. It just felt so good, swinging up and up, powered only by your own strength. Best of all, it kept your mind off things.

Things like Mike and Emma...

Susan pushed the thoughts from her mind. If she started to think about Mike, she'd lose concentration and fall again, and she was in enough pain already.

She reached the top and rested her cheek against the wall, twisting her head so she could see her belay partner down on the floor, looking small and faraway. She gasped with effort, her chest heaving, and then gave the signal that she was starting down.

"How do you feel?" Wayne asked when she reached the floor.

"A little sore," she confessed. "I smashed pretty hard on one of the holds."

"Where?"

"Right here." Susan pointed at her forehead.

"It's already turning a little dark and swollen. Does it hurt?"

When he asked, Susan realized that her head was beginning to throb and ache in earnest. She probed her temple, wincing.

"Hey, you'd better go home," Wayne said.

"I'm okay. I don't need to..." But even as she spoke, Susan wavered on her feet and felt her head beginning to spin.

"Go on," Wayne said. "Go home and get some ice on that bruise before it gets any worse. The kids in your class are gonna think you've been in a fist-fight."

"I don't want to go home," Susan told him. "The evening's only half over."

She thought of the house on Birch Drive, and wished that she didn't have to go home at all.

"Do you want me to drive you?" Wayne asked.

"No thanks. It feels a bit better. I can manage."

Susan gathered her equipment and went into the dressing room. She paused by a mirror to examine her temple. Just as Wayne had said, the skin was already starting to swell and darken along the outer edge of her eyebrow.

She sighed, thinking about her students—Jason in particular—and what he'd say about this bruise.

Jason had ferreted out a lot of information about her personal life, but he didn't know about the rock climbing on Tuesday nights. Susan realized she would have to manufacture something to keep from arousing his suspicions. If he learned about this hobby, a whole group of students would probably be here next week, cheering Susan's efforts and making loud jokes about teachers climbing the walls.

Susan's head cleared as she changed into her jeans and boots, shrugged her coat on and headed outside, where the night air felt cool and soothing on her hot face. By the time she got home, most of the aching and dizziness was gone, but the bump on her forehead continued to swell at an alarming rate.

She parked in the garage and walked through the backyard to the house, where everything was wrapped in nighttime silence. Even Buster didn't come out of his doghouse to greet her.

Mike's truck was gone, so he and Emma were still at the movies, Susan was relieved to notice. If she hurried, she'd be able to take a hot bath, make an ice pack for her bruise and climb into bed before they got back, and another awkward evening would be over.

Once such a warm and welcoming place, her house now seemed to contain only tension and unhappiness. Mike hardly spoke to her anymore. He spent his evenings on the phone, calling listings from the classified ads.

Irrationally, Susan found herself missing Mike and Emma already, even though they weren't gone yet. She missed the easy camaraderie of her relationship with Mike, the jokes and arguments and lengthy after-dinner discussions about everything under the sun. She missed his tenderness, his teasing smile, his lovemaking...

Her face twisted with misery. She paused at the back door, searching in her handbag for the key.

And she missed Emma, too. Even though Emma didn't know anything about the upcoming move, and was as cheerful and exuberant as ever, Susan felt the distance between the two of them growing. And it was a separation initiated by Susan. Although she ached to hold the little girl and kiss her, she was afraid that if she did, she would never be able to let go. She had to keep telling herself that Emma would soon be leaving. Susan would never watch her grow up, start first grade, become a teenager and then a young woman. All that sweetness and pleasure was going to be denied her.

Just the same as it had been denied Emma's mother, she reminded herself grimly.

Mike had made that decision all on his own, and everybody else had to pay. His behavior was so unfair, so incredibly selfish...

She walked into the kitchen and set her handbag on the table, then froze.

Somebody was in the house.

Susan could sense the presence. There was no noise or scent or anything tangible. Just a prickling on the back of her neck, a chill against her face, a sudden clutch of dread in her stomach.

She licked her lips and gazed intently at the empty kitchen, listening.

"Who's there?" she called sharply, then realized how idiotic the words sounded.

As if an intruder was going to call out and announce himself...

Her voice echoed through the house, vibrating eerily in the quiet. She pictured somebody listening, frozen into stillness, calculating his next move.

Susan shrank back against the kitchen door, trying to think. She could run outside, over to a neighbor's house, and call the police.

All at once, she heard a sound, a muffled thump and rattle from the direction of her room. All thought and reason fled, replaced by a hot, instinctive flood of anger. She knew she was being foolhardy, but she refused to be victimized. Susan strode across the kitchen floor and flung her bedroom door wide open, then paused, breathless and stunned.

A man crouched by the window, wearing a shabby denim jacket and blue jeans. He was dark-haired and slight, his shoulders straining with effort as he tried to raise the sash.

Despite her shock, Susan felt her fury grow. She was so utterly incensed to see this stranger in her private space, among her treasured books and antiques, she almost forgot to be afraid.

"Who the *hell* are you?" she demanded. "What are you doing in my house?"

The man gave another futile tug at the window, then turned to her reluctantly, his face contorted.

They stared at each other for a moment while the air in the bedroom crackled with tension. Susan's eyes widened as he drew a handgun from his pocket and leveled it at her.

"Just stand real quiet," he said in a low, shaking voice, "and don't try anything."

Susan stared at the gun, paralyzed, as he began to edge toward her. He gripped it so hard that his knuckles whitened and his hands shook a little.

Simultaneously, she realized several things. Susan knew she'd seen this man before somewhere. And she could sense, with a deep, sure instinct, that he was just as terrified as she was.

"The park," she whispered. "That's where I've seen you. You're in the park sometimes when I go running. You're...you're Lynnette's friend," she added, appalled at the realization.

The man's face drained of color. "Just stand aside," he muttered, "and let me out the door. Don't try to stop me, and don't call the cops after I'm gone. If you do, you'll be sorry."

The words were menacing, but Susan's fear was vanishing rapidly. There was something about his face, a look of pleading that belied his toughness. And when he drew closer to her in the doorway, Susan realized something else.

"That's not even a real gun," she said rashly. "It's a toy made of plastic. Emma used to have one just like it."

The young man whimpered and dropped his hand, sagging against the door of her closet. Susan gave him a cold, appraising look, her anger returning.

"What are you?" she asked. "Some kind of thief? What do you think you're doing, breaking into my house and threatening me?"

He raised his head and gave her a look of defiance. "I'm no thief! I'm looking for my own money, that's all."

"Your money?" she asked in confusion. "What do you mean?"

The man glanced down helplessly at the gun in his hand, rolling the clip between shaking fingers.

"What do you mean?"

His next words left her speechless with shock.

"That suitcase," he said miserably, looking up at her with a childlike look of appeal. "It's mine."

"But how..." She stared at him, bewildered. Suddenly, she recalled that evening in the park, the stillness of twilight and this young man passing her on the running trail just minutes before Buster discovered the suitcase.

"*Yours?*" she asked. "You're the one who hid it in the bushes?"

He nodded, looking down at the gun again.

"But why didn't you...why did you hide it? There was nobody around. And why didn't you tell me as soon as I found it? You must have watched me open it, didn't you?"

He nodded again, not looking at her. "I was afraid you'd turn me over to the cops. I just couldn't stand that."

"Why? Did you steal the money?" she asked, her eyes narrowed. "Did you steal it and then hide it in the bushes?"

"No!" The man took a deep breath and looked directly at Susan. "I got it from...it was my aunt Rosa's. She...she died in the hospital at the beginning of September. Just before she died," he went on, words tumbling over each other in his haste, "she told me there was something in her apartment, and it belonged to me, and when I went over there after...after she was gone, I found that suitcase full of money."

"So why did you hide it in the park?" she repeated.

The man told her some garbled story about meeting a pair of thugs in the park, and the need to hide the suitcase until they were gone.

"I still don't understand why you didn't tell me at the time, when I found the suitcase," Susan said. "There were no thugs around then. There was nobody in sight but you and me."

"You would have told the cops," he said. "And then what could I do? Rosa was dead, so she couldn't tell them where I got the money. I had no way of explaining it. The cops, they would have charged me for sure." His voice trembled.

Susan looked at him with sudden understanding. "You've been in trouble with the police before, haven't you?" she asked.

He nodded miserably. "I did two years when I was nineteen, for driving the car while some guys held up a store. I'd rather die than go back to jail."

"How am I supposed to believe this story?" she asked. "About your aunt, I mean. How do I know you didn't just break into a liquor store or something and steal the money?"

He shook his head and stared at the floor, the toy gun dangling from his fingers.

"After all," Susan went on, "I came home and found you in my house with a gun. You must have followed me, watched us all this time..." A light dawned suddenly. "It was you, wasn't it?" she breathed. "You've been hanging around and spying on us, haven't you?"

"I just wanted to find my money. I didn't want to hurt anybody."

"Have you ever been inside the house before tonight?" Susan asked tensely.

"Once, in the morning," the man confessed. "It was awful," he added with a shiver. "You were home, and I didn't know it. You came down the hall about a foot away from me to get the mail."

"My God." Susan stared at him in horror. "You were *inside* the house that day?"

He nodded. "I'm sorry. I know it was wrong. I just... I really wanted my money. I didn't know what else to do."

Susan struggled with wildly contradictory feelings of outrage and sympathy. It was horrible to think of this stranger watching them for months, even sneaking into their house. But he looked so vulnerable and desperate that her heart softened.

"What's your name?" she asked. "Lynnette told me once, but I've forgotten."

He hesitated, then lifted his hands in a gesture of despair. "Danny," he muttered. "My name's Danny Clammer."

"And your aunt's name was Rosa?"

He nodded dumbly.

"And how am I really supposed to believe all this, Danny, about your aunt dying and leaving you a suitcase full of money?"

He reached into a pocket with his free hand. Susan tensed, then relaxed when he drew out a shabby billfold and rummaged through it, the gun still dangling from his fingers.

"Here," he said, extracting a photograph. "This is the only proof I can show you. That's me and my aunt Rosa."

Susan took the picture and examined it. She saw a round, smiling woman with gray hair rolled into a bun, standing next to a much younger Danny. They appeared to be on a seaside dock, with a line of rustic cabins behind them.

"How old were you?" she asked.

"Thirteen. We were on our summer holiday at Tofino, out on the Island. My cousin Waldo had a cabin there. Rosa and I used to go every July if she could get the time off work, because it was so hot in our apartment in the summer."

"Your aunt raised you?"

Danny nodded. "Look at the suitcase," he added, gesturing with the gun handle at the photograph in Susan's hand.

She studied it, and her eyes widened. There was no mistaking the cheap suitcase in the picture. It was the one she'd found, right down to the straps and a dark crescent-shaped blemish in one corner.

"What made that funny mark?" she asked.

Danny grinned briefly. "Waldo's wife dropped a hot iron on it one day about fifteen years ago. Almost fried that plastic. Rosa was really upset, because it was a brand-new suitcase."

Susan looked at the plump woman holding the suitcase. "Where did she get all that money?"

"She saved it," Danny said, his voice trembling as he looked over Susan's shoulder at his aunt's smiling face. "I never even knew. When she was... that day in the hospital, she said she didn't have a will, but there was something under her bed and I could have it. I thought it was a photo album or a new sweater or something."

"You must have been pretty shocked to find a suitcase full of money."

"I couldn't believe it. I knew she didn't trust banks, but I never dreamed she'd have that kind of money in her apartment. She never spent anything on herself."

Susan looked at the thin young man beside her and saw that his eyes were wet with tears. He brushed at them hastily with the back of his hand.

"Look, Danny—" Susan stopped abruptly as the front door opened and closed. They heard Emma clatter up the stairs to her room.

"Go straight to bed," Mike's voice called from the lower hallway. "No fooling around, you hear? Or there'll be no more movies."

"Okay, Daddy," the little girl answered obediently from upstairs, and a series of muffled noises indicated that she was getting ready for bed.

"Susan?" Mike asked, his voice coming nearer down the hallway. "I saw your car in the garage. Why are you home so early? Did you—"

He stepped into her doorway and his face went pale with shock. He looked at Susan standing in her jacket with the photograph in her hand, and Danny next to the closet, still holding the gun.

Mike's muscles tensed. He leaped protectively in front of Susan, staring at the intruder.

"Mike," Susan began. "Look, it's not—"

"Drop that gun," Mike said harshly.

His eyes wide with terror, Danny looked up at the bigger man. He dropped the pistol, letting it clatter hollowly on the floor, and began to tremble like a puppy.

"Mike, for goodness' sake," Susan said.

Mike kicked the gun under the bed, then looked at Susan. "My God, you're hurt," he whispered, touching the tender bruise on her temple. Susan winced, and Mike looked at Danny again. "If you laid a hand on this woman," he said coldly, "I swear I'll kill you."

"Mike, it's not what you think! He didn't hurt me. Can't you see the poor kid's scared to death?"

Mike glared at Danny a moment longer, then turned back to Susan, looking bewildered. "What happened to your head?"

"I slipped while I was climbing in harness, fell away from the wall and then crashed back against a hold. It hurt so much, I decided to come home early. And when I got here..."

"You found him inside the house," Mike concluded bitterly, reaching out to grab Danny's arm. "With his gun. Right?"

Danny struggled ineffectually in Mike's iron grip.

"Let him go, Mike," she said. "He hasn't done anything wrong."

"Nothing wrong!" Mike snapped. "For God's sake, Susan. How about break and enter, armed robbery... Call the police, okay?"

Danny's face turned white and he swayed on his feet, looking sick.

"We're not calling the police," Susan said calmly, earning a look of gratitude from Danny. "For one thing, it's not a real gun. It's plastic, just like Emma's. Remember her toy gun?"

Mike shook his head in disbelief, but he let go of Danny's arm. "How do you know that?"

"I could tell right away," Susan said. "I guess I'm cursed with an eye for quality," she added, trying to make a joke and lighten the tension in the room.

But nobody was smiling. Mike leaned down and drew the quilted bedspread aside to retrieve the gun, hefting it experimentally in his hand. He gave Susan a cold glance.

"Tell me, at what point did you decide the gun was fake, Susan?" he asked softly.

She shrugged and turned away, refusing to meet his eyes.

"When he was loading the clip and aiming it at you?" Mike persisted.

"Sort of," she said reluctantly.

"God, how can you be so foolish!" Mike shouted. "You've got an intruder in your house, pointing a gun at you, and you don't take him seriously because you're sure his gun's a fake?"

"Well," Susan said mildly, "I was right, wasn't I?"

"That's beside the point," Mike said, so angry that his nostrils were white and a muscle twitched ominously in his jaw. "That's the kind of stupid behavior that gets people killed!"

"Hey, don't keep yelling at her," Danny said, moving protectively toward Susan. "She didn't do anything wrong."

Mike's threw up his hands in a gesture of outrage. "Oh, my God. Why did you break into this house, anyway? What's your—"

"He was looking for something that belongs to him," Susan interrupted. "He's a friend of one of my students."

Mike's confusion deepened. "Belongs to him? In this house?"

"My money," Danny said, looking frightened but determined. "In the suitcase. You've got my money, and I came to get it back."

"Do you know what he's talking about?" Mike asked Susan.

She nodded, toying nervously with the photograph. Danny's eyes widened in surprise as he looked from one face to the other.

"You never told him about the money, either?" he asked Susan.

She shook her head.

"How come? Were you planning to keep it all for yourself? Are you guys getting a divorce or something?"

"We're not married, Danny," Susan said gently, feeling a sudden clutch of pain in her heart while Mike looked at her in silence. "I can see how you got the wrong idea, but we're just... I own the house, and Mike is my tenant."

"Who's the little kid, then?"

"She belongs to Mike."

"Susan," Mike began in a warning tone, "are you sure it's wise to tell him all this?"

"What about Buster?" Danny interrupted. "Whose dog is he?"

"He's mine," Susan said.

"I love Buster," Danny told her with a wistful smile. "He's the nicest dog I ever met."

Mike shook his head in despair and sagged against the door frame. "This is crazy. Totally bizarre," he said. "Susan," he added, his voice hardening, "do you mind telling me what money he's talking about?"

"Later, okay?" Susan told him. She turned to Danny. "The money's never been in this house, Danny," she said. "I took it to the police station as soon as I found it. I'll go down there with you tomorrow, and you can claim it."

His face turned pale. "I couldn't...I can't go to the cops," he whispered. "They'll never believe me."

"They will if I vouch for you. You have to face up to this, Danny," she said, touching his arm. "You can't run away from it, especially not if you're the rightful owner and you have people to back you up."

The young man looked at Susan with desperate appeal. "Why would you do that for me?" he muttered. "After...after everything I've done to you guys?"

"Everything?" Mike asked with sudden alertness. "What else has he done to us?"

Susan waved a hand to silence him and turned to Danny. "Because it's fair," she told him simply. "If your aunt really saved all that money and wanted you to have it, then it should be yours."

"But the police . . . what if they . . ." Danny paused in agony.

"One of the policemen handling the case is a good friend of mine," Susan said in a reassuring tone. "If we go and explain things to him, there'll be no problem. Can you come and see me tomorrow?"

"At the school?" Danny asked, then flushed with embarrassment.

"You know where she *works?*" Mike asked.

"Both of you," Danny said, looking sheepish. "You both work over at Whittier High, and the little girl goes to day care over there . . ."

"Look, kid," Mike began, his face darkening again.

Susan laid a hand on his arm. "Please, Mike," she murmured. "It's all right. Danny, you'll meet me at the school tomorrow afternoon?"

Danny nodded.

"Okay, stop by the main office at about four-thirty, and ask for Miss Adamson. I'll go with you to the police station. Don't be scared," she added when she saw the young man's expression. "If you're telling the truth, you have nothing to worry about."

He nodded again, still looking dazed and terrified, and moved past them toward the kitchen, wincing as he drew nearer to Mike's solid, muscular body.

"I'll just . . . I'll go now," he whispered, staring at the floor. He raised his eyes timidly to look at Mike. "I took off a basement window to get in," he confessed. "I'll put it back before I leave, but I think maybe I damaged the frame a little."

Mike watched him in cold silence.

"I'll pay you for it, sir," Danny muttered. "As soon as . . . as soon as I get my money," he said, giving Susan a cautious glance as she handed the photograph back to him.

"You can pay Susan," Mike said abruptly. "It's her house."

Susan followed Danny to the door and watched while he patted Buster a couple of times. Then he slipped out through the back gate, waved to Susan and disappeared down the alley.

She closed the door and turned to Mike, who stood watching her quietly.

"I've seen that kid before," he said. "He was out in the alley on Halloween night."

"I guess he's been hanging around ever since I found . . ."

Her voce trailed off.

"The money," Mike said. "You found some money, did you, Susan?"

"Yes," she murmured, shifting awkwardly on her feet.

"A lot of money? It must be, if he's gone to such lengths to get it back."

"It's . . ." She swallowed hard. "It's a little over fifty-three thousand dollars. I took it to the police station as soon as I found it."

Mike gave a low whistle. "How long ago did all this happen?"

"Back in September, just after you moved in. The police said . . ." She fell briefly silent, then forced herself to go on speaking. "They said if the money went unclaimed for three months, I could claim it as the finder."

"And you almost got it. Is that why you were so willing to throw me out, because you wouldn't be needing the rent money anymore?"

"No!" she said, stung by his words. "The money had nothing to do with it."

"And do you really believe this skinny little guy has a legitimate claim to fifty-three thousand dollars?"

"I think so. After I tell you the whole story, you'll understand why—"

"I'm not really interested in hearing the whole story," Mike interrupted. "But I *would* like to know what he meant when he apologized for all the stuff he's done to us. What else has he done?"

"Well, he's been hanging around for quite a while. I've told you I sensed somebody around the house?"

She gave Mike a questioning glance, and he nodded.

"Once he actually broke in, that day when I was at home with my cold. I guess I almost stumbled over him in the hallway. The poor guy, apparently he was completely terrified."

The planes in Mike's face tightened and hardened again. "You'll have to pardon me if I don't feel all that sorry for him." He gave Susan a quick glance. "You knew all along that somebody was hanging around, didn't you? You were far more sensitive than I was."

"I was pretty certain we were being watched."

"Then why didn't you insist on calling the police and reporting it?"

Susan looked down at the floor, tracing a pattern in the linoleum with the toe of her boot. "I never dreamed it was somebody looking for that money. I thought it had something to do with Emma."

"*Emma!* How could a prowler have anything to do with Emma?"

Susan took a deep breath and looked up at him directly. "I thought it was a private investigator, trailing you," she said.

"Why?"

"An investigator hired by Emma's mother," Susan went on, feeling hot and reckless. "Somebody planning to snatch Emma and steal her back, just like you did."

"Susan...I don't have the faintest idea what you're talking about."

"Yes you do!" Susan said passionately, tears beginning to gather in her eyes. "You're a kidnapper, aren't you, Mike? You stole your daughter from her mother and ran away with her, and you've been hiding all these years! What you're doing is cruel and horrible."

"Susan, for God's sake—"

"Don't lie anymore! I saw that letter, Mike. I took the pieces from your wastebasket and fitted some of them together, enough to know that the police are looking for you, and the poor woman's heart is breaking. She's under a doctor's care, because *you* think you have the right to steal a child and keep her hidden. That's why I asked you to leave my house."

She fell silent, her chest heaving, her cheeks wet with tears.

"If you honestly believe I'm a kidnapper," Mike said quietly, "then you should turn me over to the police, shouldn't you, instead of just kicking me out?"

"I can't," Susan muttered, unable to meet the fierce blue of his eyes, the coldness of his face. "Emma loves you, and she has no memory of any other life. I can't be the one to take her away from you. But I don't want you in my house, either."

She wanted to go on talking. It was such a relief to confront him after all these months of conjecture and silent worry.

But it was too late. Mike turned on his heel without another word and left the room.

CHAPTER THIRTEEN

SUSAN LINGERED for a while in the kitchen after he left, making herself a cup of coffee. She watered the plants while the kettle boiled, then sat at the table with her mug and stared at the hallway in brooding silence.

Suddenly, she frowned, listening. An unusual amount of noise seemed to be coming from upstairs. She could hear thumping sounds, rapid footsteps, doors opening and closing.

What on earth was he doing?

She couldn't endure the suspense, and went to the foot of the stairs. "Mike?" she called nervously. "What's happening?"

There was no response. Footsteps passed by overhead, going from Emma's room to Mike's.

Susan climbed the stairs slowly and went down the hall, pausing in his doorway. Mounds of clothes and toys were piled on the bed, and he was neatly filling suitcases and boxes.

"I didn't mean for you to leave immediately," Susan said.

He turned to give her a quick glance, his face cold. Susan watched him quietly. She couldn't believe that this grim stranger was the same man who'd kissed her so tenderly, laughed and played and cuddled with her, whose lovemaking had carried her to such soaring heights of ecstasy...

"Where will you go?" Susan said, breaking the silence.

He shrugged. "We'll find a place to sleep tonight. I'll come back for the rest of our stuff tomorrow while you're at work, and put the key under the mat. I'll leave the month's rent in an envelope on the hall table."

"But that's crazy. Emma's already sound asleep. You can't take her away in the middle of the night."

Mike paused with a shirt in his hands and turned to look at her. "What's the problem? This is what you want, isn't it? You told me that you wanted me out of the house, and I'm going."

"But not like this! Not taking Emma away in the middle of the night, to God knows where..."

He folded the shirt and put it in a box, then placed Emma's dollhouse on top. "Having second thoughts, Susan?" he asked bitterly. "Now that you aren't going to be a rich woman, after all, you want to hang on to your tenants for a while, even though the guy's a liar and a kidnapper?"

"Look, you have no right to talk to me like that. I haven't done anything to hurt you. I'm not the one who's been lying."

He looked around, his face so full of pain that she was shaken, almost frightened.

"You really believe that?" he asked. "It shouldn't hurt me to be accused of being a liar and a kidnapper? I have no right to be upset when the woman I..."

"What?" Susan urged when he fell silent and returned to his packing. "What were you going to say?"

Mike took his drafting tools from the drawer and concentrated on fitting them into a corner of the box. "I trusted you, Susan," he said. "I thought we understood each other, and we were friends before we started to be lovers. I believed the things you said to me."

"Mike..."

"And all the time," he went on, looking up at her, "you were suspicious of me. That letter came a long time ago, before we ever went to bed together. Didn't it?"

"Yes," she said. "It did."

"And ever since, you've been convinced that I'm a kidnapper and a fugitive."

"But the letter said—"

"You went to bed with me," he said. "You held me and made love to me, made me happier than I've ever been in my life. And all the time you believed I was a criminal."

Susan was silent.

"Didn't you?" he asked fiercely.

"Yes," she whispered.

"There's no way I can spend another evening under your roof. If I'd known what you were thinking, I'd have been gone long ago. You really had me fooled."

Her head began to throb again, and indignation overcame her misery. She moved closer to him, snatching one of Emma's stuffed toys from his hands and tossing it back onto the piled clothes on the bed.

"What was I supposed to think?" she asked. "You and Emma arrived here out of the blue, with no friends or family ties of any kind. You didn't get any mail from anybody. Nobody ever called you. Emma had no memory of her family, except for you. She doesn't even know what a grandmother is, for God's sake! And then that letter came..."

"Oh, right, the letter," he said quietly. "The one you took out of my wastebasket and fitted together. What did you read that upset you so much?"

She didn't answer.

"Come on, tell me. What did the letter say?"

Susan looked at him reluctantly. "It said...that the police couldn't find you. That you were being selfish and you should bring Emma home for her own sake. That the poor woman's heart was breaking, and she'd been to the doctor..."

"So naturally you assumed the letter was from Emma's mother and I was a fugitive parent, telling you all kinds of lies."

"Be reasonable, Mike! Who else could it possibly be from?"

He turned away, picking up a pair of jeans and folding them automatically. "I told you my wife was killed when Emma was a baby. I told you the whole story before we moved in."

"I know. But I—"

"You didn't believe me," he said flatly. "You decided I was lying."

Susan looked away, reaching up wearily to rub the aching bruise on her temple.

"Look," he said after a brief silence, "I hate talking about this. I've never told this story to anybody, but I'm going to tell you before I leave. Sit down," he added with a formal gesture at the chair near the window.

She crossed the room and sat down, her hands gripped tightly in her lap, while Mike sat on the edge of the bed facing her.

Susan looked into his grim face and realized, with sudden, blinding clarity, that she'd made a terrible mistake. She had no idea what he was about to tell her, but she knew that she'd misjudged this man, and her accusations had damaged their relationship beyond repair.

At the same moment, Susan realized that she loved him. He was the man she'd been looking for all her life, and no other man could ever take his place.

The knowledge was utterly overwhelming, so devastating that she swayed and felt dizzy. She gripped the arms of the chair and forced herself to meet his eyes steadily.

For a long time, Mike gazed at the black winter sky beyond the window, then turned to her. "I told you what my life was like when I was a kid, after my parents died."

Susan nodded.

"Well, it didn't get much better. I worked like a dog at school and at my job, saved every penny and won a scholarship to medical school. All I ever wanted was to be a doctor, specializing in pediatrics. I didn't give a damn how hard it was. In college, right from the start, I worked part-time at the cafeteria to supplement my scholarship."

He gave her a brief, humorless smile.

"Do you have any idea how hard it is to go to medical school and hold down a part-time job?"

"I can imagine," she said in a low voice.

"Well, I got through the first three years of medical school in Toronto, and life started to get a little better. I was twenty-four, and I could actually see some light at the end of the tunnel. I just had a year of medical school left and then a couple of years of residency. I knew I was going to make it. Then I met a girl."

Susan tensed and stared at him, her hands still clasped tightly in her lap.

"Shelley was a student nurse in the hospital. She lived in the nurses' residence. Her family didn't mind our getting engaged, but they wanted us to put off getting married until I started my residency and was earning some money. I agreed with them, because I wanted to be a pediatrician more than anything. But then Shelley got pregnant."

Susan looked at his hard face, the beauty of his callused hands with their long sensitive fingers, and wondered how she could have been so blind.

"Her parents made all kinds of threats," Mike said quietly. "They wanted her to have an abortion, but she refused. And I was really torn. If she wanted to have the baby, I had to help her. We got married and I quit medical school, went back to construction work to support us. We went out to Alberta, and I got a job on a big project. It was a hospital," he added with a bitter smile. "The pay was really good."

"Oh, Mike," Susan whispered.

"When Emma was born," he went on, "and I saw her for the first time, it made up for all the sacrifice. I've never loved anybody the way I loved that little baby. Not until—"

He stopped abruptly. Susan looked down, her heart aching. Finally, he squared his shoulders and went on talking.

"I kept trying to save money, hoping that I'd have enough someday to go back and finish my training. Shelley was never really strong after Emma was born, but she insisted she wanted to get a job and help me. She didn't have a chance, though, because she died when Emma was four months old."

"In the bus crash," Susan said softly.

Mike looked at her for a moment, his eyes clouded with memory. "That's right. She was going to Montana to visit her sister. After that, there was no possibility of going back to school. I had Emma to look after, and we were all alone."

Tears filled Susan's eyes. She sat tensely in the chair, watching him.

"After Shelley died, her parents wrote and said they wanted to help me with Emma. I thanked them and said I could manage. I couldn't forget the threats they'd made when Shelley got pregnant and how distant they'd been even after Emma was born. Eventually, they came out from Ontario with a lawyer and a bunch of legal papers, saying I wasn't able to provide a stable home and they should be the ones to raise the baby. I told them they could visit as much as they wanted, but I'd die before I'd give Emma up. The next week, I got a notice that they were suing for custody. Emma was ten months old, just beginning to take her first steps. She'd already learned to say Dada."

He fell silent, looking down at his hands.

"What did you do?" Susan asked.

"I went to see a lawyer at Legal Aid. He told me I could try to fight it, but there was no guarantee I'd win. After all, her grandparents could offer security, private schools, music and dance lessons, every kind of privilege. All I had was a ton of love."

"But... you're her *father,*" Susan said in disbelief. "How could they possibly take her away from you?"

Mike gave her a bleak smile. "Fatherhood doesn't cut much ice in the courts. Shelley's parents argued that if Emma lived with me, she would have to go to day care while I was working. I could never offer the kind of privileged home life they were able to provide. I realized that I could actually lose her."

"So what did you do?" Susan asked.

"I decided to run. Just ignore the court summons and take off. And that's what I did."

"So Emma's grandparents got the police to look for you?"

"I doubt that they looked very hard. I had legal custody, after all. My only crime was ignoring a summons. After a year or so, letters started getting through occasionally so I assumed the police weren't all that interested in me. Just the same, I wasn't about to contact anybody and find out."

"So that letter," Susan breathed, her eyes widening, "it was from Emma's *grandmother?* Your wife's mother?"

"She's mellowed a lot," Mike said, gazing at the window again. "Nowadays, she begs, instead of threatens. I guess they're suffering, too," he added, looking back at Susan. "But it's pretty hard for me to forgive them."

"Will you . . ." Susan's voice faltered. She cleared her throat and went on, "Will you ever be able to finish your medical training?"

She looked up at his shuttered face, and realized she no longer had any right to ask him questions.

"I hope to," he said coolly, as if they were strangers making conversation. "If I keep saving, and we can find a place to live so we don't have to keep moving around all the time."

"Mike," Susan whispered. She looked up at him. "Mike, please . . . you can stay here. I don't . . ."

He shook his head. "Not here," he said. He got to his feet and started packing again.

Susan understood what he was saying. The sweet, tender love that had blossomed between them was irreparably damaged. If he stayed in the house, both of them would find the situation impossible.

She got to her feet and moved toward the door. "At least, don't leave in the middle of the night," she said quietly. "Can't you wait until tomorrow?"

He didn't turn around, just shook his head and continued packing. Susan watched him for a moment, then went down the hallway toward the stairs. She stopped in Emma's doorway and stood for a long time looking at her. Emma was sleeping soundly in the little bed, a serene expression on her face, unaware of the drama that had just taken place.

Finally, she left the child's room and wandered down the stairs, more miserable and bereft than she'd ever felt in her life.

DANNY GOT OFF the bus and walked toward the high school, his heart thumping noisily under his thin jacket. He knew he was early. She'd told him to come at four-thirty and it was only a few minutes past four o'clock, but it was impossible to wait any longer.

Classes were just letting out for the day. Teenagers streamed around him, laughing and pushing one another, sporting a bewildering array of clothing and hairstyles. Danny felt like an old man in their midst.

He entered the building and hurried though the halls to the office, then sat on a bench in the hallway to wait. Students still thronged the halls, carrying books and sporting equipment.

He was relieved, at least, that there was no chance of running into Lynnette. She had a spare in the afternoon, and she always left early to be at work before three-thirty.

The hands on the big wall clock dragged toward the half hour. At four twenty-five, he ventured into the school office, where a spectacular redhead in a cashmere sweater looked up from her computer keyboard and gave him a warm smile.

"May I help you?" she asked.

"I want to..." Danny's voice cracked with nervousness. He took a deep breath and plunged on. "I want to see Miss Adamson, please. She told me to come here this afternoon."

"She's probably still in her homeroom," the secretary told him. "Room 723, just down the hall to your left."

Danny nodded and left the office. He made his way to the door she'd indicated, paused for a moment, then knocked.

"Come in," a voice called.

Danny opened the door and saw the blond woman standing at the blackboard with a notebook in her hand, writing something. She looked as beautiful as ever despite the livid bruise at her temple. But her face was tired and drawn, and her eyes were bleak.

"Hello, Danny," she said, glancing at her watch. "You're right on time."

She sounded so sad that Danny ached with sympathy. He knew there had been a lot of tension between her and the dark-haired man the night before, and he hated to think he'd been the cause of it. He wanted them to be happy, living in their elegant old house with the sweet little girl and the big yellow dog.

Danny hesitated in the doorway, shifting from one foot to the other. He glanced at the rows of empty desks and wondered which one Lynnette sat in. Thinking about her gave him a little courage.

"Come in," the teacher said with a tired smile. "I'll put this away and get my coat."

"Miss Adamson, if you're busy, I can—"

"Call me Susan," she said, setting her book on the desk and walking over to a closet to take out a long brown overcoat. "And don't worry about me. We can't put this off any longer. It's too important."

"I'm really sorry," he said. "If I caused any trouble between you and...and Mike. I didn't want to...I mean, I..."

"It's all right," she said, giving him another of those gentle smiles that didn't ease the sadness in her eyes. "The problems between Mike and me have nothing to do with you."

He waited while she locked the door of her classroom, then walked with her down the hall and out to the parking lot.

"We'll go together, all right?" she asked.

They walked through the parking lot, and Susan gave him a brief smile when he stopped beside her car.

"We'll take my car, all right?" she asked.

Danny nodded. "I came by bus."

She got into the car and unlocked the doors, then waited while he fastened his seat belt.

"This is really scary for you, isn't it?" she asked quietly. "Going to the police, I mean."

His heart began to pound. "Yeah," he muttered. "It's pretty scary."

"Do you have that picture of your aunt holding the suitcase?"

"It's in my wallet."

"Well, then, I think they'll believe you. I don't think there's anything to worry about."

Her confidence didn't ease Danny's fears very much. He looked gloomily through the passenger window as she drove out of the school grounds and started across town to the police station.

But Susan began asking him questions about his life with Rosa, his school days and his job, and before long he found himself beginning to relax a little. He even told her about his feelings for Lynnette.

"She's really a wonderful girl," Susan said. "I think she has a pretty hard time at home."

"I know," Danny said fervently. "There's nobody like her in the whole world. I really love her."

"Maybe you could bring her over to my house sometime. I'd like the chance to get to know her outside of school."

Danny looked up in astonishment. "You wouldn't mind? I thought you'd never want me in your house again after... what I did."

"I'd like to have you come for a visit, and bring Lynnette, too."

"What abut Mike? Won't he be upset if I..." Danny fell silent.

"Mike doesn't live at the house anymore," Susan said quietly, looking straight ahead. "He's moved out."

"Yeah?" Danny asked in surprise. "I didn't know he was moving right away."

"Neither did I," Susan murmured with a little catch in her voice.

Danny was afraid she might start crying, and he didn't know how he could bear it if she did. But she got her voice under control and turned to him with a sad attempt at a smile.

"Buster's still there," she said. "And I'm sure he'd be happy to see you. I guess you two are pretty good friends, right?"

Danny grinned faintly. "I must have given him a ton of licorice the last two months. Buster really likes licorice."

"That's what... what Emma says," Susan whispered, sounding on the verge of tears once more. Danny was almost relieved when they pulled up and parked near the police station.

But after they were inside, his panic began to rise again and he would have bolted if Susan weren't holding him firmly by the arm.

Susan paused at an office door while Danny looked at her, fear written all over his face. "I can't stand it," he whispered. "I can't stand it if they—"

"They won't," she told him firmly. "Come on, Danny. We have to do this."

Numbly, he allowed himself to be led inside the room where a handsome young police officer sat behind a mountain of paperwork.

"Danny," Susan said, "this is Constable Liepert. Curt, this is Danny. I told you all about him on the phone."

Curt Liepert got to his feet and shook Danny's hand, looking at him intently. "I guess you don't remember me, do you, Danny?" he asked.

Danny stared at the policeman. He didn't remember much from that dreadful time. It was all a hot muddle of uniforms and handcuffs and clanging doors, of Rosa's sorrow and his own fear...

"No," he whispered. "I don't."

"Well, I worked on that robbery. I remember you."

Danny looked at the floor. He was dimly conscious of Susan beside him, giving his arm an encouraging squeeze.

"Sit down, both of you," the officer said. "And Danny can tell me his story."

Haltingly, Danny told all of it, starting with his release from prison and his efforts to find and keep a steady job. He told how Rosa got sick, and their strange conversation in the hospital the night before she died, and then the shock of finding the suitcase full of money and losing it to Susan. Finally, his voice on the verge of cracking, Danny told how he'd tracked Susan and watched her house, then broken in to retrieve his money.

When he was finished, he looked at Constable Liepert. "I know it was wrong. I should never have done it. I just don't want...please, I can't stand to go back to jail. I'll do anything to make up for what I did, but I can't go back to jail."

Liepert balanced a pencil thoughtfully in his hands. "Is that why you didn't approach Susan right away and tell her the money was yours? You were afraid of the police?"

Danny nodded. "With my record and a suitcase full of money, I thought you'd arrest me right away."

"Susan told me you had a picture of the suitcase. Can I see it?"

Danny rummaged in his wallet for the photograph and handed it across the desk, his fingers trembling.

Liepert studied it with a faint smile. "I remember Rosa," he said at last. "She came in to make your bail with a paper sack full of money. Said she didn't trust banks and checkbooks."

Danny nodded. "She was always that way."

"She told us you were going to be looked after," the policeman went on. "She hinted that she'd saved a whole lot of money for your future. Somebody asked her where the money was if she didn't trust banks, and she told us to mind our own business."

Danny's mouth dropped open. "Then you *knew?* You knew all along that she..."

Curt Liepert smiled. "I would have believed you, Danny," he said gently. "You caused yourself a whole lot of misery for nothing."

Danny settled back in the chair, stunned, while Liepert turned to Susan.

"You want to press charges for the break and enter?" he asked, getting out a form.

Danny looked at her in horror, then relaxed when she shook her head. "I don't think so, Curt. I really doubt that Danny's about to embark on a life of crime."

"Okay. It's your choice." Liepert put away the form and got to his feet, reaching for his patrol jacket. "Let's go."

"Go where?" Danny asked nervously.

The policeman grinned at him. "There's been enough of this keeping money under beds," he said. "I'm giving you a police escort to the bank with that suitcase, and I'm watching while you deposit it. You got a bank account, Danny?"

Danny nodded and got to his feet, still feeling dazed. "There's...it's got forty-seven dollars in it. I'm saving up to buy a Christmas present for my girlfriend."

Susan and the officer exchanged a glance. "Well, soon there'll be a few more dollars in that account, won't there?" Liepert said cheerfully. "You coming with us, Susan?"

"I wouldn't miss it. Besides, I think Danny's going to take me out afterward for burgers."

"I wish I could go along," the policeman said wistfully, giving Susan a melting glance. "Are you *sure* I'm not your type?"

She tried to smile, but Danny could see the pain that clouded her eyes.

"Sorry, I'm just not in the market for a relationship right now. Come on, guys," she added with forced cheerfulness. "Let's go to the bank."

Constable Liepert disappeared briefly down a corridor and returned with the battered suitcase, and Danny realized that the long wait was about to end. He was finally going to get his money.

Susan saw his face and smiled, squeezing his arm. He walked between her and the policeman into the fading light of the November afternoon, so happy, he couldn't even feel the pavement under his feet.

CHAPTER FOURTEEN

CRISP NOVEMBER DAYS gave way to the sleet and cold of December. Snow fell on the beautiful city by the ocean, muffling the world in a blanket of white and snarling traffic for miles along the crowded roads and bridges. The afternoons were brief and dark with cloud, but the long frosty nights were pierced by thousands of Christmas lights glistening softly through the ice crystals.

Susan went about her days mechanically. She taught her classes, had her hair cut and took Buster to the vet when he got a long splinter of glass in one of his front paws. She went to her rock-climbing and needlework lessons, had lunch with Betty, visited often with Danny and Lynnette.

She told Peter she wasn't interested in seeing him anymore, and continued to gently discourage Curt Liepert when he called. A few weeks before Christmas, she cleaned the house from attic to cellar, trying to exorcise the ghosts of Mike and Emma. But it was a futile effort.

The memories were everywhere, stabbing at her heart when she least expected them. She looked out at the snow-covered terrace and saw Emma sitting in the sun in her denim overalls, feeding cereal to Buster. In the yard she saw Mike working on his old truck, glancing over his shoulder at her. His dark hair shone, and his eyes were bright with laughter.

One bitter night when the wind howled around the eaves and sleety rain hissed on the windowpanes, Susan got up, climbed the stairs and slipped into Mike's empty bed, hugging the pillow and gazing into the darkness with eyes full of sorrow. After that, she often slept in his room, both tormented and strangely comforted by her memories.

One Saturday morning when she was doing laundry, she found a white cotton T-shirt of his wedged between the washer and the basement wall. She pulled it out and sat on the wooden stairs for a long time, pressing the soft fabric to her face. Finally, she took the shirt up to her bedroom and tucked it under her pillow while tears streamed down her cheeks.

She didn't know where Mike and Emma had moved. Eventually, Susan swallowed her pride and approached the foreman of the construction crew at the school, but he didn't know any more than she did.

"Best worker I ever had," he said with regret. "The guy quit one day without an explanation. Said it was an emergency and he had to move on, and he was real sorry he couldn't give me any notice."

"Do you have any idea where he is?" Susan asked. "An address, or anything? He . . . left a few things behind at my house," she added awkwardly, "and I'd like to send them to him."

The foreman shook his head. "Not a clue. I think maybe he was heading back East somewhere."

Betty saw her friend's misery and tried to help. "You could send him a letter at your own address," she suggested one evening, curled by Susan's living-room fireplace.

Susan looked at her blankly.

"The post office would forward it, just like they did that other letter. Right?"

Susan's face clouded at the mention of the letter that had caused so much damage.

"I doubt it," she said listlessly, getting up to poke the logs on the hearth.

She watched as a shower of bright sparks erupted in the grate and flickered up the chimney.

"God, I feel so terrible," Betty said. "I should never have interfered. This whole mess is my fault."

"It's not your fault," Susan said. "If this awful experience has taught me anything, it's that we have to take responsibility for our own actions. I should have trusted him and believed in him. I can't blame anybody else for what I did."

Betty leaned forward to take a handful of popcorn from the bowl on the coffee table, then sat back, munching thoughtfully. "So how did Peter take it?" she asked. "When you told him you weren't interested in dating him anymore."

Susan gave her a bleak smile. "Oh, he seemed to bear up pretty well. Peter always has so much on his mind, I think a relationship isn't all that important for him. If he gets lonely enough, he'll just go back to the dating service and pick out somebody else."

"How about you?" Betty asked casually. "Are you ready to take another stab at it, Susie?"

"At what?"

"The dating service. Come on, let's go down there this weekend and see if they can find a good prospect for you."

Susan shook her head. "I don't think so. I'm just not interested."

"Look . . . you really can't mope around here forever, sweetie," she said gently. "He's not coming back, you know."

Susan didn't answer.

"Besides," Betty went on, "you always said he wasn't your type. You're attracted to a completely different kind of guy, Susie. You always have been, and you know it. You really need to put Mike and Emma out of your mind and get on with your life."

Susan crossed the room and sat on the couch, tucking her feet underneath her and holding an embroidered cushion in her lap. She wanted to change the subject, before she started crying.

"You still haven't told me about your ring," she said.

Betty's face turned pink with happiness. She held out her left hand, displaying an antique topaz in a heavy wrought-gold setting. "I guess it's not officially an engagement ring," she said. "Barnaby doesn't believe in all the orthodox customs. He says it's more of a pledge."

"Well, that's okay. Pledges are nice." Susan smiled at her friend. "So, tell me, does Barnaby believe in marriage?"

Betty grinned. "He's not *that* unorthodox. I think," she added, looking almost shy, "that we'll probably get married in the early spring. Connie's moving in with her boyfriend right after Christmas, and Barnaby and I will be looking for a house somewhere closer to the city. I want one just like this."

"I'm so happy for you," Susan said. "You really deserve to be happy."

"So do you. That's why I wish you'd—"

The doorbell rang, chiming softly in the hallway. Susan's heart leaped as it always did when she heard the doorbell or the telephone. She got up and went to the front door, picturing Emma on the veranda with her kangaroo, and Mike in his clean white shirt down by the forsythia...

"Hi, Susan," Danny said when she opened the door. He stood in the porch light with his arm around Lynnette, who smiled up at her shyly. "Lyn and I have something to show you."

Susan swallowed her disappointment and hugged both of them, then drew them inside.

Danny was wearing a soft leather jacket and pleated slacks, and looked prosperous and well groomed. He seemed taller, Susan thought, gazing at him fondly. He'd shaved off his mustache, and his young face was hardening into a manly look of competence and strength.

Lynnette was as delicately pretty as ever, but tonight there was a special glow about her.

"Wow," Betty observed from her seat in the big armchair as Susan led the young couple into the room. "Look at Lynnie. The woman's positively glowing. What's up, kids?"

"Hi, Betty," Danny said cheerfully, helping himself from the popcorn bowl. "How's Barney?"

"Barnaby," Betty corrected, slapping his hand. "You can't have my popcorn. Go into the kitchen and make your own."

"You two stop fighting." Susan sat down on the antique curved love seat. "Danny, what did you want to show me?"

He turned to Lynnette, who held up her hand shyly. Betty leaned forward, her eyes widening.

"Susie, do you have some sunglasses?" she asked in mock alarm, covering her eyes. "This huge thing is blinding me."

"It's not that big," Danny said. "It's not even a diamond. Lynnette—"

"It's an opal, my birthstone. I didn't want Danny to spend too much on my present."

Susan bent to look at the ring on the girl's slim finger. "So what is it?" she asked, kissing Lynnette. "A friendship ring? An engagement ring? Or is it a pledge, like Betty's?"

"It's a pledge," Danny said proudly, putting his arm around Lynnette's shoulders. "It's my solemn promise that she's the only girl for me, as long as I live."

Susan and Betty smiled at each other. "Pledges are wonderful," Betty said.

Susan loved to see her friends so happy. But everybody was pairing off, and she felt like the loneliest woman in the world...

"Aren't you going to put up some Christmas decorations?" Danny asked, looking around at the fire-lit room.

"She's just lazy this year," Betty said through a mouthful of popcorn. "You should see this house at Christmastime. It usually looks like Santa's workshop. She hasn't even bought a tree yet."

"I know," Susan said. "I just...haven't gotten around to it. I really should buy a tree, and get the boxes down from the attic..."

"I'll help," Danny volunteered. "Whenever you're ready, Susan, I'll come over and help you string lights and everything. I'd love to."

"Thanks, Danny," she murmured, looking down at her hands. "That's nice of you."

Danny studied her thoughtfully for a moment, then got to his feet with sudden decision. "I'm going to make some more popcorn," he said, heading for the kitchen with easy familiarity. "Susan, do you think you could give me a hand for a minute?"

She nodded and followed him, leaving Betty and Lynnette together by the fireplace, immersed in a happy discussion about Betty's wedding plans.

Danny crossed the kitchen and glanced out the window at the doghouse. "How's Buster?" he asked.

"His paw is still pretty sore," Susan told him over her shoulder, getting out the popping corn. "He keeps licking the salve off. But the vet says it's healing nicely."

"That's good."

Danny measured popcorn into the popper while Susan went to fetch the butter and salt. He paused, on the point of turning on the switch, and looked at her directly.

"Susan," he said.

"How much butter should we melt?" she asked, peering into the fridge. "Lyn doesn't like it too soggy, does she? Betty, on the other hand, likes to eat her popcorn with a spoon."

"Susan," he said again.

"Yes?" She turned around, caught by something in his tone.

Danny looked at her, his face quiet and concerned. "I saw him," he said.

Susan gripped the butter dish in her hands and waited.

"I saw him walking on the street," Danny went on. "Yesterday afternoon, when I was finishing my shift."

"Mike?" Susan whispered. Her heart began to pound, and her breath stopped. "You saw Mike? Are you sure it was him?"

Danny nodded. "I followed him in my cab. Susan," he added gently, "I know where he's living."

SUSAN SPENT a long time finding a parking place. Traffic was heavy, and the sidewalks were filled with Saturday-afternoon Christmas shoppers. She sat in her parked car for several moments, looking at the brightly decorated streets and passing crowds without even seeing them. Finally, she took a deep, nervous breath, climbed from the car and went around to let Buster out of the back seat, snapping his leash in place.

The big dog leaped clumsily around her. He gazed with curiosity and delight at the unfamiliar street, and strained at the leash to sniff the base of the parking meter.

"Come on," Susan told him, tugging on the leather strap. "We don't have time for that now."

He fell into step behind her, trotting obediently at her heels as she walked down the street to a shabby apartment building. Although she'd driven past the apartment at least a dozen times in the past week, it was still almost overwhelming to be standing here, so close to the place where Mike and Emma lived. Her knees felt weak and shaky, and she had to summon all her courage to push the door open and walk inside.

At least it wasn't the kind of building where you had to ring for admittance. She couldn't bear the thought of speaking to Mike on an intercom and being refused entry.

She paused in the lower hall, breathing deeply, assailed by a blast of heat and the mingled odors of fried onions, carpet dust and pine-scented air freshener. She clutched Buster's leash and began to climb the wooden stairs.

A man came out a door in the lower hallway marked "Caretaker." He was bald and immensely fat, wearing dirty white coveralls and carrying a pipe wrench.

"Hey, lady," he said roughly. "You can't take that dog up there."

Susan looked down at him, barely seeing him. She gripped the peeling handrail while Buster slunk close to her on the stairs, looking frightened.

"I said," the man repeated, "you can't take that dog upstairs."

"Yes," Susan said after a moment. She gave him an absent smile and went on climbing. "Yes, I can."

He stared up at her in astonishment, the pipe wrench dangling in his hand.

Susan and Buster mounted to the third floor and went down a narrow, dark hallway.

She stopped by a green-painted door. Buster sniffed at the floor and threshold with sudden intense interest. His tail began to rotate frantically and he whined deep in his throat, gazing up at Susan.

"Oh, Buster," she whispered.

She looked down at the dog for a moment, then bit her lip and forced herself to ring the doorbell.

For a long, sinking moment, she thought the door wouldn't be answered. At last it swung open and Emma stood in the entry, looking up at her in openmouthed surprise.

"Susan!" Emma shouted. The child swarmed up into Susan's arms, burrowing and clinging. Susan held her with tears running down her face, cherishing the feel of Emma's warm little body, her silky hair and skin.

"Hello, darling," she whispered, kissing Emma's plump cheek. "Oh, Emma, you just can't imagine how much I've missed you."

Emma snuggled fiercely, gripping Susan's collar. Gradually, she became aware of a noisy disturbance on the floor nearby, where Buster galloped around Susan's legs in a frenzy of welcome.

"It's Buster!" the child said, radiant with delight. "Buster came, too!" She wriggled in Susan's arms, slid to the floor and flung her arms around Buster. The two of them rolled together on the carpet, a happy tangle of blue denim and golden fur.

Susan looked up, smiling through her tears, and saw Mike in the doorway.

She caught her breath, overwhelmed by him. Everything about him seemed so vivid, larger than life. He was taller than she remembered, and his eyes were even bluer. His body looked lean and hard in jeans and an old plaid shirt, his shoulders broad and strong. He stood quietly and watched her, showing no emotion.

"Hello, Mike," Susan ventured, stepping aside as Emma and Buster tumbled against her legs. She bent down to give the leash to Emma, uncomfortably aware of Mike's steady gaze.

"How did you find us?" he asked.

"Danny saw you on the street last week," Susan murmured. "He followed you and found out where you lived."

Mike gave her a humorless smile. "I guess Danny's pretty good at that kind of thing, isn't he?"

"He's doing really well these days. I see him all the time. He's bought his own cab now, and he and his girlfriend are getting quite serious. She's—"

"Hey, Susan, guess what?" Emma tugged at Susan's coat sleeve to get her attention.

"Yes, darling?" Susan smiled down at the little girl, stroking her hair tenderly.

"I have a granny. My granny's coming to visit," Emma announced. "She's coming right after Christmas. Daddy phoned her, and she's coming on the plane to see me and she's bringing a present for me."

Susan looked at Mike in astonishment.

He shrugged. "I guess a man can't keep running forever. I'm tired of running. It's already cost me everything I ever—"

He fell silent abruptly and turned to Emma who was shouting to get his attention.

"Can I take Buster into the kitchen and give him some cereal?" she asked.

"Okay," Mike said. "Don't make a mess."

They vanished inside the apartment, while Susan and Mike looked at each other in tense silence.

"May I come in for a little while?" Susan asked.

"If you like." He stood aside to let her enter, then followed and closed the door.

The room was neat and clean, like any place where Mike lived, but it was painfully bare, and the sparse furnishings were shabby and worn. A tiny Christmas tree stood in one corner with a couple of wrapped presents at its base.

"Not such a great place, is it?" Mike said, following her gaze. "But it was the best I could do on short notice."

They stood awkwardly, listening to the sounds of hilarity coming from the kitchen.

"How's Peter?" Mike asked.

"I haven't seen him for a long time," Susan said quietly. "I told him I wasn't interested in going out anymore."

"Why not?"

Susan took a deep breath and looked at him. "Because I'm in love with you."

His hand clenched briefly and a muscle tensed in his jaw, but he gave no other sign of emotion.

"I think you must be imagining that, Susan," he said.

"Why?"

"I'm not the type of guy you're looking for, re-member?"

Susan made an abrupt, impatient gesture. "That was all such foolishness," she said. "I didn't know what I was talking about."

She gazed at the little Christmas tree for a moment, then turned to him again.

"You know, I've matured about ten years in this past month," she went on. "All that stuff about 'my type,' it was just so misguided. No woman really knows the type of man she wants until she's met him."

Mike watched her and said nothing.

"All these years," Susan told him, "I've been attracted to the kind of man who's guaranteed to hurt me. When I finally met someone who had everything in common with me, who wanted to love and protect me and be my friend, I didn't even recognize him until it was too late. Is it, Mike?" Susan whispered. "Is it really too late?"

"I don't know," he said. "Are you sure you don't want one of those rich professional guys in a three-piece suit?"

"I want you," she told him simply. "I don't care about anything else."

"Even if I'm a construction worker all my life?"

"Yes."

He moved closer and looked down at her, his eyes darkening with emotion. "Do you trust me now, Susan? You don't believe I'm a liar and a criminal?"

"Oh, Mike..." Tears blurred in her eyes. "You know, I don't think I ever really believed that. I've been thinking about everything since you left, and I believe I just used all that suspicion as an excuse to keep from getting too close to you because I...I thought you weren't the right man for me, and I didn't want to..." She paused, then looked up at him with her heart in her eyes. "Mike, please forgive me. I was just so stupid."

She fell silent, hardly daring to breathe as he gripped her shoulders and pulled her close. Susan sighed, overcome with bliss when she felt the familiar warmth and strength of him, the uniquely safe feeling of being in his arms.

"Oh, it's so good," she whispered, lifting her face to be kissed. "Isn't it good?"

His mouth found hers and they stood locked together in the fading afternoon light. His kiss was tender and sweet, so richly satisfying that she felt herself rising and drifting in a cloud of happiness.

"Mike, listen to me for a moment." Susan pulled away and looked at him. "Please, darling, I want you and Emma to come home."

"When?"

"Right away. Tonight."

"Haven't you got another tenant?" He drew her collar aside to kiss her neck, then looked at her with a warm intensity that made her shiver.

"I couldn't bear the thought of anybody else living there. I've missed you so much. Mike..."

"Hmm?"

"Mike, I want to ask you something."

"What?"

"I want to know how much money you've got saved."

He arched an eyebrow in surprise.

"I mean," Susan said hastily, her cheeks warming, "if you've got enough that you could help me with the mortgage payments, then you could quit your job and go back to medical school, couldn't you? You could start right away. In the January semester, even, if you could get in, and we could . . ."

She felt the sudden tension in his hands. "What are you talking about, Susan?" he said hoarsely.

"Well, you've been saving all these years, right?" she asked. "You've worked ever since Emma was born, and saved your money. So if we live together and you use your savings to help with the mortgage, you won't have to work. I'll keep working while you finish your training."

"My God," he whispered, thunderstruck. "That's so . . . what's in it for you?" He released her abruptly and turned away. "What do you get in exchange for that kind of generosity?"

Susan smiled. "A doctor," she said, reaching out to touch his hand. "I get a pediatrician to take care of my kids when they're sick."

"Your kids?" A little of the old teasing light began to dawn in his face. "What kids?"

"Emma's brothers and sisters," Susan told him. Tears filled her eyes again, but now they were gentle and healing.

"I love you," he whispered, pulling her into his arms. "God, I love you so much . . ."

Lost in his embrace, Susan gradually became aware of a small hand tugging insistently at her coat sleeve. She looked down at Emma, who stood near them with Buster at her side. Both the child and the dog regarded them with bright, curious eyes.

"Susan," Emma asked, "why are you kissing my daddy?"

Susan bent and scooped the little girl into her arms. Mike held both of them in a warm embrace and they stood locked together, laughing, while Buster looked up at them with a happy pink grin, tongue lolling and tail wagging.

"You want to know why I'm kissing him?" Susan asked, her cheek pressed close to Emma's. "You want to know, Emma Murphy?"

"Yes!" Emma squealed, wriggling with delight.

Susan smiled mistily.

"Because, sweetheart," she whispered, "your daddy is the man of my dreams."

OFFICIAL RULES

PRIZE SURPRISE SWEEPSTAKES 3448

NO PURCHASE OR OBLIGATION NECESSARY

Three Harlequin Reader Service 1995 shipments will contain respectively, coupons for entry into three different prize drawings, one for a Panasonic 31" wide-screen TV, another for a 5-piece Wedgwood china service for eight and the third for a Sharp ViewCam camcorder. To enter any drawing using an Entry Coupon, simply complete and mail according to directions.

There is no obligation to continue using the Reader Service to enter and be eligible for any prize drawing. You may also enter any drawing by hand printing the words "Prize Surprise," your name and address on a 3"x5" card and the name of the prize you wish that entry to be considered for (i.e., Panasonic wide-screen TV, Wedgwood china or Sharp ViewCam). Send your 3"x5" entries via first-class mail (limit: one per envelope) to: Prize Surprise Sweepstakes 3448, c/o the prize you wish that entry to be considered for, P.O. Box 1315, Buffalo, NY 14269-1315, USA or P.O. Box 610, Fort Erie, Ontario L2A 5X3, Canada.

To be eligible for the Panasonic wide-screen TV, entries must be received by 6/30/95; for the Wedgwood china, 8/30/95; and for the Sharp ViewCam, 10/30/95.

Winners will be determined in random drawings conducted under the supervision of D.L. Blair, Inc., an independent judging organization whose decisions are final, from among all eligible entries received for that drawing. Approximate prize values are as follows: Panasonic wide-screen TV ($1,800); Wedgwood china ($840) and Sharp ViewCam ($2,000). Sweepstakes open to residents of the U.S. (except Puerto Rico) and Canada, 18 years of age or older. Employees and immediate family members of Harlequin Enterprises, Ltd., D.L. Blair, Inc., their affiliates, subsidiaries and all other agencies, entities and persons connected with the use, marketing or conduct of this sweepstakes are not eligible. Odds of winning a prize are dependent upon the number of eligible entries received for that drawing. Prize drawing and winner notification for each drawing will occur no later than 15 days after deadline for entry eligibility for that drawing. Limit: one prize to an individual, family or organization. All applicable laws and regulations apply. Sweepstakes offer void wherever prohibited by law. Any litigation within the province of Quebec respecting the conduct and awarding of the prizes in this sweepstakes must be submitted to the Regies des loteries et Courses du Quebec. In order to win a prize, residents of Canada will be required to correctly answer a time-limited arithmetical skill-testing question. Value of prizes are in U.S. currency.

Winners will be obligated to sign and return an Affidavit of Eligibility within 30 days of notification. In the event of noncompliance within this time period, prize may not be awarded. If any prize or prize notification is returned as undeliverable, that prize will not be awarded. By acceptance of a prize, winner consents to use of his/her name, photograph or other likeness for purposes of advertising, trade and promotion on behalf of Harlequin Enterprises, Ltd., without further compensation, unless prohibited by law.

For the names of prizewinners (available after 12/31/95), send a self-addressed, stamped envelope to: Prize Surprise Sweepstakes 3448 Winners, P.O. Box 4200, Blair, NE 68009.

RPZ KAL